HEART STONE

THE WISE ONES BOOK 4

LISA LOWELL

To Paula
Thank you for the Inspiration

BETROTHED

*T*anzaa looked up when the eunuchs came in to collect her. She had known. All the other girls in the harem glanced secretively at her with a mixture of jealousy and excitement. It was mid-winter day and one of them would be called, as was tradition, on any of the equinox or solstice days. Her best friend, Zamira smiled, for she had been selected just before at fall equinox to become a concubine at the spring festival and was only three months into her preparations. They would be together in their selection.

Tanzaa felt her stomach plunge as the tall eunuchs stopped and stood before her. She carefully set aside the music she had been studying and rose. The silence echoed among the other girls, for they envied her, but dared say nothing.

They would never know how her heart broke for the love she lost.

Obediently, Tanzaa followed the guards out of the garden room and to her bower where she would prepare to meet with the king. She bathed thoroughly, and then let her servants wash and oil hair and select her richest clothing. They wove silver beads and jeweled pins through Tanzaa's blonde tresses, to match the gray velvet gown. Unlike the current fashions in Umzulio, this draped frock allowed her free movement. Perhaps the king would request her to dance at this court review and she must be able to do so without argument. In a few moments, she would be setting fashion in the entire capital. Tomorrow the popular tight bodice and heavy skirts would fade from favor very quickly, all because she was selected to become the next concubine of the King of Demion.

When she had been prepared properly, Tanzaa followed her escorts toward the throne-room. As she walked, Tanzaa began silently composing the letter she would write to Dayvian when she returned to her rooms. He would get the note as soon as the weather in the pass lifted. Without meaning to, she glanced out the huge windows of the foyer. She saw that a storm brewed, with wind bending the trees of the palace gardens. The winter's cold sleet reflected her mood. Yet her gloom must not impact her dancing. She must never let the king know how she despised his offer to select her for his consort.

My Beloved Dayvian,...

She entered the main hall and tried not to react. Over fifty other concubines and a vast assortment of Lords along with their ladies, all turned to look at her. Their brightly colored robes flashed like summer flowers against the gray of the stone chamber. The king stood, resplendent in gold, on the dais, smiling grandly down at her, stretching forth his arms as if to invite her into his embrace. She wanted none of him. Zamira would remind her she would never want for anything, jewels, prestige, security, servants, power. She might even have a bit of freedom, as far as the demon would allow, but painful sorcery would rule her life.

Tanzaa would have everything except affection.

The one requirement of becoming a king's consort was to house a demon and take on the magic that went with such possession. Tanzaa shivered in terror at the thought but did not hesitate. She did as was expected. She held her head high and strode bravely through the gathered courtiers. Then Tanzaa knelt at the foot of the dais, her arms outstretched before the king, forehead on the running carpet. King Zathuramin owned her already. She had lived in his household, under his protection for most of her life. All her training as a courtesan was his. Tanzaa, the dancing harem girl would become Lady Tanzaa, the courtesan of the king.

Outside, the gathered storm struck, rattling the windows in the foyer, beyond the tall wooden doors.

"Ah, Tanzaa, my love," the king announced. "As lovely as ever. You wore silver and I stand here in gold. You have me under your spell, and even before you take on the power. Dance for me, will you?"

He didn't need to ask, she thought. She lifted herself off the floor and glanced around for the musicians. Zamira had not rejoined the musical group, for the choosing-brand on her wrist still prevented her from playing the lute, her best instrument. Zamira would return in a few weeks to playing, just in time for her wedding that was to take place at Spring Equinox. Even without her friend, Tanzaa knew to dance in obedience. Six other harem girls had gathered on the side steps and smiled down at her as they struck up a lively winter tune, designed to counter the dire weather outside.

Dance, Tanzaa.

She spun and sculpted the air with her arms like she had wings. Her delicate feet hardly seemed to dust the chamber floor like snowflakes flitting across an ice field. The loose hair across her shoulders shielded Tanzaa's impassive face from the awed onlookers. She twisted in impossible contortions, imitating a swan lifting free from the winter lake and fleeing into the sky. The courtiers watched, enchanted and murmuring their approval. King Zathuramin collected such stunning specimens, gifted with talents that would only be enhanced as they became hosts to demons. Oh, Tanzaa would be an exquisite addition to the menagerie, they thought.

The swan landed again on the ice and settled. The music faded and the king began to clap his approval.

"Yes, you will do," he almost whispered. "You will be my sixty-third wife, my lovely. You will dance for me...after you have healed.

Tanzaa resumed her kneeling on the carpet, with her arms in front, but she could not stop the slight tremor of fear rippling down her limbs. She struggled to get her breathing under control before the next stage of this ceremony. Tanzaa heard the tramping of the eunuchs' return. She did not struggle as they carefully stretched her legs out behind her so she lay sprawled in front of the king. She could not watch as a priest approached and the eunuchs held her down, both arm and leg.

The priest peeled her dancing shoes off and then, with little ceremony, placed the glowing red iron seal against the heel of her right foot. Zathuramin's mark on her talent. She could only dance for him. The pain tore from her throat, but she smothered it into the carpet. Tanzaa hoped her bowed head and shrouding hair hid the tears and fury she could no longer contain.

Outside, the storm raged on.

2

INVITED

*T*he circus geared up for the spring tour and Dayvian helped, lending his muscle to loading brightly colored tents and heavy ropes into the carts. The circus manager stood in the way, barking orders instead of helping, and Dayvian grumbled under his breath, about his laziness. However, he dared not let his sour attitude carry farther into the morning air. Dayvian needed this job. Indeed, he had needed it since he was six. There was nothing else a musician could do if he wanted to reliably feed himself. So, he endured his manager's laziness stoically.

"What's with you?" asked Cardin, his best friend for years and the only other musician in the company. He could tell Dayvian was at least fixating on something. "You usually enjoy loading up. It means we're moving out. You hate wintering over here in Teal. Besides, you'll get to see Tanzaa soon," Cardin added. He knew that the mention of the girl always cheered up his friend.

Dayvian looked around Teal's circus lot with its muddy grounds, just budding trees filling in around the perimeter and the long winter's clouds finally breaking up. Truly, he should be excited about the circus' departure. In one more day the troupe would depart Teal and wander through the Land's few eastern cities before departing through Ravgail Pass. After traveling another month, they would arrive in Umzulio. The capital of Demion, Tanzaa's hometown, a teaming city in the center of the exotic country. However, that thought brought no comfort now. Instead, Dayvian dripped with dread at seeing Tanzaa once again. He could never share the true reasons for his depression with his friend Carsin. No one knew the dark root of the fear in his stomach. A difficult tour awaited Dayvian and he knew it.

So instead of ruminating on his inability to resolve the true problem, Dayvian chose to focus on the issues he could address; nosy friends, lazy managers, the broken string on his guitar. That would have to be rectified before they left. He didn't have the funds to fix it, let alone purchase enough spare string to last the entire eight-month tour. Time to go scavenging.

Dayvian threw another load of props on top of the tent canvas that filled a cart to hold it down and turned around to get another armful. Abruptly he almost ran into a pretty lady walking between the other carts. He thought he knew everyone associated with the circus, but he would have remembered someone like this woman. Rich, chestnut hair, warm skin, and memorable eyes, one green, one blue, both twinkling in the spring air. Carsin, his quick eye open for any female within marrying age, moved forward boldly and introduced himself before Dayvian could even apologize for bumping into her.

"Hello, I'm Carsin," the musician stuck out his hand, laying on the charm, smiling and holding on to the lady's hand longer than necessary. "Pardon my clumsy friend here."

Fortunately, this lady knew how to handle an awkward situation. "Hello, gentlemen," and Dayvian caught how she carefully included them both. Her smile would have melted even Dayvian's depression, but he let Carsin continue bumbling through an introduction.

You're in over your head, Carsin, Dayvian thought. Surely his lady was already taken. Indeed, he doubted if she wasn't already married, for though she was dressed as a common maid, with her hair down and her rich tanned skin spoke of someone who worked outside, he doubted a dairymaid or farmer's daughter could afford the finely woven skirt and leather bodice she wore. No, she's spoken for and Carsin is going to go the entire tour pining for the one that got away.

"You may call me Rashel," she said in a sweet voice that Dayvian's musical ear could appreciate. "I was wondering when the circus was pulling out."

"Alas, my lady, that we must depart," Carsin brought her hand to his lips, "and we won't be back for eight months. I shall be deprived of the opportunity of gaining the acquaintance of such a lovely..."

Dayvian rolled his eyes at Carsin's pathetic attempts at charming a lady. Then another stranger, a tall, wiry huntsman, came around the corner of the cart and froze Carsin under this newcomer's glare. "And I'm Yeolani, her husband. Just answer the lady's questions please."

Dayvian sighed for his friend, but came to his rescue. "The circus leaves at dawn tomorrow. What can we do for you?"

Rashel smiled winningly, making Carsin's jaw drop. "We're looking for a certain musician and thought perhaps you qualified. The gentleman back at the gate said something about..." and she faded off, again smiling, her green and blue eyes flicking toward Dayvian. Was she really trying to get their attention, even with her husband standing right behind her now? "Dayvian, is there a place I can speak with you privately?"

Carsin began sputtering, but his friend got what he

deserved for flirting so outrageously. For his part, Dayvian swallowed a wave of sudden nerves. He glanced over her head toward the master, who at the moment had his back to this part of the circus lot. To the left, he knew the cook's tent probably wasn't occupied at this point in the morning, and he motioned for her to follow him. Carsin was about to protest when Yeolani clapped his hand on Carsin's shoulder and said something about helping to finish the packing. So Rashel's man knew about this private interview and encouraged it? How strange.

In the cooking tent, no one occupied the supper table which would probably be the last piece to be packed after the evening meal that night, so he invited Rashel to sit and then took a seat himself across from her, curiosity finally breaking through the sour mood he had cultivated all day.

"Thank you for seeing me," Rashel began, wringing her hands in a surprising show of nervousness. "I came here to speak with you specifically. How long have you been with the circus?"

That was a strange way to begin this mysterious conversation. "Since I was six...what is this about, ma'am?"

"It's about magic, Dayvian." Her frank expression caught him off guard. She wasn't trying to charm him now but had grown deadly serious.

Dayvian deliberately misconstrued what she was talking about. "The circus already has a magician. He does a pretty good rope trick, but his disappearing box could use some work," Dayvian tried awkwardly.

Rashel almost believed him for a moment, pausing to judge whether Dayvian was serious. "No, I mean real magic, no tricks," she replied, rolling her eyes at his misdirection. Then, without preamble, she held up her palm at his eye level. Without any distraction or magic words, a beautiful blood-red rose began to form in her hand, completely free of stem, leaf, or

8

soil. It emerged as a closed bud and then opened to summer size in the matter of a breath or two.

"There's no such thing as..." but Dayvian could not finish the sentence in the face of such beautiful and blatant proof to the contrary. He gave up completely as she handed him the rose and then began to craft a daffodil to go with it, again, with no subterfuge.

"How are you doing this?" he finally had to ask.

Rashel smiled secretively. "Because I am magic. You might call me Queen of Growing Things. I am one of the Wise Ones. Most people know me as Rashel. I have come to find you Dayvian because you are magic as well."

He watched her strange blue-and-green-eyed seriousness and forced himself to breathe. He could not think of one thing to say to that declaration. Magic...did he even believe in it? Dayvian knew it existed and not in the form of sleight of hand like the circus magician. He also knew about the demons in the court of the King at Umzulio. That type of magic he knew all too well. That demonic power was taking Tanzaa from him even as he sat at this simple table across from a sorceress.

"I am not a sorceress," Rashel insisted. "That is evil magic and in the Land, there are only the Wise Ones, the guardians of truly good magic. Vamilion, the King of Mountains lives just up the river in that grand palace that I'm sure you've seen. He is one of the Land's true magicians, as am I. My magic is mostly based in growing plants, though that is not a limitation. And Dayvian, you can also be a Wise One. It is one of my tasks to find the next Wise One that will become a guardian of magic in the Land. I will train you in your powers. You will live forever, able to do almost anything, but with a duty to serve the people of the Land."

This could not be true. Dayvian's entire experience with magic taught him such powers were wrong and evil. In his travels with the circus, he had seen demons at work in Demion. They possessed and then manipulated people. In Malornia the demon-possessed used their powers to oppress anyone without magic. He had also seen the small hedge-witches in Marwen who made the air noxious with smokes and hexes, claiming they could cure all sorts of ills. Nothing good ever came from their hocus-pocus, no matter how much a seeker paid for magical services. Here in the Land, he had not seen a whiff of magic...except, as Rashel claimed, that huge, glorious palace farther up the river. However, Dayvian never thought of it as magic; just some great Lord looking down on his domain.

Dayvian found himself standing, backing away from Rashel and her bizarre offer to train him in magic. He couldn't get away far enough from her, he knew, but he had to reject the idea of magical powers. He didn't know how to think, let alone consider it. He didn't *want* to believe in magic.

"Why do you not want to believe in magic?" Rashel asked.

Had he said it aloud? He didn't think he had. She had replied to something she must have heard in his head.

"I don't want...magic is...," he whispered and then tried it again, louder. "If there is magic then..."

"Dayvian, what's wrong? You're upset. I'm sorry. I thought you were old enough understand...who is the girl?" Rashel's eyes flashed in alarm.

She *had* been inside his head. Dayvian closed his eyes over the image burned into his mind; Tanzaa, the girl he would love forever. He tried to erase the vision of her white-blonde hair and stunning silver eyes. He wanted to unsee her graceful movements, alabaster arms around him. He must forget her shy smile.

Tanzaa had always been inaccessible, though he continued to seek for ways they could be together, but this year his dreams would all end. He would fail in his promise to Tanzaa. It would take magic to free her and yet magic was the reason they could not be together.

"Dayvian, tell me about the girl," Rashel ordered smoothly. She somehow created a pot of tea and poured it for him graciously. He took the proffered cup and he found he couldn't resist her magic voice.

Crumbling with a sudden wave of grief, Dayvian sat back at the table and put his head down on his arms so he would not have to look at anything beyond his eyes. He did not want to speak, but somehow, he had to do as he was told. It broke through the dam holding back his grief.

"I met Tanzaa ten years ago when she first became a courtesan in the Demion King's household at Umzulio. She was sold into that life as a dancer, as just a child. She had a gift for grace that the court valued. Some even said she was magical. Then our tour arrived in Demion, I saw her dancing and completely fell for her there. The first and only girl I've ever loved. Every year when the circus comes to Umzulio, I go out of my way to meet with Tanzaa, to play my music just for her to dance to, and she is exquisite. Tanzaa and I...we are a pair. I spent all my money on lessons so I could learn to write to her. She risks being beaten or killed every time I came, sneaking out of the palace to meet with me. Three years ago, when I was at Umzulio we promised ourselves to each other. We began plotting how we could marry ever since. But what I didn't know about at that time was magic."

Dayvian then lifted his head and almost snarled at Rashel as he declared, "I hate it. It's ruined my life and hers. I won't have it."

Rashel didn't react to the obvious resentment he directed toward her. He *did* believe in magic, but that world had destroyed him, and so he rejected Rashel's offer out of hand. "Dayvian...what happened?"

Although there was no magical imperative, Dayvian managed to pick up the shreds of his story. "This winter I got a letter from Tanzaa. As a courtesan, she officially belongs to the King of Umzulio, who has exclusive rights to her. Unfortunately, the King is also a sorcerer. He gets his power through demons. Tanzaa wrote to me that she has caught the eye of the king...and...and she is to be married to him at midsummer. That means she will be made a host body for a demon as well. If she refuses the marriage or fights this edict, she will become one of the blood sacrifices for his demon instead. No one, if they can help it, refuses the demons. She'll be his sixty-third wife and a demon's slave. There is nothing I can do. It's too late."

Rashel sat at the table watching the miserable young man crumble, and couldn't console him. No wonder the thought of magic repulsed him. And truly, there was little she could do to help him or Tanzaa. As a Wise One, Rashel's magic was for the Land, not Demion, a completely separate country, where magic developed differently. Demion, from time to time, even attacked the Land. Yet, offering to go to Tanzaa's rescue would not help their situation. Oh, if Dayvian took the magic Rashel offered him, he technically could probably rescue Tanzaa, but not without inciting an international incident and even then he would have to leave her regardless of the results.

"Rashel..." The voice of her husband, Yeolani, pierced silently into her mind. "What are you thinking? You aren't doing anything reckless...?"

"It won't be my decision," she replied in magical silence. "I'll leave it up to him. He has to at least know what he's giving up."

Rashel reached out across the table and shook Dayvian out of his malaise. "Not all magic is demon evil. The magic I'm offering you is in you naturally. I traced it to you here. Already it's part of you. I can give you the key to opening it and you...if you accept this gift, you will have more power than the Kings of Demion."

Dayvian gasped, sucking in his breath suddenly, and he reached out, gripping her hand. "What?"

"But you must understand, there are restrictions and you will not like them. You must be aware of this before you make your decision." Then, even if it were not polite Rashel tapped into the young man's thoughts, hoping he was in the right frame of mind to listen.

"If you accept my offer of magic, you will become a Wise One. It gives you almost unlimited power magically, but the moral restrictions are severe. You could rescue Tanzaa from the King and set her free here in the Land. However, doing so might start a war with Demion, if the King is willing to pursue her that much, and you will regret that. Also, you should know you will not then be able to keep your promise to Tanzaa to marry her. A Wise One must only be married to another Wise One. Then one of your duties will be to find the next one in our order, the way that Yeolani found me. You will go Seeking a woman with natural magic and can marry only her."

Dayvian's mind spun with the possibilities, making Rashel almost dizzy listening to his thoughts. "But can't Tanzaa become a Wise One too? What if I choose her?" he asked.

Rashel shook her head and restlessly rose to pace the tent. "No, you misunderstand. Only a few people have the Wise One gift. You do not get to select who will receive it. God does that. Yeolani had to look to find me and all he had was my name...just as I only had your name as a clue to find you. Dayvian, I've been looking for you for the last thirty years, starting before you were even born. And then half that time you've been out of the country, out of range as it were. I didn't know what kind of person you would be, what your gifts will be or how this will work out. If...if you do not choose the magic gift I'm offering you, then I will leave and move on, seeking another person named Dayvian and it could be a hundred years before I find another."

Dayvian shook his head, running his lean musician's fingers through his tousled brown hair in frustration. "Thirty years... I've been in the circus fourteen...you cannot be that much older than me. How did you..." His confusion made him still again.

"Dayvian, I'm over fifty years old right now and have been a Seeking Queen for thirty of those years. When I said you would live forever, I meant it. That's one reason you could never be with Tanzaa. You would remain as you are, and she would grow old and die."

Dayvian's wonder echoed in the air between them. Rashel was double his age and yet didn't look a day over twenty. It could not be real. "I thought you said this magic does not come with demons," he muttered, terribly disappointed. "That sounds pretty demonic to me. So why did you tell me this? I cannot challenge the King of Demion without it causing war and I wouldn't win anything by taking on this power. I will lose Tanzaa either way." He sighed bitterly. "Are there any other restrictions on this...this Wise One magic?"

Now it was Rashel's turn to look away. She carefully surveyed the tent, making sure no one else could overhear their conversation. "Many, but they are restrictions you are naturally prepared to accept if you are the kind of person God has already selected. For example, I know you are honest by nature, because as a Wise One you cannot lie. For some, the most diffi-cult restriction is you will have to leave your name behind. It will be used against you, forcing you to do evil."

Dayvian shook his head. That didn't matter to him. He had

no reputation or notoriety attached to his name, nor family to lose...only Tanzaa and he intended to keep her if he could.

Rashel ignored his unshared thoughts and doggedly continued her list. "Then there are the moral quandaries. You are facing one already. How much can you act toward rescuing Tanzaa, if you are not justified in starting a war? The answers to these restrictions come from this."

She held out to him a small globe, no bigger than a crabapple that glowed blue-white, pulsing to the beat of some-one's heart. He started to reach for it out of curiosity, but she pulled back. "No, if you touch it you are committing to become one of us. This is a Heart Stone. Each of us has one and this is yours if you dare take it. It acts as a conscience, blocking magic if you attempt to do anything unworthy of a Wise One. And it will help you judge how justified you may be in any situation. For instance, you may kill in defense of the Land or of an inno-cent, but other times you may not be permitted to act at all. It is the key to sprouting your magic."

Dayvian watched the swirling blue as if hypnotized by the Stone, and Rashel noted that his staring eyes bore the same color as the orb. She heard him taking a willful breath and then let it out slowly. "Will it prevent me from killing the king of Demion for Tanzaa's sake?"

Rashel closed her hand over the Heart Stone and broke the spell, slipping the magical globe back into her pocket, removing the temptation. "I am not the judge. That depends on the circumstances. Only you can know how your heart will lead you."

Dayvian lowered his head again, speaking into the table. It was a terrible decision. Rashel read in his mind how he felt like a man on a high cliff overlooking a lake. He intended to jump and discover if the water were deep enough to support him, but the cost of the leap would be irrevocable. He would know the answer or drown.

"Tanzaa...I need to talk to her. I will not make any decision without her input. You've looked for me for thirty years. You'll have to wait a while longer. We'll be in Umzulio by midsummer. I will decide after I speak with her and not before."

Without a drop of irony, Rashel replied, "That is a very wise decision." Then she turned and left the tent.

3

IN THE GARDEN

Two months later, the sun blazing down on his neck, Dayvian looked up the main road into the Demion capital of Umzulio with mixed feelings. He had spent the entire trip doing his responsibilities for the circus but with his mind elsewhere. Rashel's offer of magic burned in the pit of his stomach, haunted his nights under the stars, and dampened even Carsin's enthusiasm. At least Dayvian had the sense not to share his disquiet with his chatty friend. The last thing he needed was advice from someone like Carsin; bold and brainless, leaping off the cliff with no care if the lake had gone dry. All the input Dayvian wanted, he could hopefully get from Tanzaa. Her steady, thoughtful insight would open his mind to where he must go.

Dayvian ran through hundreds of ideas and possibilities buzzing like gnats in his head during the trek. Overall, they were fanciful and ridiculous, but he had nothing else to think about during the tedious traveling between tour stops. He could practically play his music in his sleep, so what else was his fevered mind supposed to concentrate on? 'What about getting Tanzaa out of the city and having Rashel protect her without me taking the Heart Stone?' 'What if Tanzaa immigrated to the Land and the King never could trace her, if Dayvian did the protecting?' 'What if Dayvian offered himself in trade for Tanzaa, and the King felt it was a better sacrifice because he was this magician instead?' All of these ideas seemed too melodramatic to even verbalize, so Dayvian tossed them aside as soon as they came through his head. He felt like an idiot considering all of these scenarios.

And then there were the nightmares; horrible dreams where he witnessed the future for Tanzaa. He woke nightly in a sweat, having dreamed of Tanzaa's dancing in flames, or atop a bloody altar, smiling manically or dancing for the king in her wedding gown, with a sacrificial knife in her heart. He never actually saw how her death happened, for he was always too mesmerized by her movements, but Dayvian woke convinced of her impending death. No, his nightmares haunted him into realizing no matter all his fanciful daytime plotting, Tanzaa would end up dead anyway. And that was if he did accept the Heart Stone magic. What good was such power if it couldn't change her fate?

As the circus moved over the mountain border between the two countries, he also wondered if someone out there was listening to his thoughts and overactive imagination. When the circus troupe traveled through Rayvgild Pass and they officially left the Land, Dayvian was reasonably sure that Rashel or Yeolani were in the company. Mysterious things kept happening. He found six spools of coiled guitar string in his footlocker so he didn't have to purchase any with his precious savings. Carsin conveniently kept getting distracted elsewhere by some lady he saw in the party, and so it left Dayvian the chance to think without interruption.

Even his music grew better despite the lack of attention he

paid to his work. He found himself improvising and enriching the melodic line effortlessly. He wished briefly that there was some way to write down the enhancements. Carsin gave him alarmed and pleased looks as they performed, but didn't comment on the strange improvements. Dayvian wouldn't have been surprised if the sheet music to their routine didn't find its way into his things with the extra notes penned in for him. That would mean Rashel or Yeolani had followed him on tour, and they wouldn't give themselves away like that, he assumed.

And now the time had come; the circus arrived at Umzulio three days before midsummer. He and Tanzaa had a standing meeting at midnight in the grove of trees in the central city park on the first day the circus came into town. Tanzaa would know when they were scheduled to arrive and would always find a way to slip out of the palace to meet him. Unaccountably, Dayvian felt nervous as the caravan came down into the capital. What if she couldn't get away, considering her changed status in the court? What if Rashel interrupted them? Dayvian didn't think the Queen of Growing Things would be so rude, but he already had the sense that he was being listened in on, and it niggled at the back of his thoughts. Like a puppet, he went about his duties, helping set up tents, passing out fliers announcing the circus for the next day and going through the motions of rehearsal, but his mind could only function with Tanzaa in his eyes.

Finally, with the circus settled in for the night, Dayvian slipped out of his cot, found his guitar in the dark and wove his way past other sleepers. As he lifted the tent flap he heard Carsin's encouraging voice. "Tell her *ardeli* for me."

Dayvian didn't acknowledge his friend's advice, but he hoped the Demion word applied. Tanzaa didn't speak the language of the Land but fortunately, traveling for most of his life, Dayvian understood them all. Now if he could invoke the words to make this tangled magical mess function in some way to bring them safety and happiness, Dayvian would be relieved. He left the circus grounds and slipped through the night, finding his way by memory to the grove of trees where he knew Tanzaa would await him.

"Do you ever regret that I didn't court you, the way Dayvian is courting Tanzaa?" Yeolani asked his lovely wife as they sat invisibly in the woods, waiting behind a shield of silence for the two lovers to arrive. "You're such a romantic; I really should have managed to give you flowers once at least."

Rashel tried not to laugh. "Flowers? Really? It's not like you'd be killing some of my friends or anything." She sighed then and put her hand in his. "No, you rescued me, so I consider that romantic enough. It isn't your style. If you brought me anything, you would have brought me...what would you have brought me?"

"I'm sure I could dig up a diamond or emerald somewhere, but don't ask me to cut and polish it."

Rashel chuckled, "A rock? No, my love, I don't need jewels or flowers. You make me laugh and that's more than I could ask for. Laughter is our kind of romance."

Yeolani unexpectedly swept Rashel off the ground and pretended to steal her away. "Or we could just go find somewhere more secluded and do some other things for a bit? Otherwise, I might get embarrassed watching this. Maybe Dayvian has some tricks that I can learn from."

Yeolani's suggestion made Rashel laugh again, but she put him off, knowing her husband's teasing nature and Yeolani put her down again. "Here he comes. Can you sense the girl yet?" They waited in their invisible hiding place as Dayvian found one particular tree within the grove, sat up against it and began tuning his guitar, playing softly as if luring Tanzaa in.

Over the past weeks, the two Wise Ones had taken turns following the circus, monitoring Dayvian's thoughts, making sure he held firm to his relationships and didn't let his emotions run away with him. As a result, they were both pretty familiar with his mind. They could hear Dayvian's growing excitement. They had also noted how gifted he was, to the point that they wondered if there might a magical component to his musical dexterity. He also had a vocal skill, singing in each performance in every village on the trek. He even proved adept at moving through multiple instruments: guitar, pipe, harp and even drum. Rashel did not doubt a magical element to his musical talents, but she didn't see how it would ever apply to becoming a Wise One. How would music and magic blend? Dayvian's gifts certainly must have bewitched an impressionable courtesan girl as well.

"I think I hear her," Rashel interrupted her own thoughts silently to warn her husband.

"It's about time. His music is getting downright lusty," Yeolani replied, wrapping his arms around Rashel suggestively, though he knew she was focused on this liason about to unfold.

They watched intently as a girl, lithe and graceful, wearing dark gauze in a vain effort to camouflage herself in the dark, came running into the trees. Her white-gold hair and pale skin stood out in the darkened grove, and her movements might have made someone casually think they had spied a fairy. She moved so quickly and with an eerie grace.

"I don't think Dayvian's the only one with a gift here. They *are* a pair," Yeolani commented, completely serious now. "Can you sense if she's magical?"

Rashel silently agreed. "She's got something. Perhaps she's blocking it. The King of Demion or some demon in his court would surely sense it. Maybe she uses this dance-magic naturally and no one trained her. She's like Dayvian. Something is different with her. He has the music; she has the dance. You are right. They are a matched pair."

Uncomfortably the Wise Ones watched as Dayvian rose from his playing and let the guitar slip from his fingers to greet Tanzaa. He enfolded her in his arms and kissed her passionately. But before they could get too far into their reunion, Dayvian stopped himself and broke into a frantically whispered monolog in the Demian language. Rashel immediately recognized a problem.

"We're in trouble. How are we going to help him if we cannot understand what they're saying?" the Queen of Growing Things muttered silently.

"All your grand plans, poof, and they're gone because we don't speak Demian. Well, I can think of something else we can do while we wait for him to have his discussion," Yeolani suggested roguishly.

Instead, they listened carefully to the words Dayvian was explaining, noting his careful thought process and occasionally hearing a word they knew; Umzulio, Tanzaa, and once Rashel. It was supremely frustrating for enchanters, accustomed to knowing most of what happened around them, to not have a mental track on potential problems. In the end, all they could do was sit back and wait.

Dayvian spoke as quickly as he could. They had little time before Tanzaa would be found missing. And then there were Tanzaa's issues with language. Raised in the court where speaking was discouraged, and often beaten out of the courtesans, Dayvian had learned to be efficient in his explanations to

Tanzaa. That she rarely spoke didn't mean she did not have a great ability to listen. She understood better than most. She held his hands to keep him from nervously rambling as he explained the offer of magic and that he would not accept the offer if he couldn't be with her as well. When he made this statement, she only had one thing to say.

Tanzaa looked down and whispered, "One drowns or we both drown."

Dayvian had to work a bit on understanding the meaning within that analogy although he had already applied the imagery of drowning to this situation once before. Analogies were one of the things he loved about Tanzaa; her intelligent use of metaphor to get across so much information. So, she felt that by rescuing her, he was dooming them both, like a drowning man was likely to pull any rescuer under and then they would both drown. He understood the logic but he didn't want to accept her conclusion. Warily he looked down into her gray eyes, growing silver with tears. He could become mesmerized and completely willing to do anything she wanted. Did she have any other suggestions?

"Split the gift?" she asked.

Could they both escape; her from the King, him from eternal life of magic duties without her. Dayvian would gladly give up the potentially immortal life, sacrificing a couple of thousand years for the right to live with her just a few years. But no, he doubted it. Becoming a Wise One seemed like an all-or-nothing option. Instead, he thought carefully about Tanzaa's analogy of drowning. What would he do if it were as simple as that; she was drowning and he wanted to rescue her? He knew for his love's sake, regardless of his swimming skill, he would jump in. One of them would be saved and one would drown. He wanted Tanzaa to be the saved one.

"Rashel?" he called into the air, startling Tanzaa. "I know you're here somewhere, watching us."

It took a moment, with Tanzaa's nails biting into his hands in her alarm, but eventually, Dayvian saw Rashel fade from the moonlight coming toward him through the trees. Tanzaa caught sight of her and faced the magician, her hackles up in alarm and oddly enough she shifted to stand between Rashel and her betrothed, protecting him. Dayvian found it charming, but he also felt it unnecessary. Tanzaa's distrust of magic was well-founded, but she didn't have the experience of someone who had traveled in the Land and had heard the stories of the Wise Ones and their benevolent magic.

"No, she won't harm us," he reassured Tanzaa.

"Dayvian," Rashel nodded to him and then added with a second nod, "Tanzaa."

"*Yag har en froga. Om vi ta mazikan, komehr vi ivayg nu? Fins der nogon moralisk instrenkning om vad vi yura?*" he asked carefully.

Rashel looked abashed, and Dayvian tried not to smile at her discomfiture. "Wise Ones aren't capable of everything, Dayvian. I don't speak Demian."

That gave Dayvian a flash of hope. He hadn't anticipated that the Wise Ones were unable to understand the conversation he had just held with Tanzaa. He hoped there might be a way to put this to his advantage, so he immediately translated for himself. "I asked if I took the magic right here tonight, could I get her away from here, with no moral restrictions?"

"Then have you decided to take the Heart Stone?" Rashel replied. "Of course, there might be issues, but there will be few limitations to your magic. You won't be able to master your abilities and skills quickly enough to do anything tonight, but with my guidance, you should be able to get Tanzaa out of the city without detection, especially if she doesn't go back to the palace tonight. She'll have to leave without saying any goodbyes and you'll have to shield her from detection for the rest of her life, but it's doable."

Unspoken in that explanation was that Demion would be justified in launching a war with the Land and that came with its issues as well. Dayvian knew that lingered like a bad smell in the night air.

Then Rashel brought the Heart Stone out of her pocket, where it filled the grove with an eerie light that could be seen by anyone else wandering the park that night. As moths to the flame, both Dayvian and Tanzaa approached fascinated by the simple-seeming globe. It looked so innocent, held up in Rashel's palm.

Tanzaa commented, *"Fro."*

A seed, Dayvian translated that for himself, understanding the analogy of how the magic would grow into a wondrous potential for so many other things. He didn't interpret it to Rashel. He had other plans that he kept hidden from her by strictly thinking only in Demian.

Dayvian unexpectedly snatched up Tanzaa's hand and placed it on the Heart Stone, making her touch the stone instead of him.

He had anticipated some sign of a change, some magic, but all he got was anger. Both women rounded on him, shouting at him in dueling languages. It might as well have been someone slapping him in the face. Both Rashel and Tanzaa glared and were talking so quickly he began backing up, unable to understand either one of them. All Dayvian knew was he had angered them both and he would be lucky if he didn't get himself turned into a frog.

Then he heard someone else behind him laughing at his discomfiture. Yeolani came out of the darkness, chuckling and holding up his hands to break up the verbal attack. Tanzaa stopped chiding Dayvian immediately, frightened at the approach of a strange man. However, Rashel wasn't finished yet. "And you have no idea what you might have done to her." Then she petered out.

As a peacekeeper, Yeolani came to Dayvian's rescue, but only just, intervening in a milder tone than Rashel utilized at that moment. "Not wise, my friend. What were you trying to do?"

Dayvian sighed in confusion. "I was hoping the magic could go to Tanzaa. She's the one that needs it. If she has magic, she can defend herself from the demon power the King will force on her. Me, I'm just a traveling musician. There's nothing I could do with magic. It should be hers."

"But that's..." Rashel began almost lecturing again, but Yeolani interrupted with a calming hand and again in a more reasoned tone. "You don't understand, Dayvian. You cannot pass it on to just anyone. Do you realize that in the entire Land there are only five other Wise Ones? You would be the sixth, and that's over several hundred years of gathering magic. What's the likelihood that Tanzaa is a person that can accept the Land's magic? It's too rare. She's not even from the Land."

Tanzaa, hearing her name in the string of foreign conversation, tugged at Dayvian's arm, demanding an explanation. In disappointment, Dayvian turned to her and hurriedly explained what he had been attempting to do. From the scowls she gave him, it was obvious she wasn't happy with his actions. Tanzaa said again, she didn't want the magic if that meant it would separate them even so. *"Drunkna bägge två."* Both will drown.

Rashel got rolling again with her diatribe, forcing Dayvian to switch languages. "And now if she's got any magical trace on her from the palace, they know she's touched a Heart Stone. They might be on their way here right now."

That got Dayvian to react. "Can you stop them?" he asked desperately, looking frantically around the grove as if he expected soldiers to come out of the shadows at any moment.

"Relax boy," Yeolani tried to reassure him. "We'll put such a shield around this grove that every demon in the palace could not get through."

Dayvian wasn't sure of that guarantee. "Tanzaa, be on the lookout for soldiers. You might have been traced," he advised.

Abruptly the world stopped. Dayvian found he could not move, though he was aware of the passage of time. He could see Yeolani on his left and Rashel out of the corner of his eye, but Tanzaa dominated his field of vision. He noted with amazement that the two Wise Ones could not move. Only Tanzaa could. He watched her and felt his alarm rise as he struggled even to breathe.

At first, Tanzaa did not recognize what had happened but looked around her at the three others frozen in the dark. Perhaps some sorcerer just outside the grove had made even the night insects grow silent. Her long blonde hair whipped around as she spun trying to identify why everything else in the world had grown still. She waved her hand in front of Dayvian's face, but he couldn't even blink to indicate he was alive. He moaned with the last rags of air in his lungs and Tanzaa gripped his arm with relief. Then miraculously, at her touch, he was released from the spell paralysis and collapsed to the ground gasping.

"What was that?" he asked, coughing, trying to recover his breath.

"I don't know," Tanzaa replied. "Is it right that I touch the others? Will it release them?"

Tanzaa, with a fearful hand, reached out and brushed the two Wise Ones on the arm. They too gasped as they were released from the freezing spell. Both Wise Ones shook their heads to clear the haze of the magic, and then both simultaneously looked over at Tanzaa, wondering what had happened.

"Someone has magic...powerful magic and froze us," Rashel stated the obvious. "Tanzaa, it didn't include you. Why?"

Dayvian nodded and obediently began translating the question. The Queen of Growing Things then motioned for Tanzaa to come close to her. With trepidation, the blonde girl came to face Rashel. Carefully, so all of them, even Dayvian could see, she prepared to cast a subtle spell over Tanzaa and explained it as she went. "This is a truth spell. It shows you as you truly are and will reveal all that is magic about you."

Dutifully Dayvian translated, trying to reassure his beloved. *"Rashel ska fortrolla day att visa hur du veldig air. Var inte red. Hon air her att yelpa os."* Tanzaa nodded her understanding and took a calming breath like she would before she began a performance.

When Dayvian fell silent and nodded, Rashel stepped forward and moved her hand just in front of Tanzaa's face. Before them all, her dark gauze dancer's dress shifted to brilliant white. Her hair that she had worn down that evening, showing silver in the moonlight, now lifted onto her head into a complicated confection, with silver and diamond pins holding it aloft. Her white silk gown, embroidered with stylized silver stitching now spilled out around her like snow and she wore gray satin dancing shoes that fit her perfectly. Along her arms, instead of sleeves, she boasted silver brace pieces that curled up to her shoulders like tendrils of wind. On her arm she even sported a diamond and silver bracer etched with a deer leaping up one arm. Dayvian felt his jaw drop. He had never seen anything so exquisite.

Tanzaa froze in alarm and wonder. She knew magic and distrusted it as much as Dayvian, but could such unexpected beauty be evil? The king's beautiful wardrobe did not rival this, and yet he used demonic power to maintain it. Tanzaa spun around trying to see the back of the gown, hoping not to spy an imp or other such creature waving at her with a malicious grin. The silken layers floated about the ground, though the front hem rose high enough not to inhibit her dance movements. It was perfect to perform in, and no demon lurked behind her.

Tanzaa looked up in relief, but it turned into disappointment. Her simple turn put a hypnotizing spell on everyone again, especially Dayvian. He found it hard to breathe, though he wasn't paralyzed this time.

Yeolani made him jump by putting a hand on his shoulder and whispered in his ear, "You asked for it, my friend."

"I...I...I didn't ask for this," Dayvian replied, his usually controlled voice trying to come out like a croak as he waved at Tanzaa's glorious garb. "What is that?"

"She is a queen," Rashel confirmed. "Those are the royal clothes of a Wise One of the Land. It's magic....her magic. She froze us all without even knowing what she was doing."

Yeolani laughed, breaking the spell of amazement they all felt at the moment. "Of all the wondrous things, it seems that she stole your magic, Dayvian. You made her touch the Heart Stone and *she's* now the magician. You better explain this to her before she faints," he added and pushed Dayvian forward.

For her part, Rashel released the truth spell she had used, letting Tanzaa return to her original appearance. Then the Queen of Growing Things stepped away from the dancer so the lovers could talk and she turned to speak privately with Yeolani.

"How could this happen?" she asked in a private mental conversation with him. "We both sensed she had magic potential, but she wasn't a Wise One before Dayvian made her touch the Heart Stone. It's his, not hers. Does this mean that I have to go Seeking again? She's not even from the Land. We've made a

Wise One of the future wife of an enemy. This is going to cause a magical war."

"Vamilion wasn't originally from the Land either," Yeolani pointed out, just as equally perplexed. "Does this mean that Tanzaa is supposed to Seek Dayvian? You don't have another Heart Stone to give him, so is it Tanzaa's task now to find a Heart Stone to give to him?"

"Maybe,...no, maybe...maybe the connection these two have, drawn to each other despite all the obstacles that stand between them, is just a manifestation of the magical bond they would have if they had met later when they were both able to take on the power. They simply aren't doing it in the order it has always been done: male first, then female, one Seeks the other. If you and I had met before either of us was given a Heart Stone, would we have fallen in love as these two? We know that some of us manifest our gifts before we encounter the Heart Stone. Honiea was a healer before she ever became the Queen of Healing. And we already think that Dayvian's gift will involve his music."

"So, what are we going to do?" Yeolani asked again, still at a loss.

4

DIVING IN DEEP WATERS

$\mathscr{I}$n the end, the four of them sat in the grove of trees until dawn began pushing in on them, trying to explain the ramifications of what had happened. As a Wise One, Tanzaa obviously could not go back to the palace where the sorcerers and demons would immediately recognize that she had changed. They would attack her, try to usurp her gift, or at least entrap her. They would covet her newly acquired magic. Demons had always sought some way to tap into the deep-rooted and limitless magic of the Wise Ones. No, Tanzaa would only be safe in the Land from now on.

But what would the Demion court think if Tanzaa simply disappeared and left for the border? Demion as a country was always on less than friendly terms with the Land. The Wall had been built over a hundred years before to solidify the border between the countries and block magic passing between. How far would the king pursue his lost courtesan? Did they know that Dayvian was involved with Tanzaa and would come after him instead? If so, his life would surely be forfeit. Would they punish Dayvian's circus for stealing her away? There were simply too many unanswered questions.

"And there's so much to learn about being a Wise One, Tanzaa should not go on her own," Rashel explained carefully. "That means Dayvian must come with us as a translator or we use magic to overcome the language barrier. Tanzaa's not an immigrant to the Land at this point, so the language spell isn't going to be effective yet."

"Language spell?" asked Dayvian with wonder.

Yeolani rolled his eyes in mock exhaustion at all the training this entailed and then he explained lightly. "There is a spell upon the Land so that anyone who emigrates with the intent to stay, can then communicate as any citizen of the Land. Our territory was sealed for ages, kept that way by the dragons. Then they invited the Wise Ones in to help them hold that spell, but it failed. The Seal was broken. Suddenly the dragons were gone and the Wise Ones needed a way to bond together with everyone who began immigrating into the Land. Language helped create a distinct culture. We needed that shared language with few barriers. It was the Queen of Rivers' finest piece of magic."

They waited for Dayvian to translate that explanation and then Tanzaa had a question. "*Griffeltavla?*" Dayvian translated - a clean slate - and then after the blank looks, he realized translating Tanzaa's actual words wouldn't be enough. "She wants to know if we both have to start fresh with our lives in the Land... and if we can be together."

The silence of Rashel and Yeolani gave an unmistakable reply. They did not know. The uncomfortable abyss of the unknown stretched across the grove of trees and even Tanzaa with no translation could comprehend something was not right.

"I have a question," Yeolani blurted out to allow Rashel time to form an answer. "Why does Tanzaa speak in riddles, even in her language?"

Dayvian's smirk caught them all by surprise, for he knew the Wise Ones could not know and do everything. "It's one of the things that first really attracted me to her. Growing up in the court, Tanzaa was taught women do not speak. In Demion's palace, females are collected like possessions so they don't have a voice. Some women are warned about gossiping and then actually forced to have surgery to remove their voice box. But Tanzaa's a courtesan, renowned for her intellect, grace, and talents. That means she must express herself but instead of rhetoric, she uses a simple analogy and challenges you to think. The court just developed that way to control gossip and back-stabbing in the harems, and Tanzaa's very good at it."

"Well, it's going to be a hurdle for being a Wise One," Rashel broke in. "A lot of the answers to her questions are tied to what kinds of changes she's willing to make. Will you please ask her if she willing to learn the language of the Land and emigrate?"

Dayvian did the translating but he knew her answer.

"*Nytt spel, samma kompis.*"

"She says, 'new music, same partner'." Dayvian let Rashel and Yeolani interpret that metaphor for themselves; Tanzaa would come to the Land and learn magic but she wanted to be with Dayvian.

With a sigh, Rashel nodded and then added to the word-play. "Then she's going to have to learn new dance moves too. Dayvian, while I teach her how to speak our language, I need you and Yeolani to go down to the palace and discover if they've found her missing. If so, are they looking for you as well? I need to know anything that will help us get out of here without an incident."

"What about the circus?" Dayvian asked, flustered, and now

tired. He felt concerned about trying to do his job today with no sleep at all while worrying about how to get Tanzaa out of Umzulio safely.

Yeolani shook his head with regret. "That's not going to happen, my friend. The circus is going to be short one musician from now on. Come, we've been given our marching orders. Let's let the ladies...umm...talk while we go see if they've put out a warrant for your arrest yet."

Bewildered, Dayvian rose to his feet. He had endangered his lady, given up his hope in magic, and lost his career in one night. In a stupor, Dayvian reluctantly left Tanzaa with a reassuring smile. He led Yeolani out of the forested park and turned toward the palace where they would hopefully find everything at peace.

Dayvian knew the city well. The circus came here every summer and remained at least three weeks. Also, most of his courting of Tanzaa had consisted of long walks about the teaming city. It wouldn't be surprising if someone might recognize him. Tanzaa had been famous even before the King had decided to make her a wife. Her gift of dance, well known in both the court and among the poorer folk, had made her a prized guest in many parties of all types. The court had even rented her services out to perform at many a well-to-do-estate to grace their ballrooms. Whenever he was in Umzulio, Dayvian had also been invited to provide music for Tanzaa and he had written several songs just for her style of dance.

"While the background is helpful, Dayvian, let's get something set up right now," Yeolani commented to his thoughts as they began approaching the main marketplace setting up for a fine summer's day of selling. "No one can know that I come from the Land, so I won't be speaking aloud from here on out. If you have questions for me, just think about them. I will do the same with you. Point out anything you see as important. We'll need to make this quick. I don't think I will be identified as a Wise One, but let's not take chances."

"Very well," Dayvian said aloud and then stopped himself and added in his head, "Sorry."

"Just remember, this is for Tanzaa's safety and yours." Yeolani's voice in his head at first was disconcerting, but Dayvian supposed he must get used to this. The Wise One continued. "In a way, you're more vulnerable than Tanzaa right now. You have no powers and you're a good enough musician to be remembered here."

"I knew it," Dayvian thought snidely. "I knew you two were following me, listening in on me as we traveled here. Did you buy me the guitar strings then as well?"

"Buy? No," replied Yeolani with a chuckle. "I kind of duplicated the strings you already had. I'm about as musical as a wooden bucket, so I didn't trust myself to know what you needed. I just 'looked' at your guitar and made more of what you had there. Wise Ones conjure what they cannot buy."

"You have to buy things? What's the use in that? You could do anything. Why bother buying when everything will come to you? Jewels, fine homes, and the most beautiful women in the world," Dayvian snarled in his mind, letting his bitterness into his mental tone. Then he realized he could never let Tanzaa know how much he resented magic, now that she'd become one of these magicians herself.

"Hold on there, bucko," Yeolani shoved back into Dayvian's mind, almost physically stopping him in the street. "That might be how magic works in the rest of the world, but in the Land, the Wise Ones start life as regular people and for the most part live like normal people. I was a woodsman and a fisherman before I ever saw a spark of magic. I still chop wood if the need calls for it. If you become a magician, you too will probably play music the way you always have, but you will also have duties that will demand things of you that others cannot meet. We don't live like the kings or the sorcerers here in Demion. We don't go around demanding taxes from others and stealing other men's wives. We are servants of the Land and we take that duty with deadly seriousness, or we lose our gift."

"Lose your gift?" Dayvian asked in surprise. He just assumed Wise One magic was almost limitless.

"Yes, losing the gift is always a possibility," Yeolani confirmed. "Our magic comes from God and He has every right to strip it from us if we misuse it. For example, we are not allowed to interfere in your choices to become a Wise One. It's immoral to take away someone else's freedom to choose. All we could do to encourage you was to make it easier for you to make this trip. I only conjured guitar strings. We left you alone because that's what you needed to make your decision, free from coercion. Unfortunately, you didn't give Tanzaa that kind of choice. If I had done what you just did, putting her hand on the Heart Stone, God would have...well, I can't speculate, but it wouldn't have been pretty."

Dayvian felt suddenly guilty and horrified at what he'd done to the woman he loved. "I didn't realize... I can't believe I did that. I just wanted..."

"Listen, I don't whip a pup for chewing on my boot." Yeolani chuckled a bit at the thought that Tanzaa wasn't the only one to utilize an analogy. "It's what comes naturally and you didn't know you were doing wrong. God is not going to blast you to a cinder for doing something you meant to save her. In a way, it has helped. You're going to get her out of Demion. It might have messed up your life permanently, but she'll be free. You couldn't have known. The consequences for your actions are going to be punishment enough. And you're not even a Wise One."

"Speaking of consequences," Dayvian thought at Yeolani,

changing the subject as they walked toward the looming walls of the grand palace down at the lakeshore. "I need to get back to the circus and at least tell them some excuse. They're going to think I ran away with Tanzaa and they'll put out the word to find me. If I'm not a magician, I need to stay a musician. I need to keep my job."

"We shall see," Yeolani said and then looked up, distracted by the walls that now loomed up before them. "How do you get into the palace without an invitation?"

"I *had* an invitation. How do you think I met Tanzaa in the first place? When I was about ten years old, the court heard about our circus and the music. The king collects talented courtiers like others collect jewels. He invited us to do a private performance. After that, I received individual invitations to come perform for the ladies, just me and Carsin. I can come at any time, but I don't have my guitar or harp with me, now do I?" Dayvian grumbled, irritated that he was failing in his duties and might be kicked out of the circus, and then where would he be?

Dayvian felt something suddenly draped across his back. He looked down and he found his guitar strap had appeared across his chest and the fine instrument had materialized at his shoulder.

"I couldn't just leave it there in the trees, now could I?" Yeolani commented. "So, how do you propose we get in here? Shall I be Carsin?"

"Can you?" Dayvian asked and then chastised himself. Yeolani could probably do anything he wanted, limited only by his rather well-developed imagination and the threat of losing his gift to some moral restriction. Disguising himself as Carsin seemed hardly a difficult stretch.

Rather than comment on Dayvian's doubts, Yeolani smiled with a wolfish grin that shifted subtly, and then the tall, lean

Wise One abruptly shrunk in height and bulked up to look exactly like Dayvian's circus friend. "He plays the drum, correct? Just please remember I still can't speak Demian, nor play a single note. Will this get us in the door?"

"There's one way to find out," and Dayvian reached out and knocked at the gatehouse.

———

Rashel sat cross-legged in the grass across from Tanzaa under the cover of the summer trees and concentrated carefully. She had never conceived of language as a kind of magic, but now she felt it necessary. The two women sat, facing each other, both trying to be patient with the other. Rashel felt if someone needed knowledge, there must be a way to attain it and magic would provide. Surely if Tanzaa was given this Wise One gift by accident, there must be some way to make it less of a burden for her. Rashel just had to figure out how to tap into it and bring that magic forward. She considered carefully how she had learned the language of trees, how the plants spoke to her, and wondered if she could give Tanzaa just such a skill. In the end, Rashel's magic emerged more as a prayer than an actual spell. Rashel concentrated, prayed, and waited until the sun parted the trees and she felt their warm embrace.

"Please help Tanzaa understand," she whispered.

The first indication she heard was one word.

"Yes?" Tanzaa's silver eyes grew large with wonder. "Words?"

"Yes! You're speaking the language of the Land now. This is magical!" Rashel had not lost her wonder at miracles over the years, but this type of magic, outside her direct talents with plants, it still amazed her. Maybe part of being a Wise One was indeed being open to new ways of doing magic, filling the need, and not expecting the typical.

It didn't take her long to recognize just because Tanzaa could speak the language of the Land, she was more than atypical when it came to *what* she said, no matter the language. The use of analogies had not changed, so Rashel found she would have to ask for her gifts of communication if she were going to help the girl understand what had happened to her and how it would change her life.

So many concepts - a sacrifice of self, honesty, righteous use of the gift, choice, knowledge, love, service, even humility were concepts tied to the Wise One ethos. Rashel had to find metaphors for each of them that would translate to someone with a vastly different background.

"I understand without analogies," Tanzaa replied to Rashel's struggles.

Rashel sighed in relief and then started what she hoped would be an introduction to Wise One Magic. "Tanzaa, you will need to travel in the Land and use your magic in Seeking. I will go with you and teach you before you can safely go on your own."

"To find magic for Dayvian?" The girl would not be distracted from her goal.

Rashel did not know that answer and admitted it. "I cannot tell. Usually, the Heart Stone comes along with the name of whom you must Seek. It took me many years of Seeking before I was given Dayvian's name and the Heart Stone for him. You might be given a Heart Stone in just a few months from now, but I have no idea if it will come with his name. There is a chance the magic will simply bypass him and you will be given another name. Maybe his name will indeed be given to you. In either case, you must be Seeking to find these things."

"Seeking?"

"Studying your magic. Let's work on defending yourself first," Rashel insisted. Sitting in the middle of a park in broad daylight, in a foreign land, where Tanzaa would be pursued, did not make her feel safe. Any defensive magic she could teach would help.

"Now, what happened here in the grove when you froze us all, that was you doing magic with no control. You were worried about the soldiers coming to find you and so you panicked. Your magic turned that panic into paralysis on the rest of us. You can also do that on purpose with some concentration. Shall we experiment?" Rashel lifted a stone magically out of the ground. "I'm going to take this stone and toss it into the air. You focus on it, freeze it before it falls but see if you can do this without freezing me at the same time. Are you ready?"

Tanzaa nodded. Rashel hefted the fist-sized rock and tossed it into the air where if it fell it wouldn't hit either of them. Tanzaa furrowed her brow, concentrating on the stone as it started its fall, and it froze, floating there like some strange moon in the morning light. She smiled at her success and then turned to see that she had frozen Rashel at the same time. With a sad sigh, Tanzaa shook her mentor back into motion. Rashel reanimated with a gasp.

"Apologies," Tanzaa whispered. Her inattention let the stone drop out of the sky.

"No matter. Can you bring the stone to me? Concentrate on drawing it toward you across the ground. It will come."

Obediently Tanzaa again stared at the offending stone and it lurched awkwardly across the ground toward them, and then skidded forward, clubbing Rashel in the knee. They both winced and Rashel picked up the stone. She was puzzled, for she remembered her own experience with moving objects magically, that she had control immediately. Why was this not coming to Tanzaa with more grace...grace? Tanzaa was naturally a graceful person. Why wouldn't that grace translate into her use of magic? She had been nothing but bumbling with this magical gift. But the word 'grace' again resonated with Rashel. She often experienced these Wise One impressions.

"Concentrating with just your mind is not helping you," she said. "You are a moving person. Use your hands to manipulate the magic. Lift your arms and move it so you'll have more control." Rashel lifted the stone as a challenge. "Again?" Tanzaa nodded and Rashel tossed the rock.

This time Tanzaa raised her hand into the air and held up one finger to instinctively stop the stone. Obedient to her magic it froze mid-air but Rashel was not paralyzed in the process. "See? You're more controlled with your hands than just with looking at it. Well done. You should practice this skill any time there's no one around."

Next Rashel addressed shields; preventing someone else from reading her mind, or attacking her and to break past someone else's shielding her out. This came easier to Tanzaa, without the need for physical movement. But this also required her to understand the ethics of it.

"You should not generally go into someone's mind without permission, especially into their inner thoughts, unless it is a matter of life and death. This is most important with Dayvian because he will not be able to block you. He's not a magician. He'll practically be throwing his thoughts at you and you might be hurt by some of the things you'll hear from him. You have never been able to do this in your relationship before, and this has kept you equals but now that has changed. I don't want you to be hurt, or damage your connection with him because you hear things that...that show that he's a human being. Doubt, resentment, even jealousy will lurk in his mind. He's only human and all of us have these thoughts. It doesn't mean any of us act on them. He will still love you. Do you understand?"

"I form a wall, but Dayvian holds the gate key," Tanzaa replied in her analogy form.

"Exactly. Now, see if you can get through my wall," Rashel challenged her protégé. They spent an hour or so dueling mentally, trying to get past each other's barrier. In this process, Rashel learned a great deal about how Tanzaa thought and recognized the analogies were a means of coping with the stifling environment of a harem. Such a culture appalled Rashel's sensibilities, but she also took the time once she broke through Tanzaa's rudimentary shield to implant some desires for freedom and an understanding that Tanzaa's life in the Land would be far different for the better.

Once during this exercise, Tanzaa managed to catch Rashel with a deliberately open gap in her shield and let the dancer sense in her public mind the worry she harbored for Dayvian and how he would manage now that Tanzaa was magical. Rashel let her concern leap to what Dayvian would do without Tanzaa as his hope. That froze the new magician in sudden fear at what she heard in Rashel's thoughts. It drove Tanzaa to ask a question.

"No Dayvian?" Tanzaa's concern danced across her delicate features and spoke far more than the single comment. Overhead storm clouds crept over the sky, threatening thunder.

Rashel sighed. "I don't know. You will have to travel alone, no matter what. He will not be safe with you, and you will not learn independence while trying to protect him. It wouldn't be right for either of you."

Rashel waited for the tears she expected to come, but they didn't. Instead, Rashel felt a shiver and looked up at the swaying trees. They shuddered as thick gray clouds began building, threatening rain.

Rashel, with an eye to the building storm, added, "And the magic might simply pass him by."

Rashel could hear her protégé process that thought. The trees almost froze with sudden fear that the Queen of Growing Things sensed in the tension. Was lightning about to strike? Then as quickly as it built, the storm seemed to pass. In Tanzaa's mind, Rashel heard the fatal thought that maybe Dayvian would be better without magic. He should not be burdened with this terrible power.

Rashel blinked in surprise. This reasoned perspective, a balance of emotion and logic meant that Tanzaa was becoming a Wise One. Rashel added something more with caution.

"Also, Dayvian has done something terrible: refusing the magic and then forcing you into it, without your understanding or consent. That's not a good thing and he might be punished. I don't know for sure. He didn't understand the ramifications of what he did and I know he didn't do it to hurt you. There could very well be consequences, but not as severe as they could be."

Tanzaa's distress at that news translated into a cold drop in the temperature. The dancer gripped Rashel's arm in alarm. "No," she whispered in desperate futility.

"All will be well," Rashel tried to reassure her. "If anyone is meant to be a Wise One, it is Dayvian. However, you need to understand, if he is not chosen...again...to be a Wise One, then you will need to... you will leave him. It's the least cruel thing you can do. You are going to live forever, and he will not. The magic will naturally guide you to desire another Wise One. You will essentially fall out of love with Dayvian. If you allow him to hold on to his love for you, it will only crush his heart. This was what he feared and why he refused the Heart Stone when I offered it to him. He would not leave you willingly. Now you will face the same dilemma, but the decision is being made for you. You must leave him or he becomes a Wise One. Those are the only two options."

The expected tears now filled Tanzaa's silver eyes, but she

would not let them fall. Rashel could hear her rage and frustration leaking through her under-developed shields, but the harem-bred self-control mastered it. Tanzaa did not say anything. Instead, she took out her Heart Stone from her pocket. She stared in mute anger at the orb with disdain and a crystal blue sky and frigid weather overhead at midsummer.

This is all wrong, Dayvian thought. He was accustomed to the visitors who typically crossed the Demion court; soldiers, cooks, porters, priests, advisors, and occasionally a flock of courtesans passing through the courtyard like bright flowers in a wind. Now it was all armed or dark-robed men. Not a single bright color to be seen, even from the copious windows that dotted the elegant palace overlooking the courtyard. The soldiers all clattered around in full armor, which was not unusual, but their eyes flicked about the courtyard, far more alertly than Dayvian remembered.

"Could it be you're noticing them more because you know there's a reason for them to be on alert? You might just be more aware of it at this point," Yeolani suggested silently.

"No," Dayvian replied. "There are no women around and far more soldiers. Let's go to the residence and see we can learn there. I trust Tanzaa's best friend will share the news."

With that suggestion, Dayvian moved to the more pedestrian entrance to the palace proper, where supplies would normally be brought into the palace. Animals for slaughter, flowers in boxes, foodstuffs, and other supplies, probably for the wedding, crowded at the doors. More armed men met them at the iron gates that entered into the basement levels of the palace. Just beyond this gate, farther along the side of the courtyard, a huge wall made from a different stone stuck out away from the main palace and must have formed a separate space beyond it.

"Something reeks like a bilge full of rotting fish behind that wall," Yeolani commented. "It's demon magic."

"I already told you they have demons here," replied Dayvian. "The King and his court get their power from them, and that's probably where they do their sacrifices."

"Do you smell anything...I mean as a non-magical person?"

"It smells like a butchery," Dayvian muttered mentally. "What do you expect?"

Yeolani shrugged in a gesture that looked exactly like Carsin, whose face he wore. "To me, it burns, like someone's been making pickles and then set them on fire. I've smelled it before, but not so intensely. Does all the magic here in Demion come from demons?"

"How would I know? I do know the word for demon and the name of the country are related, almost too obviously," Dayvian explained. "Now will you let me concentrate? I'm going to have to speak Demian and I can't speak in one language and think at you in the other."

Dayvian didn't wait to be sure Yeolani was going to give him the peace he wanted. Instead, the musician walked up to the gated portal and got the attention of the guard with whom he was familiar.

"Greetings, Purnik, we're back. What's with all the soldiers? We've come from the circus to play, but today seems like a bad time."

The soldier came forward, looked closely at Dayvian and 'Carsin' through the heavy slatted gate. "Hello, gentlemen. No, it's just preparation for a wedding. I would have thought you heard. The circus was invited to perform, but it's not for two more days."

"Of course, I know about the wedding," Dayvian replied

flippantly, "but that doesn't keep me from coming around just like every summer. May I come in?"

Purnik was accustomed to the routine and let the two musicians in. He found a page to escort them through the labyrinth of the palace to the harem quarters on the far side of the palace proper, away from the demon fumes. That did little to ease Yeolani's sense of their proximity. The elegant halls were draped with tapestries of bloody battlefields and warped demon figures in the main passageways. These then gave way to decorative landscapes and still life paintings as they entered the ladies' wing. Yeolani noted at each door they passed a huge man standing guard and asked Dayvian about them. Each guardian boasted a head shaved bald, polished leather uniform, and each carried huge scimitars. These muscled sentinels watched them closely following with piercing eyes as they passed.

"Is having an armed man at every door typical. I would think the King would be worried about...you know...male guards in the harem, a fox in the henhouse."

"I don't think they qualify as men anymore," Dayvian replied in his thoughts. "They're eunuchs...if that's the word. I don't think we have them in the Land so we don't have a word for them. They've been...um...trimmed so they don't feel inclined to bother the ladies, if you know what I mean."

"Yes, I do. I'm learning a lot from this little adventure of yours," Yeolani commented sardonically. "I've got a gift for knowing before a storm breaks and I don't feel very good about this. What would it take to get out of here without drawing notice, before we get into the henhouse?"

"Not until I speak with Zamira, Tanzaa's friend. She'll know what's going on," Dayvian insisted, and indicated that they were almost there. This final door boasted not one but three eunuchs, all of them huge, bare-chested, and suspicious of two weakling musicians. "This time of the morning the ladies are gathering for practice in their various arts, and to socialize. It shouldn't take long."

The closer he got to the door, the more Yeolani disliked what he sensed. The bitter tang of demon infiltrated this part of the palace too, he noted. It felt like brewing thunderclouds before a tornado formed. When the page they followed indicated the door and turned to leave, Dayvian bowed low to the eunuchs. Yeolani followed suit, but it felt like he was bending to put his head on the block to have it chopped off.

One of the eunuchs knocked on the door for them and then turned to open the double passage. They were greeted by a wave of perfume and bright sunlight. The room, draped with gauze, included a vast covered balcony, open to a garden several stories below and shaded with lofty trees. In the chamber easily twenty women and girls looked up as the two musicians walked in. Yeolani noted that every one of them was perfectly gorgeous, all gracefully dressed in flowing gauze in bright summery colors. Each concubine was occupied in sedate, genteel activities; embroidery, writing, plucking at a harp, or reading. Their work was overseen by four more of the silent, glaring eunuchs who eyed the two musicians with suspicion. It seemed so ironic to have such beauty here mingled with the pungent smell of demon.

Several of the women rose, smiling at their approach, but their expressions were reserved like they feared to speak. Yeolani recalled the harsh punishment Dayvian had explained for anyone who spoke within the harem. Only one girl, probably seventeen, with thick dark hair in a complicated braid and a wearing a bright yellow tunic, now carefully set aside her sewing and rose to meet them at the door. She smiled charmingly at 'Carsin' who could just imagine she was infatuated with the real character. Given the surveillance and the situation, Yeolani only nodded politely. This must be Zamira, Tanzaa's friend. Being also a courtesan, Zamira didn't speak much either, but welcomed them with a feminine bow and then leaned in close.

"She's not here," was all she whispered before she invited Dayvian to take a stool at the center of the room where presumably he would play for the ladies.

It might be an act, but if so, Dayvian was good at it, Yeolani thought. Dayvian's eyes raced around the room as if seeking the one person whom he wanted to see. He tried not to look worried and took the proffered seat, while Yeolani awkwardly remained forgotten at the doors, hoping no one asked him to participate. Only Zamira seemed to notice him, but that could be because she cared for Carsin. Then Dayvian began tuning up his guitar and asking the ladies about how things were going since the last time he had visited. How was this going to help them get information if none of these ladies dared talk?

"So, I hear there's going to be a wedding soon. Who is the lucky lady?" Dayvian asked, keeping a cool face and strumming idly, just to distract the ladies into speaking. Perhaps his music was his spell.

"Lady Tanzaa," Zamira provided, and an echo of gentle murmurs complemented and confirmed. Yeolani noted how every single eye was down, looking at the floor or their work. That reaction then was what Dayvian was hoping to reveal. Either the ladies knew that Tanzaa had run away or they felt guilty because they felt bad for Dayvian, knowing his relationship with her. Accordingly, Dayvian let an 'accidental' twang emerge from his guitar as if this news stunned him and he was trying awkwardly to recover. Then he began in tune again and sang some delightful little ditty that spoke of nothing too distressing. No one believed his ruse.

The women applauded him politely when he finished, and

then Dayvian dared to play something a little more troubling, a lost love song, and all eyes were up, all other activities set aside to listen. So, these ladies knew about Tanzaa and Dayvian, and, they felt sorry for the impossibility of the relationship now with an impending wedding. From their unshed tears, few of the women seemed to suspect that Tanzaa had run away.

For his part Yeolani kept his eyes moving, wondering if he dared look at this room with a truth spell over it, but he knew better than to try. Too much magic and he would reveal himself. Any demon nearby would instantly sense it. Wearing Carsin's face as a disguise might already be too much. The eunuchs kept their piercing glares focused on him rather than Dayvian, even though it was the handsome young man with the guitar that should have been more a threat in a room like this.

Then Yeolani caught Zamira looking at him again. This time it wasn't a look of interest, but suspicion. She rose as if to approach Carsin and the abrupt scent of lavender nearly over-whelmed the room.

"Time to go," Yeolani warned with a silent burst of thought. Dayvian looked up from his song, played a final chord, ending the melody, and tried to nod subtly, but it was too late. It happened too fast.

Zamira unexpectedly didn't step forward but back, and abruptly grabbed a fistful of Dayvian's hair, jerking his head back and put a wicked knife to his throat. She had not held that knife before, Yeolani was sure. The alarm in Dayvian's eyes witnessed that he hadn't expected this either. Strangely, none of the other ladies reacted. They too knew this was a trap. The eunuchs refused to twitch but instead turned on Yeolani and drew their scimitars.

"He is ours, sorcerer!" Zamira hissed at Yeolani, effortlessly using the language of the Land. Her tone, so at odds with her genteel appearance, made Yeolani jump. "You bring back

Tanzaa or we'll make him the sacrifice." That must have been a demon within Zamira speaking; no courtesan would dare to speak so fiercely.

With their secret revealed, Yeolani recklessly threw a truth spell over the room, heedless of giving himself away. What he saw horrified him. Half the ladies in that room were demon controlled. To Yeolani's eyes, they carried a strange creature of some kind superimposed over their normal appearance. Bat mixed with a wolf, roach with cat, a snake with bird wings, it was a menagerie. Ten demons and four armed eunuchs would be something he might fight if it weren't for Dayvian. Yeolani knew he never would be able to deal with all the demons and weapons before that single knife at Dayvian's throat did the job.

"Go," Dayvian's mind shouted at him. "Take care of Tanzaa. I'll...I'll be fine."

"Wise Ones cannot lie," Yeolani warned him in a tight line of thought. "You'll have to get out of that bad habit. I'm putting a shield over you that will protect you and take them some time to break. I'll be back for you soon or Rashel will kill me."

Then Yeolani put up his hands, showing he was backing away, not challenging this den of demons. With a heavy heart but without further argument, Yeolani disappeared into the morning air.

5

TORTURED

*Y*eolani arrived at the grove in a shift of a shadow, stumbling in on them just as Rashel was teaching Tanzaa how to conjure something to eat. The two ladies rose to their feet in alarm, scattering the breakfast dishes Tanzaa had managed to produce.

Rashel immediately knew something was wrong; Yeolani never traveled magically if he could avoid it, especially since they weren't on the plains where he could jump from place to place without retching. However, Rashel didn't let her alarm show. Tanzaa was frightened enough without getting worked up about an emergency. Yeolani caught on that thought too before he straightened up and started to explain.

"Hello, ladies," he began slowly, waiting for his stomach to settle. "We've got a little problem."

"Dayvian?" the dancer asked.

Yeolani smiled reassuringly, welcoming the news that Tanzaa could at least understand what he was saying because they had just lost their translator. However, there was no way to soften the actual truth. Yeolani didn't bother with words. He pressed the memory of what had transpired in the garden room into both their minds. Tanzaa's eyes grew large with alarm as she watched her best friend roughly set a dagger at her beloved's throat. The vision also included what Yeolani had witnessed under the truth spell; demons and mists of evil.

"Those are demons to the women," Rashel supplied, unsure that Tanzaa would recognize what she was seeing. "Probably invited by a blood ceremony."

Abruptly overhead the noonday sun fell behind gray clouds with violent weather moving in from the north. None of them noted the distant boom of thunder or the wind beginning to pick up in the tops of the trees. Tanzaa's silvery eyes filled with pent up fury, but she still would not express her feelings. She wasn't shielding Rashel and Yeolani out of her thoughts, but the run of foreign words running through her mind was fierce enough. Her friend Zamira would not be forgiven for this. Tanzaa anger for Dayvian's sake raged and a fast-moving storm followed suit.

Yeolani chose to ignore the obvious emotion Tanzaa poured over the grove of trees. They needed a plan, not just emotions.

"So, I came here for reinforcements," he continued. "They probably didn't identify me as a Wise One, but they must have smelled magic on me because of my disguise. They know Tanzaa has run away, but not that she's a Wise One. Our mistake was in having Dayvian come to visit as if there was no connection between his arrival and her disappearance. They knew we were coming. Tanzaa, they want you in the worst way. Why? What's your value to them? You weren't even magical when the palace saw you last?"

Tanzaa didn't answer but instead trembled in repressed fear and anger. Neither emotion spilled past her shields, neither one preeminent, but the clouds still gathered threateningly and Yeolani noticed the lowering dark, the impending tempest, and connected the two things.

"Are you doing that?" he asked gently, and Rashel looked up, also noticing how the air tasted. The trees around the Queen of Growing Things sensed sudden alarm and warned her. Trees dreaded lightning and even if they weren't in the Land, the trees here still expressed their worry to Rashel.

"This storm is coming in counter to the wind," Rashel noted. "Tanzaa, you're controlling the weather. It's instinctive magic like when you froze us accidentally. You've got to tamp it down or someone is going to know where we are."

Tanzaa's silver eyes grew large with surprise, but she nodded, reached up into the sky, spread her fingers open and the gray began to lighten, grew less threatening, though the clouds did not dissipate completely. The wind settled and the alarm among the trees eased.

After the sky had lightened, Tanzaa looked at her mentors and simply replied to Yeolani's question. "The king wants my dancing." Then, following Yeolani's example, she closed her eyes in concentration to craft a memory. Tanzaa shared with them her memory of her branding ceremony six months before, at mid-winter.

"No, it's not only your dancing he wants," Yeolani replied as he shook away the horrible image. "You are the Queen of Storms. They wanted you for your magic. The court knew probably since you were a child, and they aren't going to let you go easily. They will use Dayvian to ensure you'll cooperate. They knew you would become a Wise One before you did."

Dayvian tried not to think of how horrible his life had twisted on itself in the last few months. First magic had taken his beloved from him when Tanzaa became betrothed to the King. Then Rashel had come and offered magic to him, though he didn't dare take advantage of it. Next, he had given the potential Wise One magic to Tanzaa, denying it for himself so she would be free, but he lost her anyway. Now the demon magic world had swallowed him whole. He would probably die as a demon sacrifice the very same way Tanzaa would probably have died if he had not started this whole cycle.

As it was, Dayvian had passed beyond fear. Zamira or whatever demon had taken over her, along with half a dozen eunuchs bodily toted him out of the harem room and unceremoniously dragged him down numerous flights of stairs. Oddly enough he didn't feel each step as they banged him down, or when they threw him into a dank cell. His guitar, they broke, smashing it deliberately onto the unforgiving stone floors.

But not him. Perhaps Yeolani's shield protected him from bruising as well as magical mangling. It was surreal to feel each blow and bruise but he experienced no pain from them.

When the prison door closed with a clang, Dayvian was left in the cold and dark with his thoughts. Questions teamed like ants through his brain. How long had Zamira been demon-possessed? How long before Yeolani launched a rescue effort? Could the Wise Ones even help him, given their restrictions when it came to starting incidents with other nations? Could Tanzaa master her magic and then defy Rashel and Yeolani if they weren't allowed to act. Dayvian felt reasonably sure that they would *want* to help him. He wasn't so sure they could succeed at it. How many demons were in that room? He hadn't dared look around with that knife up against his throat, so he had not seen them. From the reactions of all the harem women, most had been delighted by this sudden turn of events.

Dayvian vaguely recalled, in the middle of his fear, how laughter and cheering accompanied his rudely being dragged from the room. He could still feel the cold blade up against his throat held with inhuman strength. Zamira probably still had a hunk of his hair as a trophy. Sitting in the cold and damp of the cell, Dayvian began to realize how little he knew about magic. How would this pitiful situation pan out? Dayvian now regretted how he had done nothing yet with his life. If he had felt helpless earlier this spring, considering how he would try to rescue Tanzaa, he felt utterly hopeless now.

Well, at least he would catch up on his sleep.

Or so he thought. In the uncomfortable stone cell, it was difficult to fall asleep, no matter how exhausted he felt. And then when he finally managed to drift off, he was interrupted by the clang of the prison door opening. Dayvian started awake. A silhouette in the doorway of someone loomed far taller than Zamira and robed like one of the magicians that filled this palace. With the sudden light from a hallway torch blinding him, Dayvian cringed back. He had nowhere to escape when blood-stained hands reached around his neck and dragged him to his feet. That hand passed in front of his eyes and Dayvian was instantly plunged into darkness.

Blind?

That terrified him more than being sacrificed and he thrashed wildly against the monstrous grip around his neck. He wanted to at least see his death approaching. He yearned to see the sun again one last time, but he wasn't to have any of those options.

Again, someone dragged Dayvian throughout the palace like an overlarge load of laundry, bouncing bodily on the stairs, but he felt none of the abuse. Then he was thrown into a chair and his arms and legs tied down. He tried to speak with his captors, but after someone fetched him a vicious blow across the mouth, Dayvian thought better of it even though he didn't feel the pain. He could sense the blood running in his mouth and the loosening of his teeth stopped him from trying to reason with someone that vicious and cruel.

In his blindness, Dayvian found himself relying on his ears and other senses to help him understand what he now faced. For instance, only one person, probably the priest who had blinded him, remained in the room. He could hear the gentle swoosh as robes brushed around the stone floor. He could also smell blood -- the butchery he and Yeolani had discussed came to mind -- and Dayvian wondered why he hadn't yet been strapped to an altar and slaughtered. He felt the chill of a stone dungeon. No light or breeze from a window so this room probably was underground.

"I want the Lady Tanzaa, not you," the priest replied to Dayvian's private thoughts. Had the shield over Dayvian's mind already been breached? Or was the shield Yeolani put over him meant just for his body and not his mind. That voice, unctuous and low, sent a chill up Dayvian's spine. No, anyone could easily guess what the young musician was thinking. Dayvian expected to be sacrificed and this priest probably knew that too.

"Where have you taken her?" the priest continued.

Dayvian almost laughed. "Do you think I would have come back into the city, into the harem room if I had already run off with her? I don't know where she is. I came to Umzulio hoping to meet with her, not kidnap her." It was probably a good thing that he wasn't a Wise One right now, Dayvian thought privately. No matter what Yeolani said, Dayvian intended to lie copiously, although it was probably best to mix in a bit of truth to make it seem plausible. He might not be able to feel pain right at the moment, but torture would eventually break through the shield over him. Dayvian knew he would not be able to endure it forever.

"And of what value is she to you?" the priest continued.

Again, Dayvian almost laughed. "I would have thought that was obvious. What else does a man like me see in a gorgeous, talented, wonderful woman like Tanzaa? I'm in love with her, you idiot," and he heartily mocked the priest for not seeing that as a given.

"How dare you fall in love with a concubine of the House of Demion!" the priest shrieked, suddenly no longer reasoned and conversational. He fetched Dayvian such a blow across the head that his eyes smarted and ears rang. When he could sit up again, Dayvian grinned at the priest, even though he felt his mouth had started bleeding again.

"I couldn't help myself," he taunted the priest. The pain-blocking shield was making him foolishly cavalier and the wiser part of his brain knew he really shouldn't provoke these people. However, a separate part of him that expected to die at their hands felt the sooner the better. He must goad them into killing him so the Wise Ones wouldn't try a foolish rescue attempt. He knew Tanzaa was free, that Rashel and Yeolani would look after her, and that was the most he could hope for. Why not get himself beaten to death rather than chopped up in unspeakable ways to call demons into the world?

The priest seemed to have gotten himself under control again as well and began his questioning again. "Does she feel the same about you?"

"No idea," Dayvian replied. "But she didn't run away from *me*," taunted Dayvian. That comment got him another slap and he felt one of his teeth loosen completely.

"Very well, young man, I am told that you're quite a musician. Perhaps your good looks aren't of value to you, but what about your fingers?" Dayvian felt his right hand gripped where it remained bound to the arm of the chair. Someone spread his fingers out on the arm of the well-worn chair. Then he felt his index finger held in someone's iron grasp and the question was posed again.

"Where is Lady Tanzaa?"

Dayvian began talking under his breath, trying to reassure himself that he could do this. You're going to die anyway. Your musical career is over. You've lost your guitar and your freedom, so your fingers are nothing more. The circus will never take you back, even if he lets you go. You're going to die anyway. Dayvian chanted to himself, lying unsuccessfully and feeling a sick kind of dread in the pit of his stomach. But he had to say something, anything to provoke his torturer. Something to make him so angry no demon would be called with Dayvian's blood.

"I'm better known for my voice," Dayvian said carefully, feeling the wrench on his finger tighten a bit.

"Then you won't miss your fingers," came the chilling reply and Dayvian felt his finger smashed with a tremendous blow of a metal bar. It sounded like two or maybe three joints were crushed, but he couldn't feel the pain, except for the loss. He would never play again, he was sure, even if by some miracle he survived this torture and Yeolani managed to get him away from the sacrificial knife. That thought pained, but not as much as knowing that Tanzaa was lost to him as well. Despite himself, Dayvian felt his eyes welling up, not in physical agony but hopelessness.

Rather than wallow in that, Dayvian drew breath and shouted instead, tapping into a wave of anger that had been growing ever since he'd opened Tanzaa's letter months ago. "How can I tell you what I don't know?" he roared with all his vocal might.

"You can tell us her name," the priest added.

That question stopped Dayvian's fury cold, leaving only his surprise. "Her name? You know her name. She's Tanzaa."

The query bewildered the musician. Why would they need her name? What was this? Wait, he remembered, that one of the things Rashel had told him way back in the Land when they were packing the circus. Dayvian would have to leave behind his name if he took the Heart Stone. Rashel had insisted on his leaving his name behind. Names seemed important. He couldn't remember the particulars, but there was something vital here. Traditionally in Demion, many people were given long, elaborate names that they then shortened to a usable length.

"If you mean her long name, I can't help you. It's too long to remember," Dayvian added, realizing he might save himself some grief, for truly he didn't know Tanzaa's full name. The Demion people seemed to relish complicated and unpronounceable names for just this purpose; keeping them safe from demons. Dayvian might have heard Tanzaa's full name once, but trying to remember it was a wasted effort.

"Dayvian, tell me Lady Tanzaa's true name," the priest commanded, and he straightened out another finger on his already crushed hand.

"I don't know her name!" Dayvian shouted in fury, tears of rage pouring down his face. Let this monster crush every bone in my body, it wouldn't help.

The priest seemed to understand this and with a sigh announced, "Very well, the ceremony might not be the same, but the demon will be satisfied. A half-rate musician instead of a priceless magical dancer, it will be. You have until midsummer to reconsider. In the meantime, I will derive some pleasure from the efforts of the day."

With that, the priest continued crushing and mangling Dayvian's other fingers, one by one, with precision. The torturer didn't bother with more questions. He simply beat every finger with the bar while Dayvian wept over lost gifts. Since neither of them felt anything, it was just a futile exercise in control, and when he ran out of fingers to destroy, the priest left. Dayvian sat in his blindness, mourning his broken hands, his broken life, and the one bright point in his life.

6

DEMON WEDDING

*T*he plan had to work, Tanzaa thought.

She removed her shoes so she could tread silently down the cold stone steps of the inner passageway. She knew the dungeons would be below, but she had never personally wandered there before. At least Rashel had felt her skilled enough to do this reconnaissance alone. Tanzaa was the only one who could. She knew the palace. Yes, Yeolani felt he could make the trek back to the harem sitting rooms, but what would he do there? Listen in? He could not speak Demonian. And Rashel was using her gift with plants to oversee the preparations for a wedding turned execution. Was the king expecting Tanzaa to willingly return to him or was there going to be a sacrifice instead?

Wearing the invisibility she had recently mastered, Tanzaa slipped past the guards like a spring breeze. She felt her way down unlit corridors, reaching just ahead of herself for the minds of anyone she might encounter. This magical skill had taken some practice to master. At first, when she had tried the sensing of minds, she had come in hard as a hurricane. Anyone she encountered – usually Rashel or Yeolani—in the park ended up with a splitting headache for an hour after. Going invisible had been a simple skill compared to that.

After an intense day of practice, however, Tanzaa felt she could go into the palace, listen to the minds of others around her and learn what she needed to know; how Dayvian faired and what was the King's plan for dealing with him. Tanzaa could not bear to leave Dayvian there to be tortured, even if she never saw him again. Rashel and Yeolani seemed to agree wholeheartedly. They might worry privately about starting a war with Demion, but not right now. War was so far down her priority list, Tanzaa didn't even bother considering it. War might come later, and she would fight against her homeland with a fury reserved only for demons. Let war come, but they must rescue Dayvian.

Tanzaa hoped to save him, but she was under strict orders not to attempt to rescue him at this point. It had to do with name magic. If the king or any of his minions knew that Dayvian had been escaped, they would simply kill him with his name. Any sorcerer could do this, which was why Tanzaa's parents had given her a long name and then only used the shortened form. For Dayvian, the trick was to rescue him without the Demion court knowing he had been rescued, so they wouldn't bother using his real and well-known name. Thus, reconnaissance was her only mission now.

Tanzaa had reached the lowest floors underground. She sensed the cold iron doors and the heavy stone walls that dripped with the echoed pain from previous prisoners. She dared not make magical contact with any humans down here, especially Dayvian. There might be traps and snares set to catch her. She was to sense the entrapments and see if there were a way around them, not to trigger them.

All the cells were empty but one, as far as she was able to

sense. Tanzaa placed her hand against the iron door and stretched forth her senses. She steeled herself for what she might find there. Creeping her mind along the flagstones, she could sense no fewer than three lurking demons in the only occupied cell. They hovered around Dayvian, who lay curled up around his crushed hands on a bit of hay in the corner. Tanzaa yearned to curl up next to him, but the wisdom of the Wise Ones held her fast.

Instead, she tried to listen in on his dreams, to see if Dayvian were himself still, or if demons had made it past the shields Yeolani had provided him. No, without making an obvious effort, Tanzaa could not penetrate the shielding around Dayvian's mind. Therefore, the demons could not either. This was good news to a point. Dayvian was worth saving. She would not have to kill him to put him out of his misery. Instead, Tanzaa reluctantly withdrew her sensing back beyond the iron door and turned to weave her way out of the palace. They would get to try another way.

"We will have to let him die on an altar as a sacrifice to demons," Rashel insisted, pacing between the trees. They all three had returned from their explorations. "It is the only way to get him out of the palaces and into the open. We can make a rescue attempt then, and 'fail' and they'll never know."

Yeolani reported his findings. "Well, there's quite a musical ensemble practicing for something. They've got the harem rooms all busy, but it's only ladies that have no demons in them. All the other women were elsewhere. I wasn't about to go exploring for them. It sure seems they're planning for a wedding."

"The trees assured me that something is going afoot.

They've brought in flowers in the one courtyard, and are setting up chairs and a bower. But in the other courtyard, they're laying blood on the walls in some sort of pattern."

Tanzaa nodded. She knew the signs. Tomorrow at dawn was supposed to be her wedding day and Dayvian had been in the hands of demon priests for two interminable nights, unreachable behind magical walls. Hopefully, at dawn, those priests would bring him out for the wedding, to sacrifice him for the demon that would then enter some other girl they would bring out to be the King's wife since they didn't have Tanzaa. Or perhaps they had a trap for Tanzaa and would force her into the wedding that way. Nevertheless, at dawn three Wise Ones, planned to execute their rescue attempt during the festivities. Two nights in a dungeon and there would not be a third for Dayvian. He would either be dead or with her; of that Tanzaa was sure.

All of the Wise Ones knew their roles and they had planned this rescue mission carefully. Rashel and Yeolani encouraged Tanzaa to think carefully rather than react on pure emotion. When she got upset or angry, storm clouds tended to gather, and random cloudbursts had dowsed the trio in their hiding place in the park several times already. She needed to master these emotions and use them only at the right time. She also required absolute control over her shields or she would be more of a threat to the plan then an asset. Dayvian deserved her complete concentration and every effort she could give. Even if this was her last interaction with him, she would set Dayvian free.

The morning dawned bright, but the clouds came rolling in almost with the sun, as planned. Summer thunderclouds bristled on the horizon and appeared so naturally, rising white and bright. Then when they hit a certain height they leveled out into anvil shapes and began stacking gray and threatening. No one involved in the wedding planning thought much of the possibility of storms, other than the contingency of moving the ceremony indoors rather than in the lady's garden. Those planning the festivities had no way of knowing that the bride did not plan to attend anyway. The participants that knew this, the King's inner circle, they organized for a different ceremony in the next courtyard over from the garden. Its guest of honor was only going to come up from the dungeons below. Dayvian didn't even need special treatment for his portion of the proceedings.

The eunuchs woke Dayvian from a feverish stupor. Yeolani's pain shield still held strong, but Dayvian's body still reacted to the abuse and made him feverishly ill. Lack of food or meaningful rest did nothing to help his lucidness. Dayvian could sense his hands had doubled in size with the swelling and he couldn't have used them to eat even if he tried with his bloodied mouth. Then there were the nightmares that had plagued his feverish sleep. Demons attacked him constantly, clawing and scraping at Yeolani's shield and kept Dayvian frantic, panicking at each move of foot or brush of cloth as the priest kept returning. Dayvian felt mentally under attack and that proved worse than any of the physical abuse. The blindness only increased his fear. His fever dreams teamed with demons and great terror.

So, when the eunuchs came and untied him, lifting Dayvian to his feet, he almost felt relief. At last, something would end this nightmare and he would die or be free. The eunuchs didn't bother cleaning him up or speaking to him. They carried him under the arms with his feet dragging behind, up the many flights of stairs and out into a courtyard he recognized by smell. Somewhere afar off he heard music, pleasant and relaxing; music for a wedding, but it emanated from too far away to calm him, beyond his reach.

When the eunuchs arrived at their destination Dayvian was set on his feet, but the huge guards held him upright. Otherwise, he probably would have fallen out of spite or exhaustion. Then his main torturer, the priest approached Dayvian, pulled back his head, and must have passed his hand before the musician's blind eyes again. Suddenly the brightness of the summer morning flashed before Dayvian's eyes and he squinted painfully away from the light.

"I want you to see your fate coming," his torturer murmured into his ear, showing himself to Dayvian for the first time.

The priest could have been any of the men Dayvian had seen over the years crossing the Demion courtyard, robes aflutter, but this man's eyes were black as if he had been the one trying to see in the dark. The stains of blood permanently embedded in his nails spoke of what his service to the king entailed. While he didn't appear evil, Dayvian knew that looks could always deceive. Just beyond the priest, Zamira stood wearing the stunning silver and pearl-encrusted wedding gown that had been intended for Tanzaa. In her hand, Zamira gripped the same wicked knife she had held to his throat a few days earlier. Her hair swirled up in a complicated coif mingled with a veil over her delicate features. The smile on her face looked courtesan-correct, but she held the weapon expertly. She watched Dayvian like a cat would eye milk in a bowl. He almost expected her to yawn or lick her chops just to show something other than that simpering smile.

Dayvian cast his eyes wildly around the courtyard, knowing this wasn't where the actual wedding was planned. This four-walled, open-air prison boasted no flowers, sweet music, or chairs filled with guests. The music he noted earlier still emanated from the other side of the wall. Instead, a congregation of robed priests stood around the perimeter, muttering and humming. The head priest, Zamira, and the two eunuchs holding Dayvian upright made up the main attraction in this ceremony.

Just beyond his torturer stood a stone altar that reeked like a butcher's shop. Arcane markings were scrawled across it, written in ash or carved directly into the stone itself. That block of granite was big enough to hold his entire body and Dayvian abruptly felt himself go weak with fear.

Seeing his reaction, the priest smiled wickedly. "Shall we invite the bride to the wedding?"

Dayvian fruitlessly thrashed and kicked, still not wanting to be slaughtered this way. He wanted to die before he was carved up like a pig at the butcher. He had made every effort to goad his torturer into killing him before it got to this point and he had failed. Dayvian knew his courage had limits and this scene just ripped right through them. Spending hours in the dark he had tried desperately to prepare himself for this eventuality. Now he recognized he had failed here as well. Dayvian's wild flailing did nothing. The brute force of his captors overwhelmed his efforts and they picked him up, each taking one leg and one arm, pinned him on the altar, and began lashing him down with leather straps. A bloody rag went next down his throat to muffle his screams and he even missed his chance to bite someone.

Now looking up into the sky, spread eagle, Dayvian realized he wasn't even going to get to see the sun as he had hoped. He watched the gray, looming clouds building up, hiding the light, and threatening rain. The wind picked up and the trees seemed to sigh in regret just beyond the courtyard.

Without hope now, Dayvian stopped fighting with this final fate and instead began praying privately. Out of the corner of his eye, he saw Zamira, all in silver and pearl, step up to the altar but the flash of lightning in the clouds above helped distract him from that fearsome sight.

Suddenly lightning struck a spire atop the castle, just above the compound, accompanied immediately by rolling thunder. The flash might have blinded him, but Dayvian thought the white light remained high, up on the wall.

"Zamira!" a familiar voice shouted up on the tall barrier wall. Dayvian turned his head to see who distracted the courtesan with the knife. He only had a moment to register that he saw Tanzaa, also wearing her wedding dress standing on the wall, arms raised as if to welcome the lightning to strike her down. Then a second bolt flashed and Tanzaa was gone.

Were the Wise Ones trying to rescue him after all? Hope made Dayvian thrash again, trying desperately to free himself from the iron grip of the eunuchs and their leather straps. However, he remained hopelessly pinned. The priest, undistracted by the interruption, approached from the other side and ripped Dayvian's filthy shirt open to the waist, exposing his chest. Then the demonic priest began chanting in some unknown tongue. Meanwhile, Zamira mastered herself, ignoring the challenge Tanzaa was giving her, and she now approached the altar and stood close on the other side, leaning down enough to whisper seductively in Dayvian's ear.

"She can't save you," she whispered. "I have your name."

That realization brought a new disturbance to mind; names again. What was so important about his name? The gentle, sweet touch of Zamira kissing him on the cheek threw his already overwhelmed senses beyond thought.

Then another flash of lightning brought Tanzaa to the other side of the courtyard, bristling in a wind that blew across the stained stones. "Zamira!" she shouted over the echoing thunder. When had Tanzaa ever shouted?

Zamira ignored the repeated threat and raised the knife

above her head. Dayvian watched the sharpened blade rise, and then closed his eyes, waiting for the blow to fall, at peace knowing he had seen his beloved in her power. Queen of Storms, he thought with a strange joy.

Dayvian heard the knife drive home, but not into his own heart and he had to look. Zamira stood over him, eerily like his nightmares, with the dagger plunged into her own heart, pouring red over the bright embroidery of her gown. It gushed over him as well. Zamira smiled down at him. "To release my demon into you, my dear," she said haltingly and then collapsed over him, covering him with her dead body and blood.

Something inhuman shrieked out of Zamira's corpse but Dayvian lost sight of it in the flash of lightning and rumble of thunder. Then Tanzaa's power struck again. She appeared at the head of the altar, resplendent also in silvery white. The priest, now holding a second knife up high, knew his time was short when Tanzaa's hand reached out toward Dayvian, about to touch him on the head, about to steal him away. Instead, the priest's voice was faster than the knife. "Dayvian, die."

Obedient to his name, Dayvian did as he was told: he died. He just stopped breathing, with his face to the sky, not seeing Tanzaa there to rescue him.

Tanzaa knew this would happen, but seeing Dayvian's dead blue eyes staring in terror up at the sky still shook her. She didn't try to control her grief. Instead, she funneled her tears into the storm above the city, forcing it to erupt, bringing rain down in sheets, washing away Zamira's blood from the altar.

To add to Tanzaa's horror, with a joyful look, the priest nodded toward her. "He's mine now," he chimed.

With unspeakable fury, but a gentle hand on her beloved's

head, Tanzaa surged magically and threw Dayvian's body, altar, and everything touching it toward the quiet place on the plains that the Wise Ones had prepared for this confrontation.

Unfortunately, the eunuchs, the priest, and even Zamira's body went with Dayvian too. The abrupt change of venue confused the three living men for a moment so they weren't prepared when Yeolani met them with his sword. He cut them down the instant the strange delivery arrived under storm-free skies over a thousand miles away. One dead priest and two eunuchs cut in half. Then Yeolani did a quick search to see that Zamira's demon had not been transported with Tanzaa's rescue. He saw nothing evil lingering when he placed a truth spell and so he pulled the body of the concubine off Dayvian. Finally, Yeolani signaled the all-clear to Tanzaa and Rashel who remained back in Umzulio.

The two women emerged from their magical shift to stand next to Yeolani. Rashel arrived still wearing Tanzaa's face, for she had been the one hopping about the palace, taunting the wedding guests, frightening servants with sudden appearances. The real Tanzaa had managed the storm. Now Rashel changed her appearance and then surveyed the damage. With a flick of his hand, Yeolani made the bodies of Zamira, the priest, and the two eunuchs disappear into the prairie grass, buried in this unmarked place. Then the ground swallowed the altar itself, leaving them to kneel around the remaining body; Dayvian's.

"You understand why we had to let him die," Rashel asked Tanzaa carefully. "They had to think that he was gone or they would simply do this again; kill him with his name."

Tanzaa's face was tear-streaked and ashen, but she nodded, brushing her hand gently over Dayvian's unseeing eyes, closing the stare away from the sky. Then she drew her fingers through Dayvian's hair, asking the question with her eyes. His normally dark brown hair had changed completely to snow-white.

Yeolani speculated, "I think the demons working to get past the shield did that to him. It happened to Owailion, the first of the Wise Ones as well. It isn't an old man's hair, just...just the experience."

"Are you ready? You wrote your letter?" Rashel asked, looking more to Tanzaa's emotional state than the poor condition in which Dayvian had been left. "Honiea is ready when we call."

With Tanzaa's nod, Rashel rose, conjured a thick white candle in her hand, lit it, and then held it high. Honiea, Queen of Healing would come to such a signal, especially to someplace so far away from other human habitation. They had selected this place on the prairie because no one was likely to find them here; not a magician, a demon, or even a wandering shepherd. The grassland emptiness suited them all for this sad piece of magic they must now invoke.

Momentarily Honiea arrived in the flicker of the candle and Tanzaa arose to greet this new Wise One. The Queen of Healing looked like a simple, pleasant woman, with her honey-colored hair, freckles, and common clothes, but she also took her work very seriously. She didn't ask for an introduction to Tanzaa. Instead, she knelt in the grass and began to survey Dayvian's broken body.

"What happened to him?" she asked frankly.

Yeolani explained. "He was tortured by the sorcerers of Demion after I had put a shield on him, which means he didn't feel the pain. He was held for two days in their dungeons. Then they used his name to kill him, but they always planned to sacrifice him. Most of the blood on him isn't his."

Honiea didn't look surprised, but picked up one of Dayvian's crushed hands and gently passed her own hand over it. A look of pain crossed Honiea's face as she closed her eyes and concentrated. "He grieved for this," she murmured as she must have looked back to magically witness exactly what happened.

"He's a musician," Tanzaa added helpfully, miming strumming a guitar.

Honiea smiled and nodded. "Then I shall have to be especially careful with my repairs. You are the new Wise One then? Tanzaa?"

"Tanzaa...Queen of Storms?" she introduced herself tentatively and then turned her attention once again to Dayvian, hating every bit of this. She felt ill just to look at the pain and damage inflicted on someone she loved.

"Well, Queen of Storms, you are a Seeking Queen, so this gift is yours and yours alone. I have here a Life Giver." Honiea pulled a little creature from her pocket, a purring bundle of fur without mouth, eyes, or limbs, but it rolled about in her palm, anxiously trembling in excitement. "Only a Seeking Wise One may use them to bring a soul back from Limbo. I may repair his body but only you can replace his soul. You must touch the Life Giver and then give it to him, calling him home. Are you ready to do this?"

Tanzaa had already considered the ramifications of this decision when she, Rashel, and Yeolani had begun planning their rescue. They knew that Dayvian's name would probably be used to kill him if he weren't sacrificed on the altar. The true dilemma had been whether to bring him back to life at all.

Either one drowned or they both drowned.

It had been Tanzaa's analogy for him accepting the magic of the Heart Stone to rescue her from an unspeakable fate. If he tried to rescue her by taking the Heart Stone himself, he might have successfully rescued her from marriage to a demon, but then she eventually would die of old age and he would live forever without her. Now she was faced with the same question, but with her being the survivor. Was it merciful to let their relationship die now, or fifty years in the future, after she had found another Wise One and her love for Dayvian had faded? Or should she let him move on in death to his final reward, burying with him the memory that she had loved him and that she had tried to rescue him?

"Life," Tanzaa said simply, holding on to her whisp of hope. She dreamed of finding him a Heart Stone, knowing that it could be a bitter pill if she failed.

Honiea nodded, accepting her decision and handed the Life Giver to Tanzaa. She took the creature, petted it briefly, and then set it under Dayvian's crushed hand, over his stilled heart. Then, with a heavy heart of her own Tanzaa rose, brought out a letter she had written to Dayvian, and gave it to Yeolani. She couldn't remain here, not even to see the Life Giver's handiwork. She didn't think she could leave him behind if she saw Dayvian alive again. So, she started walking off onto the plains with Rashel solemnly following after her. Tanzaa was going Seeking for a Heart Stone.

If Dayvian awoke, the only way they would cross paths again would be as equals; as Wise Ones.

7

LAUNCHED

*D*ayvian awoke to the strangeness of the unknown. Where was he? Was this Paradise? Had he died or was he still with the circus having just experienced the most vivid dream of his life? Where was Tanzaa? He peered blearily at a vaulted ceiling elegantly carved into what appeared to be marble. He lay on a bed, rich with red covers and a down mattress deeper than a bath. Where was he?

Then Dayvian remembered and held up his hands experimentally before his eyes. He recalled the breaking of his bones and saw no evidence that he had ever been tortured, let alone killed. He experimented by running his hands through a series of imaginary chords and scales and found nothing pained him. He had no idea how. He knew his hands had been crushed. Had magic restored him? If so, again, where was Tanzaa? Warily he attempted rising, sitting up in the bed so he could explore his surroundings a bit better.

The room, including the incredible ceiling, seemed fit for a king. A carved and polished mahogany table and chairs, accented with ivorywood stood to one side as if he would be welcome to eat or write in this room. Beyond it, an ivorywood tub waited to be utilized. Beside it stood buckets of water warming at a fireplace, with a low fire. Finally, beside the hearth, he saw a matching mahogany wardrobe with one door waiting open, with towels and what appeared to be a set of clothes that were meant for him.

Well, no one ever said he couldn't take an invitation. Dayvian slipped slowly out from under the covers, moving with incredible stiffness. If this was a dream or Paradise, he didn't imagine he would have been moving like an old man. He hobbled to the tub and took a bath that could have been a sinful luxury. He soaked longer than he should have and the water grew cool before he got out. At least it had done its magic and he could move better when he climbed out.

Still, he had no answers. Where was he? He had no memory of this place. Where was Tanzaa? How long had he been...been whatever he had been? Was this Demion's King pulling a trick on him? These thoughts drove Dayvian to finally move more quickly and reach for one of the towels.

In the wardrobe, he saw something that stopped him cold. On the door hung a mirror and in it, he saw himself and how he had changed. His familiar brown hair, longish, slightly curled, in need of a trim, had gone completely white. It made his blue eyes stand out piercingly, and his summer tan seemed alien. What had happened to him? Experimentally Dayvian ran his fingers through the damp strands but they felt the same as ever. Magic must be to blame, but he couldn't figure out how or why this was done to him. Still, with no answers, Dayvian hurriedly dressed in the simple blue trousers and linen tunic hanging in the wardrobe but before he could look around for his boots, he saw something else in the back of the wardrobe that stopped him in wonder more than his white hair.

A beautifully simple guitar made of blonde wood with a

fine finish and wrapped brass strings waited for him. He had never seen its like. Dayvian almost hesitated to pull it out for fear of coveting it and then discovering it was not meant for him. This must be Paradise, he thought, for no one could have given him a more fitting gift. Except for Tanzaa's hand in marriage. Who would know him so well? Irresistibly he slung the strap over his shoulder and felt the instrument's fit. He wouldn't have been able to select anything better for himself had he been given a whole world of guitars. He set his fingers experimentally on a simple E7 chord and listened to the mellow tone, perfectly in tune. Then he moved to an F, a more complicated chord, more demanding of his magically healed fingers. He was not disappointed.

A knock at the door startled Dayvian out of his fascination with the instrument. Had someone heard him? Not letting go of the guitar he went to the door and opened it a crack, fearful of what awaited him there. To his surprise, Yeolani stood on the other side grinning like he had a secret he could not wait to share. Dayvian opened the door farther and would have motioned Yeolani into the fabulous room, but Yeolani stopped him.

"You've got to be hungry enough to eat a whole prairie beast. Come on, Vamilion is waiting for us. Bring the guitar," he reassured him, and Dayvian didn't object. At the mention of food, he heard his stomach rumble and realized he was indeed hungry.

Feeling foolish about going barefoot and still carrying the precious guitar, Dayvian followed his guide out into the hall. They moved down a spiraling labyrinth of stairs, all of them lined with statues and carvings in marble that caught the eye and bespoke of powerful magic. He followed Yeolani, over-whelmed by the twists and turns, stairs, doorways, and hallways, feeling like he would be lost forever if he didn't have his friend guiding him.

"Where exactly are we?" Dayvian asked, thinking mostly to protect the guitar from bumping into something.

"I told you, Vamilion," the Wise One replied.

"I thought Vamilion was a person...the King of the Mountains, not a place," Dayvian admitted.

"In this case, it's a place, and the person is named after it. Wise Ones try not to go by our real names. That's what got you killed, remember?"

Dayvian shook his head in wonder. "I...I don't remember. So, you're not Yeolani, you're just named after a place called Yeolani? I don't understand why you have to be named something else. That priest...that priest that killed me, he was very interested in Tanzaa's name too."

Something in that comment made Yeolani alarmed enough to halt on the step and Dayvian almost plowed into him. "You didn't give it to him, did you?" the Wise One asked with an intensity that belied Yeolani's usually playful nature.

Dayvian sputtered, "No, I don't know it...or if she did tell me once, I wouldn't be able to pronounce it. What is it with names?"

Relieved, Yeolani started back down the staircase as he explained. "If a sorcerer is powerful enough, he can take your real name and command you to do anything. You might not have noticed it, but Rashel got you to share the story about your relationship with Tanzaa by using your name. That was a pretty benign use of the power, but in the hands of a demon or a sorcerer, you can be commanded to do some pretty despicable things. When he realized Tanzaa was going to snatch you from him, the priest commanded you to die, using your name."

Dayvian let his face express his confusion. "Names have that kind of power?"

"Names have that kind of power. That sorcerer commanded you to die and so you did."

That realization made Dayvian pause in surprise. Thankfully that was also the point where Yeolani was leading him and the Wise One opened a final door into a chamber where supper awaited them. Their host rose from the simple wooden table to greet him. Vamilion was a huge, solid-looking man with roughened hands and a warm smile. It surprised Dayvian, but his host was almost middle-aged, and here he thought Wise Ones didn't grow old.

"I took the Heart Stone later in my life," Vamilion said simply to the thoughts he must have overheard in Dayvian's head.

Embarrassed, Dayvian apologized. "I'm sorry, this magical world is very new to me. I'm constantly amazed at what I don't know. Thank you also for your help. How did I come here."

"We will tell you the tale while you eat," replied Vamilion and peeled the guitar from Dayvian's hands, setting it aside so he could address the meal that had been prepared. How they had known Dayvian was awake and could have the meal hot for him, he didn't know, nor did he care. Dayvian ate like it was a new trick, wolfing down dishes he hadn't explored before and loved it all. Meanwhile, Yeolani explained all that Dayvian had missed.

"While you were directly under the control of the Demion guard, down in their dungeons, we could not help you. You were guarded too well with traps and demons. But Tanzaa was learning her magic that whole time. She learned to become invisible and infiltrated the palace. She discovered where you were being held and that it wasn't going to work to get in there to do our rescue. We would have to wait until they brought you out. The King was still going ahead with that farce of a wedding. Maybe he held on to the idea that Tanzaa would turn herself over to them to save you. Either that or they were going on with the wedding to mask their failure to the guests. The king had his reputation, you know. We were reasonably sure that they would bring you out as a part of the wedding. They wanted to draw Tanzaa out to rescue you and perhaps capture her at that time. What they didn't realize was how magically powerful she is now. She's the Queen of Storms, climate, and such. When she's upset, the weather goes insane, so we used that."

Dayvian found he had stopped eating just to listen to the story. His Tanzaa was Queen of Storms? It didn't seem to fit her. Tanzaa was so self-controlled. How would the magic of storms express itself? He could remember lightning and thunder during that blurry morning when he was being sacrificed, but he didn't recall storms helped with his rescue.

Yeolani must have recognized his confusion. "We knew that even if we rescued you from being sacrificed, the sorcerers would kill you using your name. You never knew to keep it secret. The Demians are aware of name magic and routinely give their children horribly long names that they can then shorten so that no one knows their real name."

"So that's why the long, convoluted name. Tanzaa knew not to share it with me? She knew I would blab?" Dayvian speculated.

Yeolani chuckled and then continued his tale. "We needed the Demians to think they had succeeded in killing you. Rashel, wearing Tanzaa's appearance, went hopping all about the palace, appearing and disappearing with every flash of lightning. This got most of the sorcerers in the court involved in chasing her down. Tanzaa only had to concentrate on two things; keeping the storm going as a distraction and she needed to listen for when to come to get you. She could hear and understand the thoughts of your executioners. I really must to study that language. Well anyway, Tanzaa understood when the time was right to pull you away from them. She had to be there just in time - before they sacrificed you and let in the demon but soon enough for them to rush and kill you with your name. They had to know you were dead so they won't ever use your name against you again."

Well, that seemed to make sense to Dayvian in an awkward way, but why was he still alive? The Wise Ones must have had a way to bring him back as part of the plan, he thought.

"We did, obviously," Vamilion picked up the narrative. "My wife, Honiea is the Queen of Healing. Many years ago, she crafted a special way to call souls back from the dead as long as the body was still intact. It only works when a Seeking Queen or King uses it...Wise Ones not fully trained, like Tanzaa. She used this Life Giver on you and brought you back from the dead."

Dayvian had put his fork down again, trying to remember what had happened. His last memory before waking up here in Vamilion's sprawling house was of lightning and someone touching his head. That and the sorcerer telling him to die.

"Is that where the white hair comes from; being dead?" he asked, bewildered, running his hand self-consciously through his hair.

"We don't think so," supplied Yeolani. "We think that came because of the demon that was trying to get past the shield I set on you before you were taken. They must have been clawing at you for hours, a side effect of the shield on someone nonmagical. I'm sorry."

"I'm not sorry," Dayvian assured him. "It's kind of...roguish. It makes me seem artistic like a musician is supposed to be. Thank you, by the way, for the shield. Feeling no pain, that's what allowed me to get through it. He crushed my fingers." Dayvian paused and held up his hands, critically judging them, feeling the memory, missing the agony of them being mangled, but also feeling overwhelmed by the emotion he should have at recalling that torture.

"And are you able to play now?" asked Vamilion. "Honiea was very careful repairing your hands when Tanzaa told her that you were a musician."

"Oh, yes. And thank you for the guitar. It's exquisite. Was that your magic or..."

"Mine," Vamilion confirmed. "I'm a craftsman of sorts and I could not resist the challenge to work in wood on something so beautiful. I hope you like it."

"Like it!" chuckled Dayvian. "With this, I could leave the circus and make my way as a bard. I only wish..." The Wise Ones easily heard his thoughts that now followed that, though he didn't say them aloud. *If only Tanzaa were here, I could play for her and she would dance and we could change the world.*

Finally, he had to ask the one thing they had not volunteered; where was Tanzaa? To his unspoken thoughts, Yeolani brought out a letter, sealed and bearing his name in Tanzaa's graceful script. "She left this for you," the Wise One said as gently as possible.

Dayvian took the letter and noted to his annoyance that his hands were trembling. He steadied his breath, forcing his fingers to remain still and carefully broke the seal. He opened one final letter from the woman he had loved most of his life. He recognized her handwriting and knew he was going to not like what he read.

My Dearest Dayvian,

I am now called to go Seeking. Rashel is with me so I am safe at least. You know what I seek. I will find your Heart Stone. I will find a way for us to be together. Please do not look for me. It's too painful. Until the day we can come together as Wise Ones, please learn all you can about Heart Stones. They are the key to us. Somewhere in this vast world, there is a Heart Stone that belongs to you, I know it. We are meant to be together, but I will not seek for you until there is a Heart Stone for you, this I swear. Until that day, I love you. Tanzaa

Dayvian's hands began trembling again as he carefully reread the note. He folded it back up, putting it under the strings of the guitar for safekeeping. Later, when he had acquired a case, he would keep it even safer there, but until that time, it would do. At the moment he was still trying to reflect on how he felt. Abandoned seemed the aptest word. Why hadn't she at least stayed behind to be sure he recovered? Why couldn't he travel with her if they were both Seeking Heart Stones? Deep down he knew the answers but he didn't want to admit it.

She couldn't risk falling more in love with him if there was no magic for him.

Vamilion added to what Dayvian dare not think. "She must go her own way. She would be too concerned about your safety. There will be great danger for any non-magical person while she Seeks. She has never been on her own and must discover much through the trials she undergoes. Tanzaa cannot do this with you. And if another's name calls for her, she will not wish to break your heart, but she will. This is the best this way...the only way."

"How can you say that?" Dayvian tried to speak with a steady voice, but it only came out sounding bitter and resentful.

"I know because it happened to me," Vamilion admitted with equal bitterness. "When you first saw me, you thought I was older than you expected of a Wise One. In a way, I was. When Owailion gave me the Heart Stone I already had a wife and two children. I took the stone because we were under attack and I was desperate for the magic to protect us. Later, after I learned what it meant to be a Wise One, I regretted it.

For years I refused to leave...to leave my wife, the mother of my children. I was still in love with her. But she aged, grew sick, and I couldn't stop it. I remained as I am now and it slowly crushed our love. I refused to go Seeking for Honiea, denying her existence since I kept hoping that my wife would be selected to be a Wise One. I was wrong to do that to both of these wonderful women. I suffered right along with them. Perhaps your situation will be different, but Tanzaa, I don't think, will do that to you."

Dayvian lowered his head and could not think about anything but Tanzaa: not his miraculous restoration, the wondrous guitar, or the amazing luxury around him. He struggled to hold back the emotion that threatened to break him down. Instead, he slowly lifted the guitar, removed the letter from the frets, and began to play. He did not set his notes to a melody, but instead just let the mellow, sad strumming give him a voice. He had much to think on and too much to mourn over to ever manage words. Notes and chords would do for now.

8

WISE ONE LESSONS

*T*anzaa grieved and the rain fell. Although she felt grateful to be free of Demion's king, and she had rescued Dayvian, these victories did nothing to lift her spirits or the cloud cover. Tanzaa, along with Rashel as her teacher, rode horses they had conjured, across the empty landscape. The open plains where Demion met with the desert areas of northern Marwen, held no interest for Tanzaa, and she grew restless with riding in the miserable weather.

"If you stop it raining, we won't have to be so terribly wet," Rashel chided. "You're the Queen of Weather, do something about it."

Tanzaa obediently raised her arm to the cloud cover but all she got was rivulets running down her arm, inside her sleeve. She failed to persuade the clouds to leave. That inability to keep her emotions out of her magical work only exacerbated her anger...which showed up in the thicker clouds. Only when Rashel distracted her with a different challenge, did she manage to keep them dry.

"Can you sense the Wall from here?" Rashel asked. "It forms the southern border of the Land and it's manned, so you should be able to read some of the men in the garrison there before we arrive."

After trying and failing again, Tanzaa said nothing, but a spike of lighting, not a mile ahead of them on the trek made her admit it. "I cannot. It's too far."

"I disagree. You are just as powerful as I am. I've been able to hear them for days. You aren't using what you have. I listen to the plants nearby them and they then relay it to me. What can you listen to so that you can hear the minds of the men at the garrison?"

Tanzaa had not considered that. "The clouds?"

"Perfect," Rashel encouraged her. "Listen to them and ask them to listen in on the men. If it's not raining, they should be out-of-doors training. See if you can hear through that."

Tanzaa directed her thoughts toward the gloomy sky, and then, remembering movement helped her, she stretched out her hand toward the northern horizon. She could sense the piling and lifting movements of the storm front where the clouds danced. Strangely, that comforted her. She yearned to dance with them. She wanted to rise above them and feel the relief of lightness, to not care about the plodding, earth-bound men. She wanted to forget her grief for Dayvian.

"You can command the clouds," Rashel whispered far away. "Can you make them curious to listen in to the men on the Wall?"

Silly men on the Wall, Tanzaa thought. The clouds lowered, almost sinking into a fog, and suddenly Tanzaa could hear the men on guard duty, clustered around the fire-pits. The guards grumbled about the damp and how out of season it seemed.

"Bad times are coming," she heard and relayed it to Rashel. "Never seen such miserable weather. It's a bad omen."

"I don't believe in omens. There's no such thing. It's just the last bit of spring," replied another.

Tanzaa pulled her awareness out of the sky and looked over at her Wise One companion. "Do people in the Land not even believe in magic?"

"You did very well if you heard that," Rashel commented. "No, many do not believe. Why would they? All they may witness is Honiea's healing. Perhaps Vamilion has helped with rock cave-ins. I work with farmers all across the Land, but they never see me perform grand magic for them. I just encourage their crops to grow, as they would anyway. Yeolani, his work is mostly with the animals of the plains, not the people."

"That is not good," Tanzaa replied frankly but did not elaborate.

Rashel looked at her quizzically. "Explain," she ordered.

"A child can learn if there is a school. Shouldn't they go to school?"

"Not an analogy. Explain yourself," insisted Rashel.

Tanzaa sighed. This wasn't her favorite part of being a Wise One, but she would have to learn to speak up. "If you have this great magic, shouldn't the Wise Ones teach the Land about it?" Tanzaa continued. "All the other countries, Marwen, Malornia, Demion, have their magic from spells and demons. The Land does not. Magic for us is....deeper water? If we do not teach the people of the Land, they will drown rather than learn how to swim with the magic. They will not trust us to teach them to swim. Do the farmers know how to call you for help if their crops are failing?"

Rashel looked over at Tanzaa with a smile. "That's the longest speech I've heard you give yet. And a good explanation.

Yes, I agree with you. We need to teach the people of the Land that they can rely on magic here because it is good magic. However, many people emigrated from those other countries. They fled here to escape the spells and demons and they brought their mistrust of magic with them. We do not want to frighten them away from our help."

"Magic should not be frightening," Tanzaa insisted.

By dusk, the two women had reached the passage into the Land, at the southern tip of the Wall. "Should we stay here at the garrison tonight and talk to some of the men you listened in on?" Rashel asked.

Up until then, during the three days they had taken to ride out of the frontier of Marwen, they had camped. Now, entering populated areas, they might be able to stay at inns and interact with people.

Tanzaa didn't reply. She was too distracted by her first look at Dayvian's homeland, the homeland she was now sworn to protect. On her right stood the Wall, a great thick barrier as tall as the trees of Demion. The Wall traced toward the northeast and off the horizon. On her left stood a blunt and bare tower of black stone. This rather ugly fortress almost blocked the view of the Don River spreading out, flat and winding. The river delta met with the sea about a league farther on. However, the most striking feature was the graceful palace that stood in the middle of the river.

The white, gleaming castle and gardens almost filled a shallow island in the middle of the river delta. Its walls were crafted of honed marble, with faceted spires and richly carved, green slate doors. Great gardens, sculpted and filled with all variety of trees lined the island. The palace's lofty tower was lost in Tanzaa's gloomy clouds, and she hastily dispelled them just to see the top of the spires. A long green banner, with a silver arrow as its emblem, drifted in the air from the tallest pinnacle.

"It is called Right," Rashel explained of the garrison, deliberately ignoring the beautiful palace beyond it. "Owailion, the first Wise One built it to guard the flank of the Wall and to watch the river."

"No, what is that?" Tanzaa asked, pointing toward the palace.

"Oh," said Rashel. "That might be yours. Owailion made it as well. Each of the Wise Ones has a home like it. I didn't want to tell you about the palace until you saw one for yourself. That is another reason we do not rule the people. They already think of us as leaders, when we come and go from such grandeur. Do you sense anything here?"

"Sense anything?" Tanzaa echoed. "No, it's beautiful, but what am I supposed to feel?"

Rashel nodded her understanding. "One of the many things you Seek as a Wise One in training is for your home. This one is for the King or Queen of forests, we are sure. That person has not been found yet, but the decorations on the walls are all about trees."

"Trees?" Tanzaa looked around at the scenery and saw nothing but more prairie, as far as the eye could see. Other than the gardens on that island, it seemed as if there had never been a tree for leagues in every direction.

"Yes, once this area was a great forest, but now little remains. As Queen of Growing Things, I cannot understand why it died off. Owailion remembers it, but I doubt he will explain."

"Owailion? He made these palaces, didn't he?" Tanzaa could conjure things with her power now, but mostly she had created food for their trip and equipment for traveling using this skill. She could not imagine conjuring a huge building, larger than the fortress at Umzulio.

"It was one of his Seeking tasks, to make palaces for the rest of us. As the first Wise One, his tasks were far different than ours. He wasn't really Seeking so much as Creating. That is why he is called the King of Creating."

"How...How can he do that...so beautiful. No, I am not the Queen of Trees....and what is that?"

A column of soldiers marched out of the dark garrison tower and turned their march toward the ladies. These guards carried spears and swords that flashed in the twilight. Then they halted within a spear-throw, forming a tight line to block the path before the two ladies who halted their horses. The confrontation was obvious.

"Tanzaa, you get to manage this. It's your first interaction with citizens of the Land. If you feel it necessary to introduce yourself as a Wise One and help the people know they can rely on our magic, now is your opportunity."

"It is their task? To challenge any who enter the Land?"

Rashel nodded and then added, "If you want them to know you as a Wise One, you can put yourself into that costume from when you were in the park. All white, with the silver embroidery. Just surge in your magic."

Tanzaa looked over at Rashel with alarm in her eyes but then smiled with a hint of devilry. "Like being on a stage, preparing to dance."

She then did as Rashel suggested, surging by thinking of all the things a Wise One could do as if she would conjure a hurricane. Her sturdy traveling clothes shimmered into a long silver gown that draped over the back of her steed. White stitching made the bodice so stiff she doubted she could dance in it. The platinum bracings on her arms seemed the same, twining like a whirlwind up to her shoulder, and her hair was held back with diamond and pearl pins under a swirling gauze veil. She looked as if she wore the storm above her head.

The soldiers, as they saw her transform, staggered to a halt. They formed a barricade, spears at the ready, and then their leader marched a little in front of the two ladies.

"Halt and declare yourselves," he commanded.

"I am Tan..." but she could not finish the sentence. Abruptly she remembered that a Wise One could not lie, not even about their name. This did not fluster her. "I am the Queen of Storms, a Wise One of the Land," she declared.

Beside her, Rashel had also transformed her garb to a green silk gown, replete with ivy embroidery and roses in her rich hair. "You may call me Rashel, Queen of Growing Things."

The dozen or so uniformed men began murmuring. They looked at each other nervously, waiting for their leader's orders on how to react.

"We are magicians, sworn to protect the Land," Tanzaa continued. "We seek to return to our duties. Please let us enter." Then she let her magic fade and she returned to her traveling costume instead.

The guards muttered more, of witchcraft and spells, but their captain did not seem so alarmed. "I have heard of Honiea, Queen of Healing and Vamilion, of the Mountains. Are you of their Order?"

"We are," Tanzaa confirmed. "We have been traveling for many days. Perhaps we can stay at your garrison this evening, and tell you our tale?" Then she raised her arm and dispelled the looming rainclouds that had overshadowed their travel up from the wilderness. The setting sun caught the underside of the fleeing clouds with a spectacular display of pink and gold. At that, a different tone emanated from the soldiers. They rose from their ready position and rested their spears, still waiting for the captain's word.

"What sign do you have that we will know and believe," he insisted.

Tanzaa frowned at that. She would have thought her control of the weather was obvious and she struggled to keep her irritation from recalling the clouds. Even so, lightning-sparked out of the storm as it thinned north of their position.

"Do you know the Heart Stone?" replied Tanzaa in the haughtiest tone she could manage, and heard Rashel's warning thoughts pressing against her shields, but she continued. "It is the sign of a Wise One."

She then brought out the glowing blue orb.

The captain was unimpressed. "A bauble does not mean much to us here, ladies."

"Then sir," Rashel broke in, "We will not disturb you. We speak the Language, and that will be sign enough. Let us pass and go our way. We will find other lodgings." She then spurred her horse forward. The startled men parted for her, and Tanzaa followed suit, but she let the clouds return in her confusion and frustration. The guards did not waylay them, nor try to apologize with an invitation to stay.

In her heart, Tanzaa realized she had failed.

The two ladies rode on until it was too dark to see, past the village on the river where the garrison men kept their families. Tanzaa went silently, thinking about how that interaction went wrong. Rashel waited for her protégé to formulate her questions and instead began conjuring their camp tents, and a fire that burned nothing, stopping out in the open prairie. Finally, when Tanzaa made no move to ask a question or speak aloud her disquiet, Rashel invited her to sit by the fire and eat supper.

"Why did they not...understand?" Tanzaa finally asked after she couldn't swallow a bite of the fine food Rashel had conjured onto her plate. "They feel...nothing?"

"No, they feel free. In the Land, they do not have a king or a leader. They fend for themselves and so there is no need for a ruler other than themselves. In a way, they feel no need for magic either."

"Then why are we here?" Tanzaa asked simply.

Rashel looked at her friend sadly. "For the times when they do. The miners know Vamilion and all the healers in every village have a candle to call Honiea in their need. Earlier you asked if the farmers knew to ask for my help."

Then Rashel brought into the light a copper watering can. It was simple and looked like it needed a polish. "This is one of my Talismans. It's only a watering can, but it also wields magic that is not so brazen as wearing our grand clothes or living in a palace. I make tea in it for the farmers. If I serve them that tea, they tell me their tale. Sometimes farmers find it difficult to trust a girl with the difficulties on their farm. I pour a little water in their garden and it makes them more willing to talk to me."

"Talismans?" Tanzaa asked. She had heard Rashel mention them before, but could not recall where.

"Owailion made them as part of his Seeking. Somewhere in the Land a few items have been hidden that belong only to you. They will be like my watering can, or this ring of mine. They will hold subtle magical gifts. Honiea's candle allows her to be called by any of the healers in the world. Yeolani has a compass that points him to his duty. You need to Seek out your Talismans, and in doing so you will gain more magical skill until you are no longer Seeking but become a Seated Queen of the Land."

Tanzaa noticed full well that her friend had poured water into her cup from the Talisman.

"And what will that water do to me?"

"I don't always know. It simply makes it easier to share your troubles. We have had enough rain, and I want to help you solve your unrest. Perhaps it will help you understand as well."

Tanzaa grimaced, but then deliberately lifted her neglected cup to her lips and drank from the water. She didn't feel any different, but she smiled reassuringly. "I miss Dayvian. That is my trouble. And when I am upset, my magic does not work properly. I also feel like an outsider. I do not understand the Land and why the people here do not trust or even believe in magic...and I did not need your water pot to tell me that."

"No," Rashel replied, "but you verbalizing these thoughts, that's what the Talisman encourages. You need to express yourself. Now, let's address each problem you listed one by one. First, Dayvian. How often did you see him when you were in the harem in Umzulio?"

"About once a year, for about three weeks. So, I guess that means I've had my chance this year." Tanzaa realized. "I don't miss being with him, I suppose. I miss the hope of him. When I was in the harem, I knew he would come and I could spend a bit of time with him. Now, I don't have that hope."

"Tanzaa, you cannot think like that," warned Rashel. "You have got to keep hope. Your quest in finding a Heart Stone is all about hope. If you lose that, you will stop Seeking and you'll never find it. The Heart Stones come from when we make an effort and if we do not do everything we can, we don't deserve that gift."

"And how do I keep...keep from drowning?" Tanzaa returned again and again to that analogy; that one or the other of them would drown, and if they tried to rescue each other they would both drown.

"You remember that you love him and you want to have him join you. Be positive because that is how you keep from drowning. You have an eternity. What are the positive things you can do? You have a whole year until you would normally meet again. Think of that and find something that will keep your focus."

Tanzaa looked into the fire and watched the strange green flames that always made up Rashel's fires that burned on no fuel. "Dancing. That was what I was good at."

"Then find a way to make dancing part of your magic. Just because people in the Land tend to distrust magic, does not mean you cannot teach them about it through your dancing. I've seen your slightest move paralyze some and put a spell on others. You do not have to declare magic for it to be within your power."

"Is that Wise One magic?" Tanzaa asked. She felt amazed at the wisdom her mentor was providing and it didn't come just from a watering pot.

Rashel nodded. "Wise One magic is subtle. We do not need to announce our power to have mastered it. I am listening to my instincts, my dreams, my compulsions. That inspiration is part of the gifts of being a Wise One...and part of being in the Land. That garrison leader did not trust you because you did not understand his freedom and perspective."

"And is that why I don't feel like I fit in?"

"Yet," Rashel qualified. "You've not been in the Land very long. You cannot expect to understand us yet. Just know that the Wise One gifts will ease your way. Trust that. You're probably a little homesick too. You don't understand some of our ways, but you will and you'll begin to appreciate them. For instance, our not having a king."

"You don't have any rulers, not even the Wise Ones," Tanzaa pointed out in frustrated wonder. "No one will trust us."

"It's just that the Wise Ones do not want to be their rulers like sorcerers are in other lands. Power leads to corruption and fear of magic."

"But we are called Queens..." Tanzaa realized.

"We are Kings and Queens of things, meaning we have mastery over that element, not the people."

"We do not rule, we guide? Then who rules?"

Rashel did not speak for quite a while, and her fire burned low, leaving them in the dark.

"Good question."

9

GOAT OR WORM

"*D*o you want to be turned into a goat? That's what will happen," Yeolani declared.

"Really? I thought you Wise Ones were all about honor. You would never do something so petty as turning me into a goat," Dayvian replied as he stuffed an extra set of clothing into the pack he had borrowed. He was determined to leave Vamilion's wondrous palace in the mountains as soon as he could.

"Not me, but Owailion will." Yeolani flopped down on the bed beside Dayvian's bag and stared in frustration at the ceiling of the bedchamber while Dayvian packed. "He won't see you. You'll freeze to death on his doorstep."

"Not if you go with me," Dayvian replied and threw spools of guitar string on top of his clothing. "You would have a better idea of how to beg a Heart Stone than I will."

"Then why are you going all the way to that god-forsaken iceberg to talk to Owailion? He won't speak to another Wise One, let alone a heart-broken bard with a twangy guitar."

Dayvian looked sourly over at Yeolani. "Because I must. I cannot give up. Would you give up on Rashel?"

"No, she'd kill me," Yeolani admitted. "And she's got the power to do it too. Well, if I can't dissuade you and I can't turn you into a goat because of my spotless morals, I guess I had better go with you. Besides, Tanzaa will kill me too."

Dayvian, who was trying to find an acceptably safe way to sling both his guitar and his pack on his back, stopped in surprise. "You can go with me? I thought you had Wise One duties to perform."

"Do you think we sit on a throne all day, dispensing justice from our palace? That's not our style. I can count on one hand how many nights I've ever spent in an actual bed in my own palace."

"So, what do the Wise Ones do then?" Dayvian asked, setting aside the fragile guitar. He had no way to take the instrument with him as it was. He privately hoped to beg a conjured case from Yeolani if he was willing.

With a wave of his hand, Yeolani supplied a guitar case exactly like the one Dayvian had lost back in Demion, complete with scrapes and scuffs.

"We help train the next Wise One. That's what I would have been doing if you had taken the Heart Stone. Otherwise, I tend to travel a great deal, blending in with the common folk. I teach about digging wells and setting up windmills. Sometimes I ease tensions within towns. I also keep demons from forming and drive back invading sorcerers. Wise Ones are the secret defenders of the Land."

Dayvian looked in wonder at the new case but didn't question it. "I've lived here my whole life. Why did I not know this?" Dayvian found it strange that Yeolani, or any of the Wise Ones, did not display their astounding power.

"Do you recall the word 'secret'? It's easier to break up a fight and then help mend fences when people aren't begging you to make them fabulously rich." Yeolani didn't see the irony of creating a guitar case as he said this.

"But you're going with me to ask Owailion about finding a Heart Stone? You don't think he'll help me, and yet you want to come with me?"

"Ha!" Yeolani barked in his joking tone. "I don't *want* to do that, especially since I can see your planned route. But like I said, if you die on this trip, one of those two ladies will skin me for leather."

Three weeks later, Dayvian peered with a wise eye at a boat rocking at a dock on the Laranian River. He knew he was not going to like this next leg of his trip. Dayvian and Yeolani had already argued along the whole trek out of the mountains to the small shipping village of Lolar on the eastern shore. Now they needed to stop arguing and decide their next step.

"Wouldn't it be easier to walk cross country to my palace?" Yeolani asked. "I do ships about as well as I do guitar string."

"I thought you were a sailor back...back...when you weren't a Wise One."

Yeolani sat down on the edge of the dock and kicked at the weathered hull of the scull they might sail aboard to go north toward Owailion's home. The sailors loading the ship for the trip upriver ignored the two men hovering. Dayvian had hoped to speak with the captain, but he wasn't there overseeing the cargo.

"There's a very good reason I'm not a sailor now. We could walk...or ride horses even. I can find us a couple, not difficult out here. Anything but a boat."

Dayvian looked at his friend with a knowing eye. "Seasick?"

"And I've no doubt you get seasick too," the Wise One muttered. "It's one of the curses of magic...thanks to R....the Queen of Rivers."

Dayvian's eyes dipped in puzzled curiosity. "There's a story there."

Yeolani sighed and explained since there was nothing more to do while waiting for the captain. "Back three hundred years ago, the Land was Sealed. Did you know that? The only humans within the Seal were invited inside by the Dragons, who managed all magic here. The first two humans were Owailion, King of Creating, and his wife, the Queen of Rivers."

"Owailion, who will turn me into a goat? He had a wife? What happened?" Dayvian asked.

"Yes, her name was..." and Yeolani looked around to be sure they weren't overheard. "Raimi, Queen of Rivers. She had a gift for working with deep spells. She's the one who crafted the spell that allows immigrants to speak our language. Well, she was being haunted by sorcerers that came near the Seal. They knew her name and were using name magic to have her manipulate the Land without her even knowing. They invaded her dreams. She suspected someone was pulling her strings, so she instinctively needed to push them away. She crafted a deep spell that made every magician in every country so seasick they would never come to this Land. It has become one of the simple signs of magic potential...even in people like you who don't even wield power yet."

"So why don't I know that story either?" Dayvian accused again.

"Because Owailion tells no one. He had to tell Vamilion as part of his training, but he doesn't know I even know. And Vamilion trained me. It's why we learn not to throw names around like we're skipping pebbles. You cannot tell anyone. You cannot use her name."

"Why...well, I know that sorcerers out in other lands that will use it, but why haven't I met Ra...the Queen of Rivers. Couldn't she help us move up the river faster?"

"She probably could, if she were alive. She's the one who broke the Seal because she was forced to by the outlanders. She was so ...well, she decided that the only way to stop hurting the Land and Owailion was to remove herself. She commanded herself to die."

Dayvian was about to ask another question, but then realized he did not dare. The pain of that kind of end drowned any query he held. Dayvian only sat there, listening to the gentle slosh of the river against the hull and dock. Finally, he observed, "No wonder Owailion is going to turn every visitor into a goat."

"It does tend to make him a bit cranky," Yeolani replied. "Let's go get a room at the inn. The captain is not coming any time soon. These crewmen are thinking they're going to be loading all night. He's probably drinking at the inn anyway."

The two men hopped up and strode into town, such as it was. Lolar was a port town, several miles up the delta, with hardly any population, except for the few that supported the ships and crewmen. The village was built on pilings sunk into the marshy land. Even the roads were made of stone brought in and set paces apart. It only boasted one inn, full of sailors awash in ale and sea stories. As they entered, Dayvian went to the innkeeper before Yeolani could conjure money to pay for two beds.

"I'll play music for beds, two for the night and two meals," Dayvian offered the innkeeper.

Yeolani glared at him but sat down at a table to see how this would turn out, and to his disappointment, the innkeeper began to haggle. In a few moments, Dayvian moved back towards Yeolani and laughed in triumph. "Well, I've got my room and supper, but you must pay for your own. He's also got the name of the captain leaving at dawn tomorrow, sailing as far as Meeting."

"We could still walk," said Yeolani. "It would save us both an awful lot of vomiting over the side."

Dayvian chose to ignore further argument on the topic, and instead went to the main hearth of the common room, pulled a stool from the counter, and began tuning his guitar for a night of entertainment. Yeolani had heard his protégé tinker with little songs every night as they had walked out of the mountains, but he still enjoyed his friend's skill. Now, with a full audience, eager to hear songs of the world in this backwater village, Dayvian put some extra intricacy into the tune he was crafting.

And crafting it, he was, Yeolani realized. Dayvian hadn't played this song before, and as he listened in on Dayvian's mind, he heard the young man creating the rhyme as he went, letting his fingers echo a phrase while he thought up the next line. The melody floated addictively across the flagstones and tables, like a mist. Every ear was attuned.

Laying down their heads, the Dragon slept
Into their caverns each one crept.
Till Owailion held the Land alone
Heir of all the sovereign o'erturned
With magic's secrets entrusted to learn.
A Lady stepped from the river's flood.
Shining like fire in the midsummer sun.
Bearing power in her outstretched hands
A Queen of water yet flesh and blood.

"You're going to get yourself turned into a worm instead," Yeolani projected silently into Dayvian's head. "You cannot make Owailion's pain into some ditty to share in every inn we pass."

Ignoring that warning, Dayvian launched into a rousing chorus.

The Wise Ones are watching over us.
Their power and gifts none can see.
But guarding the ways of the Land they will come
From their palaces, they rise one by one.

Dayvian didn't expand on the song but repeated the chorus several times before changing to a sea chanty that these men probably sang in their sleep, familiar and enthusiastic. Yeolani sat at his table and glowered. It was one thing to teach Dayvian, who might have the chance to become magical, about the Wise Ones. It was something quite different to teach others. These sailors would spread that charming tune all over the Land, and perhaps farther afield.

Yeolani dreaded what that would mean.

"We're not a passenger ship. We're going home, up to Meeting for the winter. What have you in mind?" The captain gave Dayvian and Yeolani an appraising look, probably wondering if they would work the poles, pushing the barge upstream.

"We can't pay, but we won't eat either, trust me. We'll be seasick the whole way, but when I can, I will entertain your men. I'm a bard and traveling north to Fallon, and we need to get off at Lara. Can you take us that far?"

The captain scowled. "I do not need a bard. Can you pole?"

Yeolani sighed in poorly hidden irritation but took up the

persuasion. "As he said, we'll be seasick the whole way, but I can try some,"

The captain looked them over doubtfully. Neither of the travelers was a big burly sailor. After weeks of tramping out of the Vamilion Mountains, they probably had lost weight off an already lean frame. At least they were willing to try. Shaking his head with suspicion, the captain agreed. "Leave your things with me and help with the on-load and I'll find you a berth."

Four days later up the river, the captain had to admit they had not lied about them being sea-sick. Yeolani poled and puked over the side as he walked the deck trying to keep up with the six other men on his side of the barge. When his fellow sailors complained about his constant episodes of being sick, the captain admitted defeat and sent him to his berth. Dayvian didn't fare any better on his side of the deck. He didn't come out of his hammock for two whole days. He could almost keep water down. When he managed that, he played a few rowing songs up on the deck. As promised, all they did was occupy space and didn't bother the men or eat their food.

Then at dusk of the fourth day moving upstream, Yeolani rolled over in his berth and reached out for Dayvian. "We are getting off this ship. Take my hand."

Dayvian looked over at his friend with a bleary eye. Before he could comment or argue, his hand reached out, and Yeolani grabbed his wrist. There was a shudder of the hull, and every-thing seemed to blur. When his eyes focused again, Dayvian found himself standing upright in a meadow with grass growing up to his knees. Yeolani stood next to him blinking in the lowering sun shining off the river they had just departed. The barge continued, unaware it had lost two of its crew.

"I had to get off that tub," Yeolani heaved a sigh and then turned around. "Besides, I wanted to show you something."

Dayvian pulled his eyes away from the sunlight and turned

around as well. And gasped. They stood in the middle of that field only paces from a Wise One palace. Its gates of gold blazed like fire in the sunset and the white walls around a courtyard rose higher than any of the trees in Umzulio's forest. Carved into them in bas-relief were herds of horses racing across finely carved fields of grain. Through the gilded posts of the gate, Dayvian saw fountains and gardens protected from outsiders. The inner building, with gold spires and green banners, rose so high it almost touched the sky.

"My home," Yeolani admitted. The sea-sickness had completely faded and Yeolani's smile broadened. "I want you to meet Brundi." He walked forward a few paces to the gates. He reached out to touch the gold bars and pushed them open effortlessly.

"I thought there would be a town here," Dayvian commented. "There's one at Vamilion, and near all the other Wise One palaces I've seen in my travels."

"What? Three?" Yeolani looked back at him dubiously as he led the way into the gardens. "Most of us are far in the north, in the Great Chain. No, these homes either attract a town because the Wise One trains others there, like Vamilion, or because it's a perfect place to build a town, like at the base of the falls on the Don River. As I said, I'm never home to encourage any of it. And who would listen to me?"

"I would," said a voice in Dayvian's mind.

Around a bend in the path through the fragrant gardens, a golden horse came into view. Obviously magical, this horse was mechanical, like an automaton, shining in gold filigree. Like it was a statue come to life, it clanked up the pathway. However, the horse lovingly nudged Yeolani in the chest like a natural horse would do.

"Brundi, this is Dayvian. Dayvian, may I introduce Brundi, my friend and mount." As he spoke, Yeolani caressed the noble neck of the metal beast, and the creature's appearance shifted, shimmering and then changing into that of a natural, palomino horse.

"He's beautiful," Dayvian whispered, but the trepidation must ring in his voice.

Yeolani looked up from grooming Brundi and smirked. "I know you dislike riding horses, and that's why you insisted on taking a boat. However, that is not why I am bringing you here. I want you to hear Brundi's story. You need to understand how magic works in the Land."

Dayvian nodded, uncomfortably. "And a horse is going to explain this?"

"I am a Talisman," Brundi replied.

The horse kept flickering between metal and flesh every time Yeolani brushed his hand down his flank. The distracting transition reminded Dayvian oddly of how bewildering Tanzaa's dancing could be.

"A Talisman is something crafted by a Wise One. When something in nature is trying to turn into a demon, a Wise One will direct that tendency," the horse explained matter-of-factly. "The magic of the Land warps nature and twists it, allowing it to become demonic. The King of Creating found a demon forming from a thorn bush and an actual live horse. He molded the two down into something else and then reformed it into an automaton, into me. He then imbued it with the power of the demon's magic. Finally, he hid me in a glacier, awaiting my Lord of the Plains."

"You are telling me, Owailion hid an entire horse in a hunk of ice?"

"No, he hid an entire spur in the ice." Yeolani laughed, "Please show him, Brundi."

The horse huffed an irritated sigh and Yeolani took his hand away from the animal's back. Brundi made a strange clicking noise, like when a thorn bush in a storm beats against a window. Then his metallic form began to fold in on itself. He fell to the paving stones with legs suddenly shorter than a cat's and his neck shifted down into his chest. With a swish of his barbed tail, he circled his withers and squeezed down into a round shape with spikes of the original thorn bush around the outside edge and then all that remained of the full-sized horse was a copper spur, fit for Yeolani's boot.

Yeolani bent and picked him up. "This is Brundi as a Talisman; a magical item that looks normal, but inside are magical gifts waiting to explore. Brundi, being a non-living horse, can travel at incredible speeds across vast distances. However, no one would know he isn't a real horse when I ride him."

"And that's why you were interested in riding rather than sailing," Dayvian concluded. "You do know, I don't have a copper horse."

"I can make you one."

"Yes, you probably can, but can you turn me into a decent rider?"

Yeolani looked at Dayvian dubiously. "Only if you want to. When I first got on a horse, I knew it fit me because of who I am, King of the Plains. We don't know what you will be King of. That's as open as dandelion fluff. You could be King of Animals and simply become a horse. Whatever you become, you have to explore it into being. Which leads me to my real purpose in stopping here. I wanted you to explore by introducing you to Brundi. I found him in a glacier at the top of the world because I *wanted* to. Desire and passion are the coins of the Wise One world. Without the desire, we can do no magic. Unfortunately, that is why it is so important that you cut yourself off from Tanzaa. She will not have the desire she needs to Seek and find her Talismans if she is looking after you. She will not test and expand her powers if she is worried for you."

Dayvian had thought he was done hearing about Tanzaa's abandonment. Arguing about going to see Owailion or whether to take a boat had easily replaced that more sensitive topic. Now Dayvian felt anger bubbling back up in his throat. "You....you think that she doesn't have the desire to find me a Heart Stone? That I don't have that passion as well? You're a fool," he muttered at his friend. "I will show you passion and desire, and so will she."

He whirled around and began marching out of the gate. Before he could reach to the passageway, the bars clanged closed in his face.

"You cannot go like this." For once Yeolani's voice sounded gentle and caring, without his customary sarcasm. Dayvian turned back, about to throw an epithet back at him, but Yeolani continued. "If you do not want my company, I understand. It was offered in friendship. I will give you a horse, or put you back on the boat. Tell them I jumped in the river and drowned rather than spend another minute aboard. Just don't go angry."

"I can't with you holding the gate closed."

Yeolani sighed with regret and walked to Dayvian with something in his hand, a pot he had just conjured. "Don't go angry and don't go empty-handed. Trust me that I have reasons why I am parting ways with you here. Take this pot. As long as you are nowhere near anyone who can see you, this pot will conjure anything you need on your trip...within reason. If you use it near people who might see, the spell will be broken and you will only be carrying a hunk of iron."

Dayvian took the pot with trembling hands as his anger burned itself out like a flame in the rain. "Thank you, but...why?"

Yeolani allowed a strange look to pass over his face that Dayvian could not interpret. "There are dangers you know nothing of, and I have kept you safe from them. If you go now, ship or horse, you will make it to Owailion's, whether I go with you or not. Will you make it before winter, that is the most pressing question."

"I will, and I will find my Heart Stone," Dayvian said, but his voice sounded like he was trying to convince himself.

"Then I will let you go," and Yeolani opened the gates. "Ship or horse?"

"Ship. Your caldron cannot provide me the will to learn to ride."

Yeolani looked out at the river that flowed nearby. The ship they had taken had passed beyond their vision, and the night had settled. "Very well. Good luck, my friend. Use the caldron carefully and I hope Owailion treats you well."

With a flick of his wrist, he put Dayvian back in his berth on the barge ship.

And so Dayvian was not able to see how quickly Yeolani changed his focus, threw Brundi's spur on the ground, and waited impatiently for the horse to emerge from the Talisman.

10

BLOOD LILIES

*H*er entire life Tanzaa had been coddled and cared for like a rare hot-house flower. Her clothes, rich and embroidered by servants, her food provided by exquisite cooks to expand her palette, and her tutors were the brightest minds in Demion. She had not appreciated those advantages as she should have, she thought.

She had also anticipated a rough life being married to a traveling musician. She and Dayvian had hoped to start their own troupe, with dance and music rather than tricks and acrobatics as the centerpiece. So, she wasn't dismayed by the idea of living on the move. However, that had always been with the understanding that Dayvian would be part of her life, not the one thing in the entire world she would be denied.

None of that prepared her the rustic inn at Too.

"Make your shields impenetrable, physically as well as against magical powers," Rashel warned in a tight mental voice.

Tanzaa ducked instead. Crockery flew across the common room and the brawl expanded when someone disagreed with a tankard of ale dumped on his head. The innkeeper and his disgruntled customer grappled with each other and tripped over the hearth, almost landing in the fire. The other guests either cheered on their favored contestants or cowered under the tables and benches. Rashel just stood in the doorway, watching with a smirk on her face as Tanzaa waded in, hoping to stop the brawl. Rashel had declared it was Tanzaa's responsibility to resolve, so Tanzaa had gone in.

"What are they arguing about?" Tanzaa cast toward Rashel on a private thought. "They're making no sense."

Rashel just chuckled from the safety of the doorway. "That's what you've got to determine."

Tanzaa couldn't even get near the actual central fight for other patrons crowded in, shoving to get a better view of the melee. These bystanders took objection to Tanzaa's efforts and one even put his hand on Tanzaa's shoulder to push her away as she tried squeezing between two brawny men.

"Unhand me," Tanzaa growled at the man, and he obeyed, not at the tone, but her cool glare and the magical flash of lighting in her eyes. Meanwhile, a chair lifted into the air, about to come down on a patron's head.

"Oh, this is ridiculous...ENOUGH!" she bellowed.

The word came with Tanzaa's magic quelling all movement. Everyone stopped and she didn't care at that point if they also could not breathe.

"You'll have to let them get some air. This is going to take you some time to parse out what's going on," Rashel said.

"Should I care if they suffocate?" Tanzaa asked as she squeezed between the bystanders now unmolested. She removed the chair from someone's grasp and put it down. Then she agreed and allowed everyone to breathe once she got to the central contestants. However, she still didn't trust anyone to move just yet. Carefully Tanzaa concentrated on the bar-keeper and reanimated just him.

"You, sir, what is the problem here?" she demanded.

When the bar-keeper ignored her and used his freed limbs to try to swing at his opponent, Tanzaa froze him again. She then turned toward his victim and reanimated him instead. Perhaps he could be more reasonable now that both of them, if not the whole room, knew magic ruled the chamber.

"What is the problem...in your opinion," she asked this trader.

The man seemed more hesitant and straightened up from the gut-punch he was about to receive before Tanzaa's inter-ruption. He shook his head, doubtful of explaining himself, especially to the delicate woman glaring up at him. Tanzaa wished briefly for a bit of Rashel's tea, but something else slipped into her mind and she knew instinctively to wait. The answers would come.

"Is this you giving me patience?" Tanzaa asked of Rashel, sending silently to her.

"No," the Queen of Growing Things replied. "It's the Wise One instinct. Listen to it. It will guide you on how to deal with this."

Meanwhile, the subject of her interrogation finally noticed that the whole room had been frozen and everyone awaited his reply. "We have a....misunderstanding," he muttered.

"I saw that much," Tanzaa said with a tone the king of Demion might use. Then a more reasonable impression came on her and she realized that her temper would not help this situation. Indeed, she might have alienated the entire room with her sharp reaction and all-encompassing magic. She quietly allowed all but the innkeeper to move again and there was a collective sigh of relief from the on-lookers.

"I'm sorry, I lost my temper. Go on," she apologized. "You had a misunderstanding with him over...?"

"The inn," the combatant answered. "It's mine."

The still-frozen innkeeper made a disagreeable sound in the back in his throat, protesting even still. Tanzaa had no intention of letting that one move until she had heard this side of the story.

"And why is it yours if he is the innkeeper?"

The trader sighed in irritation and rubbed his cheek where a bruise had begun forming. "He's my brother. Our father left me the inn when he died, but I was not here. I was away on a trading run. Odel never wrote to tell me that our father had died. He simply began to run the inn. I was to take it over when I returned, but Odel will not let me even come in to talk to him about it."

Tanzaa thanked the man and then stepped in front of the angry innkeeper, so he would have to hit her before he could reach his brother to continue the brawl. "Is he right?" she asked in as gentle a voice as she could manage, given her anger. Then she carefully peeled back the freezing spell she had set on him.

"Not at all," the innkeeper bellowed. "He lies. Our father left the inn to me. Frey abandoned us to see the world. He did not want the inn and our father would never have given him a thing after he betrayed us."

Tanzaa stood between the two men and could not judge. "Is there anyone here who can tell who is speaking the truth?" she called to the whole room.

One man who had been betting on the brawl looked down at the coins in his hand and then admitted, "Their father, he was the magistrate. He would know the right of it, but he's dead."

"And was nothing written down?" Tanzaa asked in desperation, swallowing her awe at how backward these people were. Not having a king had rippled down to this backwoods brawl and left them no recourse. She looked up to see if Rashel had some input, but the Queen of Growing Things had slipped out of the inn, leaving the door open in the night.

Tanzaa had to deal with this on her own. Part of her wanted to just warn the two men to stop fighting and then walk away. However, the Wise One part of her knew that would be a betrayal of her duty. There had to be a way to solve this impasse. Like she had been taught, she centered herself in the skies above her where the passing clouds calmed her soul. She tapped into the earth beneath her feet, where her world stage awaited. The Wise One instinct would tell her what to do. It would show her the truth. If only there were a way to know...

Tanzaa's silvery eyes opened and she looked at the two men. Their appearance changed but the gathered crowd did not seem to notice. No one gasped at their transformation. Only Tanzaa saw that the brothers both had black blood running out of their mouths. Their tongues hung out as well, with a split in it...a false tongue? Had she set a truth spell on them? If so, it showed them both as liars.

Suddenly Tanzaa knew what to do.

"You both are not telling the truth. I suspect your father never made his wishes known at all. Therefore, neither of you can be trusted. Instead, I have something better to say."

She conjured a chain that bound both men at the wrist. But this chain was made of the most exquisite lilies, white as the snow on the mountain tops. And each one bled a drop of scarlet blood.

"This chain is of your father's making. He loved you both. He would not want you to fight. He wanted you both to have the inn. Your feud only pains his memory. From now on you will both work the inn, and you will both be the magistrate of this town. If you do not agree to this, you will see the lilies bleed again. All these people are a witness. They will know if you are not keeping the pact. Do you understand?"

The innkeeper began to complain immediately. "Do we have to remain bound like this, all our lives? We cannot work with this...this chain around us." He tugged with contempt at the lilies that became stone hard at his touch.

Tanzaa gently touched the chain as it stretched between the two men. It fell in two and she wrapped the fallen ends around their respective wrists. "It must stay, as a reminder of the bond you have with each other. It will gradually fade, and it cannot be removed."

"And if we do not want to hold the inn together?" asked the other brother. "What if I decide I do not want to be bound to him, even by this much?" and he held up his beflowered wrist.

"Oh, I think you will have that choice eventually. For now, you must stay and work it out together. Perhaps in the future, you may want to split the duties. One might be more content as a magistrate and the other as an innkeeper. You will know. For now, you must find a way to work together, until you love one another again."

Then she let the truth spell fade. No one seemed to notice it. Tanzaa turned around, looked at the audience she had garnered, and smiled to reassure their solemn stares. "You will be my witnesses, won't you? If you see their lilies bleeding, you must call me. The flowers might tighten if they are squabbling again. Keep an eye on them."

"And how will we call you, my Lady Witch?" asked the barmaid, as the spokesman for the amazed crowd.

Tanzaa shuddered. "Do not call me a witch," she said. "I am a Wise One, Queen of Storms. If they start to fight again, tell the clouds and I will know."

With that, Tanzaa walked out into the summer night, seeking Rashel. She did not like how she felt, and thunderstorms brewed in her mind. Tanzaa found Rashel standing at the bridge that crossed the river to the village of Next on the other side. Both women considered the night and what had happened at the inn, where they probably would not be spending the evening.

"Why would you be upset?" asked Rashel, who had heard her protégé's unrest. "You did very well there. You are starting to listen to your Wise One impressions."

"I lost my temper. I was so angry at their...pig-headedness. Is that a word here? I am supposed to provide a better example. Instead, I yelled at them. A courtesan never raises her voice."

"You are no longer a courtesan," Rashel said.

"Well, a Wise One should never raise her voice either."

"Perhaps. And it will be difficult to regain their trust if you have frightened them. Some of those villagers may not forgive that. Others will. We are not perfect, Tanzaa, but we have to try. Your solution to their feud was one inspired by the Wise One gifts."

"Would you have done differently?"

Rashel smiled back at her. "I am not you, my friend. My teapot would have been of no use if they will not drink. You, however, can quell a storm without thinking. I suspect that many would believe they are under a spell, just by being near you. You used a truth spell without knowing. You did that entire interchange without resorting to analogies. You are no longer Tanzaa, the dancer. They will call you the White Witch, and it is a title that you should take on."

"Witch, it is not a good thing."

"What do you care? In the Land, perhaps a witch is a good thing. And so, I must depart. You are ready to go alone now, I think."

Tanzaa gasped. A thousand thoughts of inadequacy flooded her mind, threatening to drown her.

Rashel's look rejected them all. Instead, she gave Tanzaa an analogy. "You must now learn how to swim in the deep waters alone."

And with that, Rashel disappeared.

Tanzaa understood the metaphor perfectly, but she did not like it.

Two days later, Tanzaa still felt uncomfortable in the deep water, but she was swimming. She wondered anew at the world she had entered for she now approached a second unoccupied Wise One's palace called Chiasm on the map Rashel had given her.

Chiasm looked like a crystal mountain carved out of a diamond at the base of a whole range of mountains. The spires glittered gold and high walls surrounded a vast courtyard the size of a small city. All around the outer walls, the grasslands teamed with horses and other animals attracted to it like metal to a magnet.

It must belong to a king or queen of animals, Tanzaa thought. The antelope and horses wandered right up to its seal. She still couldn't imagine why a Wise One would need such a grand place. No one here respected the Wise Ones because of their mansions. She knew these palaces were a symbol of power more than an actual home.

"Why?" Tanzaa managed to ask herself. Then she recalled her intervention at the inn a few days prior. She could not help there if she had been hiding in a palace somewhere up in the mountains. She turned away from the castle that was not hers and looked back downriver.

Her eye caught again a tremendous waterfall that marked the end of the Don as a navigable river. She felt attracted more to the waterfall than to the palace built just above it. I will be drawn to things, Tanzaa recalled from Rashel's lessons. That was how to find the Talismans or the pendant that opens the palace. No Wise One could rest until they had found all this Land hid for them. That included the Heart Stone for the next Wise One...for Dayvian. Then I will be Seated, not Seeking.

So why was she fascinated with a waterfall? Might a Heart Stone be hidden there?

Just below Chiasm, the river plunged into a crevasse, in a hundred span waterfall, almost as broad as it was tall. The roar of the torrent reminded her of thunder and the smoky mist kicked up by the river cooled the late summer heat.

Tanzaa spurred her horse right up to the bank of the river, with the waterfall above her, looming and impressive. Little knowing what she was attempting, Tanzaa lifted her arms as if she were going to dance. Nothing happened, but she felt the prompting to explore grow stronger so she slipped out of her saddle and walked right up to the riverbank. She swung her arms and now felt the response of the water. It swayed to her direction as the clouds did. Instinctively Tanzaa began dancing with the waterfall, watching in amazement as the river parted for her. It allowed her to land dry-footed right in the middle of the water, with her arms up, parting the waterfall over her head like a light gauze fabric, rather than a heavy pounding torrent.

Tanzaa could sense the tremendous weight and pressure of the waterfall, but as long as she continued dancing, it wouldn't crush her. Leaving her horse behind on the shore, she skipped her way through the water. Somehow Tanzaa knew something waited to be discovered on the backside of the fall. Please be a Heart Stone. Obediently, the water parted for her as a stage curtain and she danced beyond the torrent with barely a misting. The light grew dim and she nervously created a glowing ball in the palm of one hand. She could continue to dance but still see where she was headed. The slick stones, moist from the river mist forced her to remain light-footed and the chill reminded her of a dungeon, where Dayvian had been beaten mercilessly. That memory would haunt her forever.

Rather than be distracted by the past, Tanzaa forced herself to deal with the empty dark she faced in a cavern behind the waterfall. Now past the actual force of the water, she stopped dancing and lifted her hand high for the light and caught the flash of quartz against the dark stone. The dazzling cavern glittered and shifted color, like the sun sinking, gold, pink, lavender, and then blue. The roof wasn't high; perhaps double her height and the smooth inner walls only pushed back under the earth about a hundred steps. The floor of the cavern seemed littered with the broken marble and debris left from quarrying for the Wise One's palace right above her head. Some boulders even appeared roughly chiseled. Stones cut only on one or two sides dripped with moss, making the cavern appear like a lush, soft garden for giants.

So, what was she doing here, for she had been drawn irresistibly? She stepped around stones, moving toward the back of the cavern, wondering what secret lay hidden here. No one could have entered this cavern without magic enough to go through the waterfall. Rashel had explained that the Talismans would demand higher and more complex magic from the Seeker. That thought reminded her that she was alone and she turned back toward the white curtain behind her, wishing for Rashel's company.

However, the mere act of spinning around lightened something in the ceiling of the cavern.

Curious, Tanzaa studied the roof of the cavern, wondering at the light that flashed there when she spun. Experimentally she performed a pirouette and was rewarded by a spinning light moving up into the ceiling. It looked, for all she could judge, like water falling *up* into a drain. When she stopped her turn, the 'water' froze and she could see how the phenomena pierced into the ceiling. What waited there for her?

She would continue the dance until she found what was hidden for her up in the roof, trapped in seemingly solid stone. Tanzaa checked carefully to make sure she had free space and then began a set of fouetté turns. Moss and slick stone hardly made an optimal stage, but she could manage.

Tanzaa turned, keeping her eye mark at the point where the waterfall met the wall, ignoring what might be happening overhead. She did notice the cavern getting progressively brighter. She spun faster although that seemed impossible. She had never been able to make this many passes before she'd become a Wise One. This dance invoked magic here, and only her movement opened this vortex above her. Tanzaa reveled in it.

Then something clattered onto the stones behind her and Tanzaa stopped her spin. It took her a moment to reorient herself. A hundred passes would make anyone dizzy, but now above her head, the whirlpool had closed and the ceiling returned to solid stone. Instead, Tanzaa looked down to see what had interrupted her dance. A simple metal object rested on the mossy floor of the cavern. She recognized it instantly and bent to pick up the silver bracer she had seen on her arm on the day that Dayvian had made her touch the Heart Stone.

With one hand exploring and the other providing light, Tanzaa traced the doe and intricate scrollwork etched into the silver steel. She didn't dare put it on; not here or before she could talk to Rashel about her discovery. She suddenly felt exhausted and struggled with a sense of disappointment. She had found her first Talisman but had come no closer to finding a Heart Stone for her Dayvian.

Regretfully Tanzaa turned back to the waterfall, used her arms to part the water, and walked away from the hidden cavern, trying to focus on what she had just learned about her magic, about herself, and what keys this would open in her new world.

11

AT GANDOY

"I'm sorry you had such a miserable trip," the ship captain admitted. "We'll make Lara by mid-day tomorrow. What are your plans now?"

Dayvian looked at the man with bleary eyes, still feeling miserable and ready to retch. "I'm looking for someone up north," he admitted.

"Well, that's going to be good. Don't come south any time soon. You probably didn't hear the rumors. When we onloaded at Lolar, we heard that there's a war brewing in the east."

"War?" Dayvian gasped, suddenly wary. Was that what Yeolani had been protecting him from? "War with whom?"

The captain shrugged. "I heard a bit in Gardway and then when we docked at Lolar the workers had all kinds of news brewing. They are recruiting soldiers at Gardway. I don't know exactly the particulars, but I didn't figure you for one joining a draft. They're calling for soldiers at the Wall as well. That means it's either Marwen or Demion. Something about a stolen lady or something. Anyway, it has one of the outland kingdoms all up in arms. It's also got the Wise Ones involved as the battles are magic too."

Dayvian didn't dare comment until he knew his voice and face were completely under control. "Why didn't you say something earlier? I might have wanted to join up."

"Boy," the captain chuckled, "You're doing the right thing. You're too scrawny to be a soldier and have no dog in a magical fight. You're going north where they'll appreciate a bard. Stay there until the war's over."

Given how he felt, Dayvian had to agree. That didn't mean his heart didn't sink. He *did* have a dog in this fight. Demion started a war with the Land to get Tanzaa back? He was horrified but carefully he thanked the captain for the news and lay back in the hammock hoping to get some sleep, such as it was. And when he did sleep his mind wallowed in guilt. War plagued his dreams.

The next day the barge paused long enough to let Dayvian row over in their lifeboat to the bank where the two branches of the Larinian River met. He stepped ashore and almost immediately felt better. The barge pulled back its lifeboat, turned up the river, and moved beyond his view. Why the motion of a ship always made him ill, Dayvian couldn't fathom, but solid ground made him want solid food. He sat right there on the shore and started a fire ring for himself.

As he wandered away from his camp to gather wood, he found that just beyond the trees that lined the rivers stood one of the palaces of the Wise Ones, but this one was sealed. He couldn't approach nearer than a hundred paces. Its owner had not been found yet, he realized with a start. Maybe that's Tanzaa's. The gleaming marble and high walls seemed to fit her somehow; graceful and pristine. However, the cold strength and silence chilled him. These walls certainly didn't speak to him and he turned away with his armful of fallen branches.

Out on the open of the riverbank, far from the nearest inhabited village, he could bring out his gift from Yeolani. He had promised he would not use it around other people and he had been true to his word. From his pack, he brought out the simple iron pot. Dayvian couldn't help but think it was a witch's cauldron, though this cauldron didn't brew potions. He closed his eyes and concentrated on what he wanted and then reached in and pulled out a dead rabbit all ready to skin. He next pulled out a potato, onion, and carrot so he could make himself a soup. He even brought some more substantial firewood so he wouldn't have to go off the shore to hunt for more fuel than he had gathered to that point. All Dayvian had to do was wish for that thing and the caldron would provide. It even worked pretty well as a cooking pot too. He couldn't ask it for anything complex, like the soup itself. He felt sure he could get anything he needed on the road. The gift of the pot made him realize that Yeolani at least had hoped he would eventually become a Wise One. He wanted Dayvian familiar with the magical capabilities and the restrictions involved. Either that or Yeolani simply didn't want him to starve on the trip, even if he didn't think he should go to Owailion.

Vamilion had been the one who had given him enough information to select Gandoy as his next goal. Taking Tanzaa's challenge to learn everything about the Heart Stone, Dayvian had asked both Yeolani and Vamilion frankly what they knew about the key that had given them their magic.

"Curious are you?" Vamilion had commented. "Well, I don't know the answers. It could be that God creates them. He selects who is the next Wise One, I know, but Owailion is the one to ask. He has dealt with the Heart Stones before any other men came to the Land, hundreds of years ago."

"Then how do I speak with this Owailion?"

Yeolani shook his head vehemently at that point, but

Vamilion didn't seem reluctant to share what he knew. "He lives in the far north..." and Vamilion had conjured a map, spreading it out to show Dayvian. "Here, beyond Jonjonel. It will take you months to get there and you'll be facing winter at best. There are no villages beyond Savone so you'll need to carry your supplies."

"Why all the concern suddenly?" asked had Dayvian curiously. "You aren't thrilled that I'm going on Tanzaa's little mission rather than getting on with my life. Why now?"

Vamilion had shrugged. "I just don't want you to be disappointed."

"I won't be," Dayvian had assured him. "I have faith in Tanzaa more than Owailion, but Tanzaa asked me to do this and I'm bound to try. When I'm done speaking with Owailion I'll come and speak with you again.

"If you survive," Vamilion had murmured and then left him. He had not seen them off before they had walked out of his home, heading west the next morning.

Now looking back on that parting, Dayvian wondered again. Had Vamilion known about the war already? Was that why he wanted Dayvian to leave? Had he known what greeting he would receive when he arrived at Owailion's palace in the far north?

In two months Dayvian had come halfway on this trek. He now stood beneath the shadow of a sealed Wise One's palace named Lara on the map, and Dayvian felt tense. He sensed the autumn chill in the air. Overhead clouds threatened and he wondered if the cauldron could provide him a tent, or at least some way to keep the rain off his head.

Tanzaa, wherever you are, he thought, you're skilled with the weather. Please keep winter at bay a few more weeks. Please? No one answered his request, but then he never expected she would.

Over the next few weeks, autumn descended like a furious lion, blustery, rain-driven, and bitterly cold as he walked through the Fallon Forest. Thankfully Dayvian's magical cookware included plenty of warm winter furs and a tent. These carried him through the Fallon to Savone on its northern verge.

The town, pressed between the start of the Great Chain and the Fallon Forest, made a fine living working in mining and timber. Now, with winter driving the miners from the mountains and lumberjacks from the forest, Savone filled up with restless and loud men. Dayvian went to the first inn he found and immediately begged work as a bard. The innkeeper gladly paid him room and board as well as a coin a song. Anything to keep the men from starting a brawl during the long evenings. There Davian sat by the fire and played new songs into being, as he considered his next move.

For one thing, he worried that his name would carry to Demion, even here. With a war brewing, he knew his name and actions were at the root of it. Many of these seasonal workers might travel west to the ports and sail around to join the war. Would they carry with them the word of a musician as they migrated? Davian started introducing himself as Dayo, just in case someone recalled him later.

Another worrisome development; his music still improved without his actively concentrating on it. During the days, sitting in the inn's finest room, he wrote down the new songs he crafted each night. He easily added new verses to the Wise Ones song, one for Vamilion, Honiea Yeolani, and Rashel. It had become a popular tune. A verse for Tanzaa did not come easily, so he did not try for that. However, again he worried that bringing the Wise Ones to mind might stimulate an interest in going to war.

The power within his new songs scared him. Why was this happening? Was it because he had come so close to becoming a

Wise One himself? He wondered at the skill that blossomed from the end of his fingers. His reputation around town spread with the sadness of his voice as he tapped into his loneliness and longing for Tanzaa. It rippled into his music to the point that he could easily make an audience of hardened, half-drunk miners and lumberjacks weep into their ale. Young girls flocked to whatever venue he had booked and flirted with him shamelessly. He grew rich enough with his tips and earnings, but he wanted none of it.

Davian felt only the winter cold and a terrible longing. He knew there was magic in the music and it haunted him. Nowhere on earth could he play any music that didn't magically call to Tanzaa. He felt driven. His only hope was that she would hear his music on the stormy winds.

And so, Dayvian determined to leave Savone, telling no one. He abandoned a flock of innkeepers and admirers with no answers. With his earnings he'd purchased a compass - his cooking pot probably couldn't manage something so complex - and a few private lessons in orienteering before he set off into the uninhabited lands north of the mountains.

After only a week of slow trudging, trees grew sparse, the hunting almost completely disappeared and Dayvian survived solely on the contents of that pot. He stubbornly moved across the terrain in the near-total dark. He used the stars as guides because the sun lightened the horizon only for a few brief hours a day. When storms blew in, he huddled in his tent and waited it out, playing songs for the wind and not bothering to write them down. Then after the storm passed on, he moved across the crust of blown snow once the sky cleared enough for him to see the northern stars.

In such a way he trekked for over a month. Then, at last, Dayvian saw something strange in the flat, gray world of starlight on snow. It looked like another mountain, but with its slopes so sharply set and so tall he could see it from days away. The northern lights snaking overhead reflected in its crystalline stone. Sometimes they flashed like diamonds off its spires. Snow drifts built up by the wind piled against one side, marring its symmetry, but otherwise, there was no mistaking it: Gandoy, the home of Owailion, the King of Creating and the first Wise One to walk the Land.

Dayvian, at last, arrived to ask a question.

In the half-light of the stars, Dayvian wondered if he was going to catch someone in bed asleep. Not that it mattered. Someone who lived in this white world would sleep whenever they felt the need, regardless of the light. Surely someone as powerful as Owailion had anticipated his guest. Or at least Dayvian hoped so. He walked right up to huge doors made of some kind of crystal; not ice nor glass. The pattern cut into the door faces fascinated Dayvian, like a piece of music he couldn't read, ups and downs that bewildered his ear. Every time he thought he recognized a pattern in the sculpted walls, something broke it like an accidental note off-key or an odd time change amid the regular rhythm. Don't let yourself be distracted Dayvian told himself. He pounded his fist on the crystal doors.

No one came for at least an hour and Dayvian could just imagine Yeolani's sad eulogy once they found him frozen to death on Owailion's doorstep. Here died Dayvian, the frozen goat. Pounding on the door kept him warm. When he tired, Dayvian sat down in front of the door and played a few songs, bemoaning the cold that set his strings out of tune. Maybe the sour music would make it to Owailion's ears. Then Dayvian pounded on the door some more.

Finally, in the midst of a painfully out of tune love song, Dayvian heard something creaking and he scrambled to his feet. The crystal doors opened a crack and he felt a wave of warm air blow out at him.

"Well, don't let the heat all out," he heard someone bark at him.

Dayvian obediently slipped through the opening in the enormous doors that promptly closed behind him with a boom. No one was there to meet him. Instead, Dayvian found himself in a warm courtyard open to the sky. The space teamed with strange equipment and odd contraptions that might have been mechanical but almost looked alive. The heat in the courtyard, after weeks of bitter cold, felt almost strange. Dayvian could see the open sky still icy with stars above his head, yet this yard felt spring comfortable. Magic opening doors and balmy weather reassured Dayvian but he would have preferred to see his host as well. Without permission to come nearer, Dayvian began weaving his way through the graveyard of metal projects. He made for the great looming building on the other side of the courtyard; the palace itself.

As he approached, Dayvian spied doors identical to the ones on the outer wall that lined the courtyard and they too began opening as he approached. Now, at last, he saw his host, or so he presumed. Owailion stood in the doorway wearing a week's worth of beard. He too boasted shaggy white hair like Dayvian's but his gnarled hands, work apron, and folded arms were anything but inviting. Owailion's face, burned by the cold and wind, looked like aged oak bark as if four hundred years carried more grief than he deserved. Dark eyes glared at Dayvian as he approached and the musician reminded himself again, he wasn't going to be intimidated just because this man possessed more power than any person in the Land. Owailion certainly didn't look the part.

"Looks can be deceiving, Dayvian of Teal," Owailion said. "You've come a long way just to ask me a question."

"You're the only one who might have answers," Dayvian replied.

Owailion only grunted and turned, walking into his house, expecting Dayvian to follow. The foyer of the palace glistened like ice, but the warmth within made Dayvian strip off his furs and piled them on his arm before they disappeared, back into the cauldron. He followed Owailion up a flight of glass stairs and into a room full of globes of crystal. Dayvian gawked at orbs the size of his fist, each with a misty, unclear picture inside. Some rested on a desk, while others occupied the chairs and even floated about the room like massive soap bubbles in water. Near the ceiling glowed several orbs to provide light and the frosted windows kept out the cold starlight. When Owailion swept away a few orbs from off the glass desk they floated rather than fell. Hesitantly Dayvian cleared a carved crystal seat and sat across the desk from Owailion. With no hint from his host, Dayvian set his things aside and felt a sense of relief when they didn't vanish as his coats had gone.

Owailion didn't say anything but just propped his head upon his fist and stared at the floating orbs beyond his guest. Dayvian decided that was close to an introduction and so he began the carefully prepared topic he had come two thousand miles to discuss.

"I need to know everything I can about Heart Stones. I assume you know that Rashel offered me one, but I gave it to Tanzaa instead and it made her into a Wise One. Is there anything..."

Owailion interrupted in his gruff, windblown voice. "You're a fool. You toyed with the order of things and now you want to avoid the consequences. You want me to clean up your mess."

Dayvian reeled back at the accusation. He had not expected to be praised for his sacrifice but neither did he feel he deserve so severe a lecture. It took him a bit to regroup, but he came back with as humble a tone as he could manage.

"No sir,...I mean yes sir, I'm a fool and I want to know if there's any hope for me to clean it up for myself. I can sense that magic is still part of me, in my music. If there's a Heart Stone out there, I'll Seek it, but if there's no hope...it's better that I know now. Rashel, Tanzaa, even myself, can any of us possibly find it, if it exists."

"And what would you do, boy, if I told you there is no unclaimed Heart Stone *ever* and they always have a tie to one person, the one who touched them. You've lost your chance boy."

Dayvian sighed, but not with regret. He still did not rue his decision to force Tanzaa into being a Wise One. It was better that Tanzaa become the magician and he would just be better off as a bard. He had spent the better part of four months thinking about just that scenario.

"Then I will move on with my life the way Tanzaa has. I'll become the greatest non-magical musician the Land has ever known and when I die, she'll still be able to dance to my songs forever."

Saying those words aloud made Dayvian's eyes ache and he felt the regret at the back of his throat, but he meant them. He would move on, striving for the rest of his mortal life to leave behind the music that would lend grace to his love for an eternity.

Finally, Owailion made eye contact and dropped his fist, looking at his unwanted guest with a new glare. The Wise One might be taking him seriously at last. "Well, at least you've got the right attitude. It's not your fault that you two met before Rashel found you. It never should have happened that way."

Dayvian puzzled over that comment a moment and then

gave up and asked. "How so, sir? Loving Tanzaa has been the most amazing thing that has happened to me."

"And it would have been perfect," the Wise One replied. "It just happened in the wrong order. As a Wise One, you would be drawn to her, but only after your magic was firmly in place. We are meant to be with each other, to form these bonds. Unfortunately, you two found each other before the magic found you and it should have been in the other order. Now it is ruined and you'll both be lonely, you for your lifetime and she for eternity."

Dayvian didn't want to hear more recriminations. He hadn't known any of this back when he made that fateful decision to give Tanzaa the Heart Stone. Now he had come all this way to find answers, not more reminders of how foolish he had been. "So I'm doomed to remain a lonely curmudgeon like you?" he growled under his breath.

Owailion grunted. "You didn't think of that when you put her hand on the Heart Stone, did you?"

How did Owailion even know about that, Dayvian wondered. Did all these globes floating about the room tell him the past?

"I didn't know about magic back then," Dayvian tried to defend himself. "I wanted a way to solve her immediate problem and the magic did that. Now I want to solve the next problem. Is there a Heart Stone out there with my name on it? Will Tanzaa find it and give it to me, or must I find it myself? Is it possible for me to become magical? That's all I want to know."

Owailion thumped his fist on the desk, startling the crystal orbs away with his forceful blow. Then he rose, pacing about the room. "Boy," he barked, "You've asked three separate questions with separate answers....no, no and maybe. Does that satisfy you? Of course, not. Next, you want to know how. Well, that will take more time than someone with a limited lifespan will allow. I've been alive for sixteen generations and still do not understand Heart Stones myself."

Dayvian was still trying to go back to his three questions to understand why they wouldn't have the same answers. First, is there a Heart Stone with my name on it; no. In other words, the one he was offered was meant for him, not Tanzaa. Will Tanzaa find another Heart Stone for me; no, but that could mean someone else, perhaps Dayvian himself could find one. And finally, is it possible for him to become magical? Maybe was the answer. Well, demons gave magical abilities to their hosts, but Dayvian rejected that idea out of hand. Demons simply craved pain and evil. They only took their hosts over to achieve those ends. He could not love Tanzaa with that kind of magic within his heart. Another possibility was people in other lands who had native magic and could be trained to develop it. Such gifts never achieved the results seen in a Wise One, such as immortality.

"You think too much," the Wise One grumbled. He undoubtedly heard every word that wandered through Dayvian's brain. Owailion glared and sat back down before he continued. "If you want to understand the magic you must be willing to learn, to practice, to train, to struggle, and perhaps fail. It is the only way you *might* achieve what you seek. The discipline demanded must be self-imposed, not by me or God or anyone else. I cannot give it to you."

"But you can teach me?" Dayvian affirmed.

"Teach, no. Expose you to the information, yes. Only an open mind can be taught. Can you be taught, Dayvian of Teal?"

For once Owailion's blazing black eyes leveled on Dayvian and he felt that he had the Wise One's undivided attention. It sent chills down the musician's neck. What had he gotten himself into? Only the future would say, but Dayvian would leap off the cliff and into the lake of magic, knowing he might drown. There was no shield over him now to protect him from the torture Owailion was about to inflict. Yet, Dayvian said the only thing he could.

"Yes."

12

DEMON WRANGLING

*T*anzaa looked out over the view from the first mountain pass and marveled at the village squeezed into the dale beyond. In Demion they had no peaks this high. She wondered how she could ever search them all. The Great Chain, a swath of tremendous mountains that cut across two thousand miles of the Land made an impressive barrier. These vast mountains, so tall they would not support trees, hid beneath snow even in the summer. They seemed alien and beautiful to her. She had been riding across open plains toward the mountains for two days since she left the river and had finally reached the base of the Chain.

Now her true fear began to kick in. She had to face people again and this time without Rashel beside her.

Tanzaa could sense these village people distrusted outsiders, and they didn't even know she was a magician or Demian. These were simple mountain folk, cutting wood, hunting, and struggling to farm between the rocks. When a fine lady rode out of the pass everyone gathered to find out who she was coming up off their narrow trails to visit them.

Tanzaa fingered the bracer she had won behind the water-fall. What were its gifts? She still did not know. Talismans were individual to each Wise One. Nothing Rashel had taught her helped to discover the bracer's purpose. That meant she must Seek answers alone there as well. Perhaps it would help her face down her nerves when she spoke to the crowd that gathered like flowers turning toward the sun, in the town square to see her.

"Greetings, I am the Queen of Storms. I'm visiting all the palaces around the Land," she explained to the silent crowd. "I am sharing about the Wise Ones."

"Queen of Storms? Welcome to Timberline." The town's head man approached. Tanzaa could hear his silent suspicion echo through his mind, but he was polite enough. "We have no inn for the night. You are welcome at my house. If you come in peace, you may have my peace."

Part of Tanzaa wanted to refuse, preferring to move on up the mountain, not bothering with the suspicious group. They did not need her help, not that she could tell. Their biased minds pressed against hers, forcing her to block them out. They didn't want or need any help.

But just because they wanted nothing from her did not mean she should not be polite. It was only a stage where she must dance. She had new music to dance to. The gift must be honored and used.

"Peace," she declared accepting his offer of a room for the night.

The invitation to the simple house soon included someone from every family in the village. Tanzaa tried to enjoy the festivities as they unfolded. Supper was awkward. Everyone stared at her to see if she liked what she had been served. Excited dogs, cranky children, and the over-warm room made for an uncomfortable stage. They had heard of the Wise Ones but never met one, as far as any of them thought. An old gentleman came forward to ask questions about life on the plains since he had once gone down to the towns of Next and Reflection. This made him the widest traveled man in the village. Then a young woman claiming to be a musician brought out a battered harp and played a few simple songs while everyone watched Tanzaa rather than listening to the music.

Thinking of the melody made her miss Dayvian again. Tanzaa found her eyes filling with tears she would not allow herself to shed. Above the thatched room, she could sense clouds closing in. Unseen under the table she let her hands lilt to the music, trying to dissipate her stormy emotions. Her hidden hand almost danced to it and that little spell relaxed the villagers, if not the clouds. She bound them to the music rather than to Tanzaa's presence. Even a little movement on her part could bespell a crowd and she needed that in this awkward setting.

The next song had just begun when something strange happened that twanged against Tanzaa's Wise One instincts. One of the children who had sat restlessly in his mother's arms the whole evening began to squirm and fuss, groaning and hissing. The mother didn't take him away but began holding him tighter, pinning the four-year-old's hands down firmly.

"I'm sorry, he often gets this way," the mother apologized. "He has thrown himself in a fire, run away ranting and it does no good to keep him away from people," the mother was saying.

Then the child turned his big brown eyes on Tanzaa and snarled.

The sound startled her. Curiously, she looked more closely at the child who blinked at her with glistening eyes. The Wise One in her wanted to understand. She recalled the spell she had set on the quarreling brothers. Her magical sight needed to know exactly the nature of the child's unrest.

Tanzaa closed her eyes and concentrated. Carefully she grounded herself and focused on having the room speak truth to her eyes. She added a layer of shielding over everyone else so they would not be alarmed by what they might witness. This spell was only for her to see. Let me see what is truly there to be seen. Then Tanzaa spread the power about the crowded room.

As she opened her eyes, the scene sent a chill down her spine. Thankfully it remained invisible to others. No one bolted or cried out in alarm at the demon that was latched firmly on the neck of the boy. Slimy and hissing, an alien creature appeared to be a mix of fish with a rat. Its rodent teeth sank deeply onto the child's neck. Pink and red gills gasped behind whiskers and instead of arms, it boasted fins. Its tail snapped whip-like, scaled, spiny, and hairless like a rat tail. Tanzaa squinted back at the creature's evil eye. Where had it come from? Could she rid the child of the pain and danger without harming him? The demon didn't look large and it didn't speak at her, though it appeared to notice her scrutiny.

Little understanding what she attempted, Tanzaa stood up and approached the mother of the child. She held out her arms to the little boy, inviting him to come to her. Instead, he cowered away from her, still hissing in the voice of the fish/rat demon. No one else could see what she could, but Tanzaa didn't care who saw her work now. Instinctively she began moving; a flick of a finger, lift of the wrist, curling through the air, letting the demon see every move. Its hissing changed to a hum of contentment. The mother marveled.

"He never settles like that," the woman commented.

Tanzaa ignored her. She knew the child was not the problem, but the demon. Instead, she began swaying, putting a dancing spell on the swollen-eyed creature she saw. She hoped to persuade it to leave the child's neck without hurting him more. The whiskers twitched with pleasure and Tanzaa thought she had it controlled.

"What is your name?" she asked the demon silently.

"Erildew," the demon thought back at her, still unblinking, still hypnotized by her continuously, gentle movements.

Dare she try this? Rashel had never explained how to deal with demons, only insisting that they were a Wise One's primary duty. Therefore, it must be something Tanzaa could face and conquer. She simply did not know exactly how to go about it. The demon had already given her its name. Just a little dance movement had bewitched the demon enough for her to have that key piece in her possession.

"Erildew, leave him," Tanzaa commanded aloud.

The dinner crowd gasped, not comprehending what they heard, but understanding at last that magic was afoot. Tanzaa had almost bedazzled them as well. The people at the dinner table began softly muttering and whispering to one another. What they saw, however, Tanzaa could not guess. She had to concentrate on the magic that held the demon spellbound.

Reluctantly the demon's teeth lifted away from the child's flesh, snapping and gnawing on the air instead. Tanzaa then conjured a little wooden box, having nothing else to fit the purpose. This act of magic, visible to all the villagers, made the crowd grow still with wonder. Tanzaa lifted the lid of her box and then ordered the demon inside. "Erildew, you will enter this box and never leave it again until I tell you so."

According to command, the mesmerized demon floated off the child's shoulder, its rat tail swaying as a fish would, and it entered the box with angry eyes and gnashing teeth but could do no harm. Tanzaa snapped the lid down quickly and wrapped the edges of the lid with a wax seal she conjured for the purpose. Then, as if nothing magical occurred, Tanzaa addressed the mother.

"He should be fine now. The demon is gone. Has anyone a spot of land, like in a graveyard or under a tree that will not be disturbed where we may bury this box? No one will want to touch it again."

The stunned villagers in the crowded room said anything, not even the child who now curled up against his mother's shoulder and drifted peacefully off to sleep. Tanzaa turned about the room, seeing the blank faces, open jaws, and wondering gazes of a people who had no understanding of magic. In Demion what she'd done seemed matter of fact, but not here in the Land, or so it seemed. Demons were rare and acts of magic rarer still.

Finally, the head-man rose. "There's a loose stone in the kitchen midden. Under there. Lady, are you a witch?"

"Witch?" Tanzaa gasped, thinking of all the evil that word invoked. "No, I am a Wise One. The great palaces in the Land, they are our homes. I do good magic to help all."

It still amazed her that these people did not understand the powerful magic that the Land utilized. Among the harem and court of Demion, the magic of the Land was almost legendary; elusive, hard to duplicate, and certainly enviable. Tanzaa had thought the people of the Land would appreciate what they had just experienced.

With trembling hands, the head man took the box containing the demon off to the kitchen. His departure seemed to loosen the tongues of everyone else, all chatting about what they had witnessed. There were thanks but also whispers behind hands. Tanzaa remembered the hushed conversations in the harem after she had danced. Had the other ladies there known something she had not about her gift? That she could put demons under a spell with her dance? At the time, as a little girl it had not impacted her, but now it began to make sense. Had the other concubines been jealous...or afraid of her?

The mother of the child she had freed didn't seem to fear her but approached with a smile. "There is one of those grand palaces of the Wise Ones up in the mountains, beyond the Lorion Pass. Are you going home?" she asked innocently enough.

"Perhaps," Tanzaa replied, wondering if it was true.

It must be, for she no longer could lie. She didn't know what to say more, but she also knew she dare not sleep here this night. The whispers might be appreciative now, but she somehow doubted they trusted her, despite the good she had done. Now she feared to stay in the village any longer. Without further answers she rested her hand gently on the little boy she had rescued, and left the house, walking out into the night.

She did not care that anyone saw her path. Tanzaa looked up into the mountains, oriented herself, and began moving up toward the unknown Lorion Pass. Something about that name resonated with her and if she had learned anything about being a Wise One, she must follow that prompting.

As she walked through the winter mountains over the next few weeks, Tanzaa thought hard about many things; Dayvian, demons, name magic, Heart Stones, her bracer, and her powers in general. None of these were settling into safely solid clear weather in her mind. As she left settlements behind, she created her own path. She no longer rode on a finely conjured horse. No one up in the mountains would believe a rich lady was going on a winter ride this deep into the mountains, so why bother?

Instead, she conjured herself some warm boots and a thick

cloak and began trooping up the trail. One thing she thought about while making this trek was the weather, which she deliberately controlled, refining her precision within the clouds and temperature. Winter descended all around her except directly over her head. She experimented with snow everywhere but right over where her trail took her. Slowly she grew more confident in manipulating the weather. She asked the wind to sweep aside snow from her trail, rain in certain spots while snow dominated elsewhere. She even tried a bubble of warm tropical air to follow her on the way up the paths she created. However, this only made the trek muddy and she abandoned the effort as a waste of energy.

Another thing that occupied her mind was the bracer. Apparently, she needed a guard against hurting herself if she ever used a bow or carried a weapon when she'd turned into that princess? Why a bracer? She didn't know how to shoot an arrow, so it seemed silly. She was magical; why would she need to protect herself from a little physical discomfort when firing arrows? Surely as a Talisman, it had greater gifts than keeping her from being scratched. Her fingers often traced the doe that stood alert, etched into the burnished steel. She wondered at the symbolism. Its head stood regally, ready to run if anything startled her. What could that mean? That she needed to stay alert and needed protection? Or was she fragile and flighty?

That thought brought Tanzaa face to face with her true longing; Dayvian. If she wanted protection, she would naturally gravitate to him. In actuality, she should be guarding him. He boasted no magic and the sorcerers of Demion knew his name. All it would take is one of them to see him again and they would kill him without a thought. Storm clouds gathered at that notion and she had to quickly douse the idea or she would be buried in a blizzard of her own creation. She missed

Dayvian terribly and wanted to let her mind drift across the Land, reaching toward him.

It wouldn't be difficult. Tanzaa felt reasonably sure that if she half tried, she could find his thoughts somewhere on this continent. She could easily hear Rashel and Yeolani, off in the west if she intended to do so. Dayvian couldn't be farther than that, and she was far more familiar with his presence than anyone else in the world.

Try as she might though, she couldn't justify her curiosity. The Heart Stone would stop her cold. She wanted to know how was he faring. Had he joined in another traveling company? He wouldn't dare go back to any troupe that left the Land. Perhaps he had found a measure of fame in one of the larger cities, a position as a court musician, or one making nightly performances for an audience that would applaud and demand an encore. She wanted that for him. Back in Umzulio when they had performed together, she had always received far more accolades simply because she was upfront on stage, while he played his music off to the side of the platform. He probably didn't need the fame and appreciation to feel worthwhile, but she still wanted it for him; compensation for his other losses.

Resolutely Tanzaa forced her thoughts on to other things, just to avoid her pain. She thought about all that had happened at Timberline, with her using movement, almost a dance to put a spell on that demon. Could the other Wise Ones use a spell on a demon as she had? Rashel had not mentioned it, only telling her of one incident when Yeolani had driven an invading army of demons out of the Land. That had not included removing the demons from the person they afflicted.

She had not been discrete with her magic the way Rashel insisted was best, and that made her cringe a bit. Magic in the Land needed to be subtle, if not invisible. Removing a demon from a child in front of an entire town was anything but subtle.

Yet Tanzaa still felt she had done well. What kind of stories would the villagers of that town spread about her because of it? Would they trust her about keeping that box buried deep and undisturbed? Would the box control and contain the demon adequately? More unanswered questions.

Without meaning to, Tanzaa threw her mind back down the mountain trail, seeking the little boy and his mother. In her mind's eye, she could see them, together with two other siblings and the boy's father. The child seemed happy, playing and laughing, not endangering himself. He no longer dominated his mother's entire attention just to see he did not harm himself or others. All seemed well and Tanzaa felt a sense of accomplishment she never had enjoyed when she danced and heard the applause of an audience.

As the weak sun set and it grew difficult to see the trail before her feet, Tanzaa drew her mind back to her present location. She started her magical camp for the night. She swept the snow aside from her chosen spot, conjured a tent, coaxed fire out of the winter-wet wood she gathered, and brought into existence all she wanted to stay warm and content. She even felt a bit more comfortable now on her own, except for the missing memories of Dayvian and his music.

As she worked at fixing a camp meal for herself, Tanzaa wondered at how much she had changed. She no longer felt she had to control herself rigidly as she had in the harem where a wayward glance or a slouching shoulder would be reprimanded. Now her emotions and dance expressed themselves in weather and magic, with amazing but fearsome results. Challenges pushed her into considering new scenarios that the old Tanzaa could not have imagined or prepared for. She didn't need outside control. She could do it for herself. It just didn't mean she *wanted* to be alone. She could live alone and she would not drown but no one should have to swim in waters over their head forever.

But as she lay down in a warm bubble of magical weather, she thought again of that doe, ready to bolt at the least thought. The deer seemed a weak, flighty creature. No one would fear such a token. Why would a deer be her symbol? These thoughts followed into her dreams, haunting her in the night.

The doe stepped to the edge of the pond, head erect, alert for danger. The thick, rich trees just beyond the clearing remained still as sentinels on a wall. The wind brought no alarming scents to her sensitive nose. Her sharp ears caught no hints of a hunter or predator. Was it safe to drink? Reluctantly she lowered her head to the crystal pond, every nerve aquiver and tense, ready to leap away. Danger stalked her always and only great need forced her out into the open like this.

Suddenly a tremendous splash disturbed the pond and she lifted her head in alarm just in time to see a hand straining in the water. Someone who wasn't there before fell under the waves caused by his own drowning. The doe bolted away from the shoreline before her mind could register the sight of someone sinking. The ripples on the surface spread out from the drowning man. Moments before all had been undisturbed and now the doe leaped away, frightened, unwilling to face any conflict.

Tanzaa bolted awake, gasping in the animal's terror. She staggered gracelessly, confused at being standing at all. Everything had changed around her. She had been asleep in her tent up in the mountains. Now she stood somewhere out on the plains, near a river, knee-deep in snow, wearing only her night shift. There was no sign of her tent or mountains or the trail she had followed for weeks.

Without thinking she conjured herself a warm cloak and boots on her feet as she turned full circle to see where she'd arrived. No trail of her footprints marred the pristine snow-fields all about her. Had she been dropped here by the stars? The night remained overhead but the clouds and threatening snow she had anticipated in the mountains had disappeared in favor of a cold crisp night. A whistling wind crested the river and formed ice on its shore.

How had she got here?

She had been dreaming of a deer. When the deer bolted, she had been transported to this empty place. Could she have moved here or had someone else's magic brought her? A third idea occurred slowly. Had it been the drowning man that had thrown her into this new location? Was she still dreaming? Was she supposed to rescue someone here? The river before her eyes and the pond in her dreams had very little in common.

Experimentally Tanzaa decided she would have to test out what she had learned. She pictured the doe in her mind and then imagined herself leaping away just as it would. A destination never occurred to her. Instead, she felt for somewhere peaceful and leaped as if she danced. Her eyesight blurred for a moment and then when it stilled, she saw again the whirlpool, like the one that formed in the cave behind the waterfall. This one appeared before her instead of above. Fearlessly, she leaped through it, feeling pulled in.

Her leap ended and she saw forest again, this time beside a lake. It was still night but off in the distance dawn had light-ened the sky. She didn't recognize the place and no village or even a simple cabin lining the water. Fearfully, she looked out over the lake, wondering if someone drowned there and she was meant to rescue them. No, in the starlight not a ripple on the water disturbed the scene. So she assumed the dream of the drowning man was just a disturbing nightmare.

Was it symbolic, like when she had told Dayvian that he needed to let her drown? Would they both drown? At the time she had been preparing to become a bride to an evil man or becoming a sacrifice, dying to defy the demons. If Dayvian had tried to rescue her, he would have died as well. Now the analogy had flipped, drowning him and she couldn't rescue him, pulling him back to the surface. She couldn't give her lover the magic she held and she had lost him. The drowning man symbol followed her even to this lake.

Or perhaps the symbol was only the doe. She had learned how to travel magically and the body of water changing was only her dreaming mind bringing back the imagery of the drowning man. Would it interfere with every night's rest she experienced as a Wise One? Well, she could ignore it. Instead of seeing the drowning man, she needed to study out this phenomenon of the leaping doe and this time with some intent.

Tanzaa deliberately pictured someplace she knew well; the grove of trees where she and Dayvian had their trysts every year. They had carved their name into a tree there. Winter in Umzulio would be far milder and her chilled legs could thaw out. Carefully she pictured the place and then imagined the deer leaping toward the park.

Her mind spun with the imagery, and the risen sun blinded her. She had forgotten that it would be daytime that far east. The bare oaks and dancing conifers of the manicured park greeted her opening eyes. Curiously she reached out to find 'their' tree and looked to see the words Dayvian had carved there. It made her smile, not only because of her new skill but also the innocence of the memory. That tree would live another thousand years and even if Dayvian never gained his Heart Stone, this tree would be a memorial to their love.

Regretfully she turned away, finished with her melancholy experiment. Could she find a way back to her camp on the mountainside? This time she envisioned her shelter, the skyline with mountains, and her pack full of magical items awaiting her return. It would still be dark, she was sure, and cold, with snow threatening. Then she invoked the memory of the deer and leaped into the imagery. With relief, she landed at the foot of her tent and found nothing had changed; no disturbance because of her midnight wandering.

Tanzaa smiled shyly, for she now possessed a magical form of travel. The deer had become her symbol, she thought as she climbed gratefully back into her bed. She no longer felt that the deer might be a helpless, fidgety avatar, but a swift and clever guide to her work as a magician. Tanzaa felt no shame in it after her nightly wanderings. Now, maybe it could lead her to finally understand the drowning man. She considered this as she drifted back to sleep.

In the morning she considered her next move, now that she had discovered a faster way to go Seeking. Could she travel from place to place if she had not seen the place she intended to go to? With the map Rashel had given her in her hand, Tanzaa thought over her options. She had been traveling by conventional means for months, but how far could she go with this magical leaping? It was over a thousand miles from the mountains in the Land to Umzulio's park, which confirmed distance and borders were not an issue. Could she direct her path without needing to dream the leap? Where could she go?

Her thoughts were drawn back to the waterfall at Chiasm. It wasn't too far behind her. With careful precision, Tanzaa drew an image of it in her mind and then brought in the doe to leap. Without a flaw, she'd arrived at the base of the falls and felt the mist on her face. This leaping worked beyond her dreams then. She abruptly felt deflated. She still had no one with whom to share her success. It was an unfortunate heritage of the harem, along with analogies and a desire to prove to everyone that magic existed.

Rather than dwell on her weaknesses, Tanzaa redirected

herself. Could she leap to a person rather than a place? Immediately she thought of Dayvian, but she dared not. She had sworn not to seek him out and as a Wise One, she could not break that oath. Rashel...? Tanzaa stretched out her mind, seeking across the plains, and found a lone tree along a nameless creek. Then she crept into the winter thoughts of the leafless sleeping oak. She tickled it awake and used the awareness of its existence to sense where Rashel was in this deep cold world.

Tanzaa found her fellow Wise One in a farmyard somewhere in the south where a farmer had mold in his hay stores. Rather than interrupt important work, Tanzaa looked around the farmyard through Rashel's mind. Then Tanzaa leaped to a spot behind the barn to wait until her mentor had finished her work.

"Tanzaa, what are you doing here?" Rashel asked as she came around the side of the barn after she finished speaking with the farmer. "I felt you moving in my mind, and now you are here. You're learning magical travel?"

"You're safe. You're not Dayvian," Tanzaa replied.

Rashel smiled grimly. "I understand. I think you're doing wonderfully. Magical travel...it sometimes is very hard. Yeolani went years as a tornado before he found his Talisman horse. Vamilion still often feels limited hopping only from mountain to mountain. How have you mastered it?"

Tanzaa took a few moments crafting images of the deer and then with judicious use of magical memories and a few words, showed Rashel what she had accomplished. She wasn't yet ready to share what she had done with the demon in the box, but there would be a time when she would be more comfortable.

After Tanzaa was finished Rashel sighed, looking up into the skies. "That is perfect. You seem to have no limits on your travel, which is good. As Queen of Growing Things, I suspect you, Queen of Weather, and I are going to be working closely. It might require you to go to some very out of the way places... like here. I don't suppose you can concentrate a little on the storms down here. We're getting rain daily and it's promoting mold in the grain and hay," Rashel distracted her.

"Where is here?" Tanzaa replied, looking out over the flat land with scrub grass and a few farm buildings under low gloomy clouds. She had sought out her friend, not the location.

Rashel laughed and they spent a few minutes dealing with the weather down at the mouth of the Laranian River. Tanzaa concentrated on moving away the moisture and allowing a good hard frost to descend on the area, hoping that would cure the mold problem. It comforted Tanzaa that she could use weather magic to improve things rather than distract or hurt.

Then, as she was about to leave Rashel, testing out another leap location, her friend stopped her.

"Before you go, I don't know if you've heard, but...but there have been some rumors stirring. Demion is arming for war. They are claiming you were kidnapped and that is their justification for taking military action."

Tanzaa gasped, suddenly sick at heart. The clouds overhead loomed. "Is that why you left me so soon?"

Rashel nodded. "You were ready, but I wasn't sure if I should tell you what I had heard. I did not want rumors to distract you from what you should be Seeking."

Tanzaa mastered the storm of reactions and questions brewing behind her eyes. Should she go confront the king? She wouldn't want anyone to go to war simply because she had run away from the prison of being the king's concubine. What could she do to prevent this? Could she dampen Demion's efforts with some weather to make a military campaign difficult? Maybe she could dance the demons out of the king and he would change his mind or at least listen to reason. How could she serve? She would gladly go back to Umzulio and confront the king if that would help.

Rashel placed her hand gently on Tanzaa's arm before she could offer to travel there. "No, not yet. We don't know how they will come or even if they *will* come. Vamilion and Yeolani are there investigating right now. They'll be able to tell us more when they return. For now, just be aware. Demion is always looking for an excuse to cross the Wall. This has nothing to do with you. My main worry is that Dayvian will hear of it and think he must get involved in the war. If he does, he'll be recognized and your sacrifice will be for nothing."

"Where is he?" Tanzaa asked, not daring to seek him for herself.

Rashel smirked, "He's with Owailion, about as far from Demion as you can get. He'll be safe there until this war has passed. You don't need to worry."

Tanzaa let out the breath she had been holding in a hidden fear and nodded her thanks. She could not set aside the overwhelming thought of war, but she could pretend. Avoidance was a skill she learned long ago in the harem. This too was out of her magical hands. She would just have to be patient and see how Demion would act. In the meantime, there were other Wise One palaces for her to visit. Hiding her distress, Tanzaa bid goodbye to her friend and leaped away.

GRUELING

"*Y*ou cannot earn a Heart Stone but perhaps you can prove to God that you are worthy of one," Owailion had said on the first day he began training Dayvian. "You can only earn one by witnessing to God that you are doing all you can."

That had been Dayvian's only hope. He clung to that idea throughout the grueling lessons the Wise One set for him. Hoping was the only way to prove that he was worthy of a Heart Stone. It was his magical key that would open the door back to Tanzaa.

"You said I can't create a Heart Stone," Dayvian had pointed out logically on the first day Owailion began working with him. "I'm not magical."

Owailion shook his head, rejecting that notion. "You misunderstand. A Heart Stone is not magically given to any of us. A Wise One must prove themselves by working hard and exploring their abilities, but it is not an *act* of magic that reveals the Heart Stone. They must prove sincerity and that allows them to receive it. It is not for ourselves. Always it has been for another. We only dream of the next Wise One and the Heart Stone was given. I dreamed for weeks before she came. I had to show that sincerity to God. Only then did the Heart Stone appear. No act of mine made it appear. They aren't like Talismans that require magical skill to reveal."

"And then your wife, the next Wise One, she dreamed of Vamilion?" Dayvian had the temerity to ask, knowing he was treading on sensitive ground.

"Yes," Owailion confirmed. "She dreamed that he would come down at the delta of the Don River. But by then she was under the influence of evil magic. She knew she could not be trusted and so she gave me the Heart Stone to give to him. I had to make some bitter choices. I had to wait for Vamilion to come while my wife dealt with her demon. It was a deliberate choice to let her go and I remain watching for him."

"Your wife..." Dayvian murmured. He knew the story lurked there, painful and festering in Owailion's past. The bard in Dayvian longed to tell that story, but he wanted Owailion to give it to him. The King of Creating would never share the tale until Dayvian pressured him. The answer to the riddle of this bitter hermit lurked here.

"I'm not a hermit, boy," Owailion snapped in reaction to Dayvian's unspoken thoughts. "And you will not make my pain into some little bar ditty. I will share it only so you will understand the fate you've left your Tanzaa. She too will suffer as I have, if you do not succeed in earning God's favor in a Heart Stone."

Eventually, as part of his lessons, the King of Creating had shared his story. "I was not taught about name magic because no one knows my real name, not even me." Owailion began. "I was brought to the Land, not born here. The dragons knew, but they never told me. So when my wife came to the Land, I did not know to warn her. We never thought to keep it a secret since we were the only ones here. I made the mistake of traveling to Malornia. There an outlander sorcerer learned of her name from my foolish lips. Later, he sailed right up to the Seal and invoked her name in her dreams. She tried to fight him and misdirect him but it did not work long. He coveted her power and meanwhile she had a Heart Stone for Vamilion. She gave it to me and asked me to find the new Wise One because she literally could not predict what her torturer would have her doing next. We were torn; protect the Land and its future in magic or protect ourselves."

Dayvian didn't dare take notes but he memorized Owailion's words as the King paced across the workroom where he conducted his lessons. The young bard knew he could easily craft a song that would lament this story, for he knew that pain for himself. Owailion had loved Raimi, Queen of Rivers, and if he had not covenanted to protect the Land, this story would have had a far different outcome.

"I wasn't fully aware of how much she was being manipulated," Owailion continued. "But when the Seal came down and Vamilion crossed the border I knew something had gone very wrong. Raimi – my wife, the Queen of Rivers would never have brought down the Seal unless she had been commanded to do it. She had no choice. She would rather command herself to die than harm the Land more. And so, she did...the only one of us to die. And I live the rest of my eternal life without the woman I love until..."

Owailion stopped, leaving his young pupil hanging. "Leaving me with nothing but these blasted globes to look back on the past," he finished awkwardly. "Now you know what will happen to your Tanzaa if you fail."

Owailion's tale haunted Dayvian for weeks, making sleep difficult and it demanded he reflect on how painful this knowledge must be. If he couldn't sleep, what must it be like for

Owailion, even after four centuries? The more romantic side of Dayvian's imagination filled in details the King of Creating would never admit. Perhaps these elaborations he added for himself were true, but Dayvian would never dare ask Owailion how accurate his portrayal might come.

An outlander sorcerer from across the sea had watched the two lovers flit about the Sealed Land, like children in a paradise garden. This sorcerer must have grown jealous of their tremendous power and innocence. The nameless outlander saw a way to break the Seal, to crack their happiness, and force the two lovers apart. He perhaps coveted Raimi and her innocence almost as much as he coveted her magic. And Owailion never knew how much she was being manipulated until it was too late to save her.

At first, it must have only been Raimi doing odd things, unexplained and out of character. She might not have understood or remembered what was happening to her in her dreams. Then Raimi began hurting herself and the Land and had no explanation as to why. She had been forbidden to speak of it. Some of the betrayals ventured into the realm of evil, something she would never consider doing of her own accord. Rather than continue, rather than hurt Owailion, the Queen of Rivers had revoked her right to her magical gifts and elected to die.

Owailion remained devastated, Dayvian was sure. The King of Creating had searched the world and still continued to do so, Seeking a way to bring her back. He had surely battled the sorcerer that had stolen Raimi's name. He had learned of name magic, but it was too late. Now alone, for several hundred years, Owailion rarely left his home and could not bring himself to fight dark magic any longer, leaving that duty mostly to the Wise Ones who had come after him. Instead, he remained up here in the north, far away from people for which he had no patience. He sat here tinkering on strange contraptions and machines, trying to find a way to bring her back.

Over the weeks of training, Owailion heard Dayvian's embellishments to the story and eventually told him off in magical fashion. On midwinter's night, Owailion threw his voice into Dayvian's mind as he slept.

"And if your Tanzaa does not move on and find the next Wise One and is not drawn to him, she too will become some withered crotchety hermit? I've foreseen it," Owailion warned. "She will seal herself off from others and will not leave her palace. She will create a paradise but only for herself. She will let no one in. She will walk in her garden but never leave it."

"Don't say that," Dayvian whispered in his dreams, more upset than he cared to admit. He could not imagine the graceful dance of Tanzaa stifled and crushed, not shared, and celebrated.

Dayvian recognized Owailion probably still possessed a heart if he would willingly share Raimi's story if only to prevent it from happening to Tanzaa. Perhaps Heart Stones were another area of study Owailion wanted to explore in his never-ending mission to restore Raimi. He could only bring her back if the Heart Stone appeared for Dayvian because he would have to find another one for Raimi if she were ever returned to the Land.

The stories Owailion told of his past and the ethos of the Wise Ones constituted only one phase of the lessons Owailion set for Dayvian. Others required such mental concentration they seemed impossible for anyone not magical. Since he at least had the potential, Dayvian might be able to become a magician, even if he didn't gain the title Wise One. Owailion's lessons would not make him immortal, but maybe Dayvian could become less vulnerable to demons and other acts of magic that would threaten him if he tried to follow Tanzaa's life.

First Dayvian had to master blocking others from invading his mind and then attempt to break into another's mind. That his sparring partner in this mental skirmish was Owailion, the King of Creating, did intimidate a bit, but if he could put a single chip in the Wise One's armor, maybe he could feel some sense of accomplishment.

"You're daydreaming, not trying," Owailion barked at him again on their third week of lessons.

"Don't tell me what I am not doing. Again," replied Dayvian, though he was dripping with sweat and trembling with effort.

The two of them stood in one of Owailion's crystal walled rooms now emptied of its globes. They stared each other down, one with dark bitter eyes and Dayvian with his blue eyes piercing, despite the brutal battle he lost continually. He refused to give up just as much as he refused to think of landing hard on his rear once again with another bruise for his effort. Instead, he closed his eyes to concentrate. He forced his mind into a spear of thought and launched it at the wall that he imagined around Owailion's thoughts.

The King's mind wall made of ice and stone rose higher than the mountains. Nothing Dayvian could envision could pass over and into the Wise One's mind. Every time he tried, Dayvian found himself physically thrown down, slammed against a literal wall on the other side of the room.

"Your imagination is a valuable asset, musician, use it," Owailion advised as he looked down at his student sprawled on the floor, making no effort to help him up.

Dayvian grumbled because he *was* using his imagination. He had crafted his thoughts into a spear and Owailion's mind shields into a wall, but how do you get over a wall so high? A spear seemed a weak weapon against something as formidable as a wall where he couldn't even see the top. So maybe Dayvian's imagination crafted the wrong kind of weapon. He abruptly changed tactics. He scrambled to his feet and then closed his eyes to concentrate again. He melted his thoughts down into a single question, a stone he could possibly throw up and over the wall of Owailion's protections.

In his mind's eye, the question became a stone he hefted and Dayvian carefully judged his trajectory. He leaned back and with all his physical and mental might he threw the stone up at where he hoped the top of the wall awaited him in the clouds. He lost the vision of his stone when it entered a cloud bank looming above his head. He could not hear that the stone hit anything or clattered as it collided against the barrier above him. But when it came falling out of the cloud at him, Dayvian dodged the mental rock and he didn't get thrown back into his real world as he had before.

"Better, you're trying." Owailion's compliment surprised Dayvian.

The bard leaned down to pick up the stone again, wondering what would happen with a rope attached. Could a hook do better? What would hook Owailion? Dayvian thought about it for a moment and then realized he had to be heartless to get any leverage against his master. He changed the stone in his mind, altering it in his imagination into a dove, and about the bird's neck, he tied a bit of flaxen string. Then, holding the creature gently, he launched his thought image up against the wall of Owailion, letting it fly for itself.

"Would you let Raimi in again?" It was a simple question, a gentle dove but one that would strike a chord, he was sure.

The bird came back, no longer a bird, but a spear again, sending Dayvian dodging away from certain death. It threw him out of his imagination and across the floor of the room, but not before the young man saw something in his mind's eye he did not expect. He saw a woman, lovely in the sunlight, with coppery gold hair and eyes as green as a summer river, lined with light. Her skin glittered as gold and Dayvian quaked at the sight of a queen in power. Raimi?

"I'm not the only one who is heartless now, am I?" Owailion growled at him. He then turned his back on Dayvian, walking out of the room, leaving his pupil sprawled on the floor gasping.

At last, he had reached the top of the wall. Now all he had to do was see what was on the other side, but he feared that somehow, he had gone too far and the lightning of Raimi's eyes would strike him dead where he lay.

14

AVALANCHE

*T*anzaa wasn't keeping track of the map very much. Instead of leaping from place to place, she practiced using the weather patterns she sensed. She moved as something in the wind, formed from snow, crafted of the cold. She hardly ate, rarely camped, or spoke to the people she encountered in the villages. She wore a cloak so heavy no one could see her for what she was, a ghost of the night. Tanzaa moved with the winter, and the winter was at war.

War loomed like an avalanche on her mind. She could not bear the thought that she had caused it. She carried with her a pang of frantic guilt like lead weights. It grew heavier with the idea that Dayvian might become embroiled in the fighting. She had already sworn to cut herself off from him, and she must keep that oath. Still, she worried for him all the more, thought of him constantly, and longed for his music to ease her depression. At that point in her Seeking, she felt possibly it would not be worth separating from him. A niggling part of her wanted to leave the civilized world, go to wherever Rashel had hidden him away, kiss him one more time and die. Tanzaa could do it, she was sure. She knew about how Owailion had lost Raimi and she felt tempted to give in to the same solution.

But dogged stubbornness also was part of her makeup. Forged in the harem, Tanzaa knew how to persevere if she wanted to survive at all. Something would open up a small sliver of light in her life and she would drive an imaginary knife of stubbornness into that light and pry magic open to give her hope and she would smile charmingly while doing so. She would not give up. Dayvian hadn't yet given up so neither would she. The music continued so she would spin and spin, dizzy with exhaustion but she would dance.

Would this loneliness ever ease? Could she forget Dayvian? Could she move on and find another love as deep, as perfect? It didn't even need to be as beautiful as it was with Dayvian. Please, something worthwhile at least. She could not hold the sun of his love in her arms, but perhaps could she warm herself a little by the fire at a hearth of love somewhere? Every time she thought she had mastered being alone, she heard the fall of snow or the cracking of ice in the trees. It reminded her of a particular melody in Dayvian's music. She grew desolate once again. She longed for a spring thaw or a summer garden to erase that feeling.

Winter in the mountains seemed interminable, but she could sense its end approaching. The heavy load of snow on the ridges threatened to come tumbling down over her path every day. Finally, the bitter cold began to ease and the dirty gray of the sky lightened on the day she arrived at a small town tucked up at the base of yet another mountain. This village boasted stone walls all around as if it were a fortress against wolves as well as invaders. Had the Land ever been invaded this deeply? Wolves made sense up here in the forest. The great wooden gates into town were open as she arrived. The sun had not yet set, so no one bothered manning the door. Instead, village woodsmen led carts full of their handiwork in on sleds or marshaled sheep into protected folds within the walls. Meanwhile, children ran to and fro on errands for their mothers. No one noticed her coming in with the day's end traffic.

The inn, such as it was, had grown crowded by the time she arrived. She found a seat in the back, away from the bar. She sat hooded and cloaked so no one would question what kind of person she was, nor question her. She ordered the meat pie being served but kept to herself as the locals came in for the evening. Most of the patrons were men who had already eaten their evening meal at home but had come out to hear the news and gossip. And apparently, there was much to discuss. Tanzaa listened in with half-hearted interest, hearing both sides of a lively discussion.

"The dog must be put down. He's a menace to everyone," said one of the men at the bar. "Too many mountain goats have been scared off and then there's the matter of the sheep he's attacked."

"Would you have the avalanches down on us instead? The dog's uncanny with predictions. We dare not put him down," replied another older man.

"Not to mention my children, they'd be devastated. Shotzi's part of the family. He's done no harm..." announced a third man, presumably the dog's master.

"No harm!" protested the first man. "I've not been able to bring down anything in weeks and my family's going to starve if something doesn't come into the pot. I'm convinced that the goats are being brought down by your Shotzi rather than the wolves. Wolves would eat the carcass, not leave it in the forest to rot and freeze. Your dog's bringing down the game and not eating it. Besides, he's probably half-wolf in the first place."

The argument threatened to grow heated and the barkeeper tried to calm them all by passing another round but it did little except getting others not already in the disagreement to join in, taking sides. Where was the magistrate, Tanzaa wondered? Or perhaps this town was too small for a magistrate. A rabid dog, a family pet, warning of avalanches, and scaring off winter game, these sounded like serious accusations, especially in a town that survived only hand to mouth during the winter. Although she had precious little experience with animals, having been raised in a grand, metropolitan palace, she knew enough to be concerned for these people and their dilemma. That, however, didn't guide her to know on which side she would fall. She only hoped this didn't come to blows or she would feel obligated to get involved.

Tanzaa listened to the heated debate until someone suggested that the dog in question be fetched. The owner went to do just that as if this were his best opportunity to exonerate his companion and helper. More townsfolk, women, and even a few children came into the inn with the master's return, bringing with him a huge wolfhound on a rope. The dog was big enough for the children to ride like a pony, shaggy, and affable. His tongue hung out of his mouth, making him look like he wore a perpetually foolish grin. When the master told him to sit, the hound sat politely, even though he yearned to greet and wag his tail for all the assembly that now turned to survey him. Who could resist such a friendly hound, Tanzaa thought?

Then the Wise One in her kicked in. She set a subtle truth spell on the beast, wondering if he had actually done what he had been accused of; killing mountain goats for the fun of it or worse, attacking a domesticated animal. That was no small matter. Tanzaa suspected if the hound had found a taste for sheep, no amount of training or guidance would dissuade the dog from trying again. Tanzaa had not meant it, but she realized it affected her too when her cloak shifted from dark gray to brilliant white. No one else seemed to notice, except the dog, who turned back to look at her with glowing eyes, and instead of his lolling tongue, his fangs dripped with blood. Was it demon-possessed or 'going demon', where something natural began to shift toward evil magic? She could not see the demon in him, but something said the cur had evil blood.

So focused on the dog was she, Tanzaa did not notice when the townsfolk turned toward her until someone approached and spoke to her. "You, Stranger, could you help us make a decision?" asked the innkeeper. In his thoughts, she could read how he sensed some power in her bearing and dress.

Looking up Tanzaa sat up straighter, let her truth spell fade, and pulled off her hood. She sensed a flood of surprised thoughts as the townsfolk recognized her as not only a stranger in their town but a woman and somewhat mysterious. Tanzaa blocked out the wave of nonsense speculation their minds sent at her and stood up. The innkeeper's thoughts now spoke loudly of how he regretted that he had brought her into the discussion. She was just a young lady and would probably hold no real thoughts about the issue. However, he could not take it back now without offending her, so he continued.

"We've got this dog that some are accusing of chasing off the mountain goats and attacking herd animals. But he's a house pet as well and has a reputation for knowing when an avalanche might strike. Can you help us, impartially that is, decide how we should deal with the hound?"

Tanzaa looked at the dog, once again lovable and grinning, at the townsfolk. Were they willing to take her edict? She realized this too must be part of being a Wise One; making judgments simply because she was an outsider. They wanted her decision and while they did not know she could enforce it, she would not impose it on them unless the dog was truly going demon. They wanted her not for her magic but simply because she could be impartial. Tanzaa stalled by reaching out to the hound and scratched his ears. Then she threw a truth spell over the entire common room. A few of the townsfolk changed subtly: split tongues of liars and one man sported a bloody fist as if he had been in many a brawl, but none of these people were evil. Only the dog looked like he would harm anyone.

"Avalanches?" she asked carefully.

The dog's master explained helpfully. "Not long before an avalanche, he sets to howling long and loud. It's a fine warning of an avalanche to come and we all hurry behind the walls if we can manage in time,"

Tanzaa almost laughed. Were these people so superstitious that they didn't recognize what caused the snow-slides that threatened their precarious perch up here in the mountains? Well, that made her decision easier. Other than companionship this dog provided no services to this community in the least.

"Kill him. He *causes* the avalanches," she proclaimed.

Howling not unlike the dog, half the gathered townsfolk cried out in wonder. They had not considered such an idea. Meanwhile, the other half of the crowd cheered. As if to add to the mayhem, the dog began to howl too, tugging at his leash to get outside, away from the inn-patrons. Tanzaa kept an eye on the beast, wondering if this was deliberate, for most of the people at the inn were all for taking the dog out into the night and killing him right there and then. Others, afraid of the predicted avalanche seemed reluctant to act. Tanzaa could not afford to not act.

She pulled up her hood and went out into the street, looking into the mountains. The dog's howls continued, barely muffled by the walls of the inn and his owner's efforts to clamp his mouth closed. As the townsfolk began to realize that she had left the inn, they filed out as well, curious about her actions.

In the blurry sky, filled with a mixture of stars and clouds, with little light but that streaming out of the opening doors of the cottages, she couldn't see. Instead, she sensed the tension with her weather gift. Snow, heavy and melting underneath waited on the ridges. The dog's continued baying set her hackles on edge as she waited. It would come, she was sure, and it would be her responsibility to keep these people safe.

The wind picked up and Tanzaa's sense of weather did not feel the right of it. Therefore, this was coming from somewhere else. She assumed the collapsing snow pushed the air ahead of itself. She watched the trees, expecting that would be her next clue as she turned to face the strange wind. The people around her turned as well. The rumble came next. It felt like an earthquake but with an ocean's roar accompanying it. Only then did she see movement in the trees up above the city's walls. Their trunks fell over like stricken soldiers, their feet cut out from under them. The power and sheer weight of the snow barreling toward the town terrified her, but Tanzaa knew what to do instinctively.

She lifted her arms and felt her clothing shift back into the royal white and silver. Her cloak blew back from her, revealing the bracer on her arm. She lifted it high under the influence of a magical premonition. With her other hand, she prepared to direct the snow like she was some music conductor, but it was almost unnecessary. Her bracer created a crystal barrier large enough for the entire town. The wave of snow and debris it carried flowed up and over the walls, rumbling, roaring but arching over as if the town existed in a bubble she created. The howling of the dog died behind the rush of wind and the whoop of the snow cascading over the edges of Tanzaa's shield. Snapping tree trunks echoed farther down the mountainside.

Only when the air was still again, did Tanzaa lower her arm.

The winter settled into a tense silence. When she looked

around, Tanzaa saw the entire village surrounding her in the middle of the street, staring at her in wonder. Even the master of the dog looked at her in appreciation. He had wound the rope around the hound's muzzle several times to keep him silent.

Tanzaa looked again at the dog who still struggled to free himself from the restraints, and a strange emotion passed across its expressive face. It dared her to intervene. Almost on instinct, Tanzaa lifted her arms and began dancing, swaying for that singular audience of a dog. It growled and tried biting its way free. It lifted its muzzle to bay, but the howl went inside its hide rather than out into the frozen night air. Tanzaa spun and arched in a dance, and magically the ropes binding the dog became metallic. The master dropped them like they had become a poisonous snake. Before it could take advantage of the freedom, the dog and its bindings shrank and writhed in the snow at the master's feet. He stepped back with a gasp. Finally, with the sound of a clink, the dog, its rope, and all snapped into a coiled shape, frozen in silver. In the snow rested a new bracer, stylized like the other Tanzaa wore, only this one featured a hound leaping across the filigreed shape.

Had she made a Talisman of the hound?

The speechless townsfolk barely breathed. Tanzaa had no words either. Instead, she reached down, picked up the new bracer, and fit it onto her other arm. The Hound and the Hart, she thought. None of the townsfolk knew what to say to her, just as she had nothing to say to them. Finally, the innkeeper stepped forward to break the uncomfortable silence.

"Lady, how can we thank you? What is your name?" he asked helplessly.

Tanzaa didn't have a name for herself yet. Frankly, she could continue with her shortened name, but Wise One tradition leaned toward naming yourself after the land where one's palace resided. She still had no idea where her home might await her so she said nothing.

"Are you the Queen of the Garden?" asked a wife of one of the inn patrons, "You know, the one up at the top of the pass?" The woman pointed up toward the trail Tanzaa had not yet finished.

Queen of the Garden? She remembered her daydream, yearning for someplace to close herself off from the world to mourn and forget Dayvian. There was a garden here in the mountains?

"Perhaps. I am a Wise One, the Queen of Storms. You should be safe now. I will go now." She could tell by the looks and the overly loud thoughts that while the villagers were grateful for her intervention with the dog and the avalanche, they would all feel far more comfortable if she took her magic far from their walls.

Leaving behind no further explanation, Tanzaa magically leaped from the town, above the avalanche area toward where the woman had directed her. She had to find her home, where she knew she would plant her bracer and protect it the way she had protected that town. Maybe with the bracer, she could also protect her broken heart.

15

MANIC MUSIC

*D*ayvian slept like the dead every night he worked with Owailion. The exercises like trying to break past the Wise One's wall or trying to keep the same type of mental attacks out of his own mind required little actual physical exercise in reality. However, Dayvian found himself bodily exhausted every night. He also awoke so sore he felt like an old man the next morning creeping out of bed, hobbling and wincing until he loosened up. He wondered idly if Owailion would have been as hard on him if he was a true magician.

After Dayvian had been with Owailion about a month, however, things began to change. Owailion spent more time locked in his globe rooms, staring at the orbs and ignoring his guest. That suited Dayvian well. When he wasn't battering his mind against impossible magical obstacles Dayvian wrote songs. He frantically hoped to prove to God that he wasn't wasting that part of whatever magical potential he possessed. He couldn't write the notes fast enough as they came into his mind.

Unexpectedly, after a few days of watching this effort,

Owailion took pity on him and provided him with a magical quill. It would write out on parchment whatever he played on his guitar as long as he didn't play too quickly and didn't write more than one part at a time. The problem was that the songs came to Dayvian's mind faster and with more artistry than he could ever recall experiencing. His guitar wasn't enough of an instrument and Dayvian found himself wanting to enrich his music with drum, harp, horn, and pipe. He thought of getting his magical kettle to produce these missing instruments, but Owailion's presence made that a breach of the agreement he made when given the caldron, and so he didn't dare. So how could he add to the orchestration without the instruments with which to experiment?

Finally, Dayvian asked Owailion for his help with instruments as well as quill and paper. Within a day the Wise One had produced a hand-carved pipe and a small hand drum. He even muttered something about a harp taking a little more work as it was a more complex instrument. When Dayvian asked him why he made them without magic, Owailion had only grunted something about "effort makes the Heart Stone, not magic."

Dayvian had no way to interpret that except as criticism of his work effort. It took a little time for Dayvian to think about it before he realized that Owailion might be trying to show effort on his part to be gifted with another Heart Stone himself. He wanted to earn it and be worthy of a Heart Stone, to give to a resurrected Raimi.

As he worked on his shielding and songwriting during the day, Dayvian found that his dreams flooded with music at night. He could almost hear the new songs before they ever came out of his fingers. He dreamed of lyrics and felt his throat sore in the morning from singing in his sleep. He had never done so before, that anyone would have pointed out to him.

Could you even sing in your sleep? It made sense given the expansion of all his other musical talent, but he could not recall the lyrics until after he first wrote down all the notes. Then the words came to him fast and dripping with emotion.

The one melody that he dared not share with Owailion was the song that, unlike the others, emerged gently in his dreams, not in frantic form. It was a sad and poignant ballad telling the story of Raimi, Owailion's dead wife. Dayvian wrote it one night without much accompaniment and left it in its barest form. It had started as the song about the Wise Ones but went on to tell Raimi's story more fully. And it gave her name.

The dragon lay down in the dusk
Alone Owailion walked the Land
Alone he wandered magic's path
Seeking an unsealed hand
Taking up the dragon's trust.

Raimi came, mid river's flood
Gleaming in the summer sun
With magic in her outstretched wings
From God's hand, she had come
A Queen of royal flesh and blood

Together they turned demon's tide
Cherished and burnished their love
They glorified the Land
From the mountains up above
Down to the delta's sandy side.

And spoke of plans and whispered names
Outlander's bitter lust stirred
Lady's name and magic swore

A subtle knife he slyly bore
And drove to everlasting shame

Elude the tide? She could not see
The river's sweep washed her away
The sins of cursed evil she bore
Harm her Land? Her love held sway
To die might find a way to free

A shattered seal was her last curse
Lady fell by her own magic's hand
Owailion's grief the Land withstood
Demons floods now westward spanned
Leaving still he who was first.

Keep sacred all the Wise One names
And bring the people to Land's shores
Defy the evil that now enticed
Wise Ones will fight their battle sore
Until sweet Raimi comes again.

Once Dayvian got the lyrics written, the maniacal musical drive eased a bit. He could refine the words or notes and then sleep for a few hours. This routine continued for weeks, throughout his training with Owailion: wake early, write frantically, train most of the day with the Owailion and then collapse in bed to dream songs that he would write the next day.

After two months at Gandoy, Dayvian had completed a dozen full scores all written with orchestration and ready for performance. He yearned to hear them someplace other than in his head. He had no way to play all the instruments at once and would need the services of the kinds of performers he could only find Outland. He imagined Tanzaa moving as part of the music and it made him weep in his sleep to think of her choreography. And the songs, almost with a mind of their own, wanted to be set free. Yet Dayvian had no audience, no stage, not even a single listener for them. Owailion would not listen; probably out of spite. Dayvian knew he had to find a way to set them free. They were like wild birds put into cages, yearning to fly, withering if he didn't discover a way to let the music out.

"What kind of post do you have here? Does anyone ever come here, traders? Trappers? To share news or letters?" he asked on the first day when it was light enough to see the edge of the sun on the southern horizon.

Owailion had laughed but said nothing.

"Well, what do you know of the war? Surely you follow what is happening." Dayvian tried to make his motivations in asking a little less selfish.

"I know what is happening, I assure you. Now guard yourself," Owailion ordered and closed the topic with abrupt severity by continuing the lesson.

In other words, Owailion's magic would not send the songs to someone who could spread them to others. The nearest person Dayvian knew who was not magical would probably be Carsin. Presumably, he was wintering over with the circus down in Teal. Dayvian didn't dare contact his old friend. That part of his life was dead, and he so would he be, if he considered it. So how could he share the music? God wanted his effort, so why let the music go to waste in his notebook up here in Gandoy's icy tomb?

The person he truly longed to share the music with could be even more dangerous. He couldn't mail it to Tanzaa even if he left Gandoy and went south to Savone. She could be anywhere on the continent and probably not staying still long enough to be found. Owailion would never do him the service of sending the precious music to her. The Wise Ones wanted him to forget his love and move on with his life.

Dayvian didn't want to disobey the Wise Ones, but he knew his compositions contained magic. Tanzaa would be uniquely qualified to judge the power within the music if anyone in the Land could. He must manage to get the scores to her and not violate his oath to her. Yet he also did not want to anger the powers that be. If he were going to earn a Heart Stone he had to be on his best behavior. He had already run afoul of the ethics of the Wise Ones just by forcing Tanzaa's hand, making her take the original Heart Stone. He didn't dare press for more. These twisted dilemmas followed Dayvian to bed each night and perhaps into his dreams. He didn't remember them specifically, but he knew he dreamed.

Inside that hazy world, he first spied a deer leaping over a waterfall and then jumping to the top of a mountain. The snow flew behind her as she bolted magically back and forth across the Land, vaulting rivers, spanning swamps, tripping briefly through villages at night. Finally, the doe stopped, alert and wary, perched on a ridge high in the mountains and looked down into a deep valley. Despite the heavy snow-laden elevation, below her the sheltered dale teamed with a lush garden, filled with tropical plants unknown in the Land. The doe took one hesitant step toward the garden and stopped, blocked momentarily from entering the paradise.

With a start, Dayvian woke from his dream of the doe. He sat up in the dark of the frosty room afraid to try to go back to sleep. At least he had not dreamt another song into being. A different dream should have been calming, reassuring, but something dangerous niggled at his mind. The doe was trying to enter a Sealed Land. Dayvian remembered that his entire homeland had been sealed at one time when Owailion wandered it alone. Then Raimi had found her way into the

Creating King's life. But with Raimi's death, the Seal protecting the Land had been broken. Was the deer a representation of Raimi? Why was he dreaming of the dead Queen? He had finished the ballad about her already. That should have been enough to ease the tension in his mind.

Then Dayvian recalled the disturbing conversation he had with Owailion when he had first arrived at Gandoy, about Tanzaa's fate. "I've foreseen it," Owailion had warned him. "She will seal herself off from all others and will not leave her palace, where she'll create a paradise but only for herself. She will let no one in. She'll walk her garden but never leave it."

No, thought Dayvian, the doe is Tanzaa. He felt the conviction that she has found her garden and now was trying to get inside. She would seal herself off just as Owailion had foreseen. With a chill, Dayvian recalled the one time he had seen Tanzaa in the park at Umzulio with all the regalia of a Wise One. He remembered the bracer she wore on her arm and the stylized deer on it.

The doe was Tanzaa's symbol.

Dayvian's conviction in this interpretation grew as he thought more about the beauty of that garden. It fit her grace and most poignantly, her isolation. How could he stop her from entering? She must not go in or she would never come out. He would be too late.

Why was he dreaming of this? Dayvian couldn't stop her. What was the purpose? He was not magical enough to do anything about what Tanzaa might decide. She had only to take one more step and become a myth of the Land, lost to the world. He had nothing to offer her, nothing to keep her away from that beautiful, garden where no one could disturb her. He had nothing...

Abruptly Dayvian remembered his songs. They were on tangible paper but also in his mind. He could not send the paper to her, but he could try the mind instead. There was nothing to lose in the attempt, he thought. He would cast them as he had done with the bird in his training against Owailion's wall.

Dayvian sat up against the headboard and his imagination reached for a magical guitar of his own creation, made of ice and time. To do this, he would have to utilize pure imagery, projecting his memory of the songs. Dayvian visualized that he could see the dream deer, stepping through the snow and peering longingly down into the warm valley below her. He guided his thoughts toward the doe's great silver eyes. He could almost reach out his hand toward her, but he knew instinctively she would bolt from him. Instead, he began to play one of the pieces he had composed for her. He need not worry that he only had two hands and one instrument. He could hear every rich note in his mind and imagined it wafted through the winter air toward her.

Dayvian begged her with the mystery and beauty of his songs to not go into the valley. When one tune ended, he continued to the next, playing his fingers raw, his mind lifted. He understood now the purpose of all the songs he had been crafting in his loneliness. They would draw her back, begging her to stay in the Land for him, to give him just a few moments more. He was trying so desperately to find a Heart Stone. Wait for me, please, they whispered.

Unbidden the dream image of the drowning man came into his imagination. It interrupted and shifted him back into his cold room in Gandoy. The chamber's walls then blurred and became a deep lake with steep sides too sheer to retain snow. Ice had formed almost across the lake. The ice imagery in his mind remained smooth and eerie. Far from shore, he noticed a ripple as an arm broke through the ice. It struggled to bring the drowning victim's head to the surface. Dayvian felt himself creeping across the ice to reach for the drowning victim. He lay down on his stomach, crawling out toward the straining hand thrashing in the water.

And Dayvian's arm froze. The drowning one stopped reaching, frozen as well. Which was he now? Drowning victim or rescuer? Neither was splashing or trying to reach. In the hand he poised over the water, he found the sheet music rolled up, held out for her. Both would drown? He still did not know. He would rescue her or drown trying to pass her the music. Would the songs keep her from entering the Garden and leaving him in the icy lake's wasteland?

Dayvian made up his mind. He used the drowning man imagery to pass along the scores, hoping they would draw her away from the next step into the paradise where he could not enter. She would not drown, even if he would.

With a start, Dayvian woke gasping. He had turned his imagination into dreams. How could he have fallen asleep while trying to send Tanzaa his music? The bedsheets were scattered and his guitar lay face down on the cold stone floor. Most perplexing of all, the actual physical paper music was gone, torn roughly out of his notebook. Dayvian rose and searched, but he could not find a single note.

Had it worked? Had he been able to pass her the physical sheet music? Would it be enough to help her see that he was making progress? Would his words of love and loss be the key to break through her willingness to drown and not accept his reaching hand? Or would they help her make other, more painful, and permanent decisions?

Horrified, Dayvian then remembered what he had written in the Ballad of Raimi, of the Queen of River's suicide. Growing up in Demion, she would not be familiar with that story of the broken Seal and he doubted any of the Wise Ones would share it with her. However, the despondency, the magical frustration could not help but resonate with her. Tanzaa would rather revoke her magic than hurt those for whom she cared. Too late he recognized how Tanzaa would feel so much like Raimi. What a foolish thing to send to her. Please, he thought, do not follow Raimi's example. I'm trying. See how far I've come? Don't do anything so permanent, please.

More upset than he cared to admit, Dayvian dressed quickly and bolted out of his room to find his host. Owailion might not be the best listener, but he had to hear him now. Dayvian clattered down the crystal steps of the palace to the workroom where Owailion most often could be found, even at obscenely late hours, tinkering on his machines or crafting some crystal ball with arcane purposes.

It was no different this time. Dayvian burst in on the Wise One who held up a globe of glass filled with gray mists and a glimmer of light like the sun straining through storm clouds. The instant Owailion saw him, the globe grew opaque and dull, no picture to be seen. Owailion lowered his hand. The stormy look in the Wise One's eyes might have been irritation at the interruption, but somehow Dayvian understood. Owailion was in pain.

"I'm sorry to interrupt but..." Dayvian started but then recognized that the storm clouds also brewed in the air above Owailion's eyes, and no flash of sunlight was going to ease the Wise One's anger.

"It's started," Owailion muttered, completely ignoring Dayvian's interruption. "I'm away. You have the run of the place. Lock the doors before you leave."

And the Wise One started for the door, scooping globes up off the floor magically and making them disappear as he went.

"What's started?" Dayvian gasped and shifted to block Owailion's departure, stunned by this turn of events. He had not yet learned nearly enough to understand Heart Stones. He needed help in interpreting the dream. He wanted some way to make sure that Tanzaa wouldn't go into the Garden, nor take the Ballad of Raimi to heart too much. He had been a fool to send her that song and now he wanted some way to stop what he'd started.

"That seems to be a recurring theme in your life, Dayvian of Teal," Owailion growled, standing nose to nose with the musician. "What do you think I'm doing? I'm fighting the war you started by giving her the Heart Stone in the first place. You need to learn to clean up your own mess." And with that Owailion disappeared in a flash of light, leaving Dayvian in a workroom still full of blank globes of crystal with no idea what he had done.

16

REACHING

anzaa looked down from the top of the world and knew she had found her home. Surrounded by mountains and impenetrable but by magic, she saw a lush green valley filled with summer flowers. Waterfalls, ponds, pools, rivers, and springs glittered in the winter sun. In the very center of the valley stood a white marble Wise One's palace. The edifice called to her unlike the other two she had visited. Isolated and graceful - it was hers. That conviction rang like an echo from the mountains. She marveled at the magic that kept a summer garden so bright and warm amid the perpetual winter here. How long had it been waiting for her here? She could not fathom the magic required to create and maintain such wonder.

She took one more determined step toward the edge but found herself blocked. How was it still sealed? Her hands reached out to sense the barrier and again felt in awe of so much power. She would not be allowed to enter until she was done Seeking? It required her to find all her Talismans and the pendant that opened the seal. Regret brought Tanzaa back another step and she returned to the winter snows.

How could she bear to leave this place, letting go of another thing she longed for with all her magical soul. First, she lost Dayvian and now her wondrous home? She didn't want to leave it. She would rather drown than keep swimming in this hopeless effort to wait gracefully for things to fall into place. She was Seeking but never actually finding hope within reach. It felt so out of her control.

Tanzaa sat down the snow, unwilling to dredge up the energy to fight the cold. She didn't conjure up her tent, or even some barrier between herself and the icy elements. The depression descended like a storm, stripping her of the ability to think. How long she sat in that stupor, she didn't know. She recognized the stars rose above her head and she'd drifted off into dreamless, restless sleep. Then she felt something stir in her hand. The wind was picking up and something rustled, waking her from her daze.

She grasped delicate, inexplicable sheets of parchment in her hand. They struggled in the wind to free themselves from her strangling grip. They fluttered in the dark like birds, unreadable, so she lifted her free hand and crafted a globe of light that danced over her shoulder. Then in her magical light, she spread the parchment open on her lap. She gasped in joy.

Dayvian's music. How had it come here? She recognized his style and writing, though none of the sheets bore a signature. She held twelve separate pieces, all of them originals. Yet she recognized his penmanship, his craftsmanship, even the keys he selected that fit his vocal range so well. Frantically she looked at all the titles and noted with pleasure each was well developed and set to full orchestra, with multiple parts and rich arrangements. Without thinking about it, now with something to draw her out of her malaise, Tanzaa conjured herself a tent, a fire, and defrosted herself enough to truly look at the gift she held. Each represented something more precious than a newborn babe to her.

While she didn't have Dayvian's skill in reading music, she could follow the line of the melody. The choreography for each song leaped to mind easily as she instinctively planned dance movements to the major themes. She longed to hear the fanfares as it was written with full performance, as they were meant to be heard. If only she weren't on the edge of a mountain, but back in civilization with a troupe of musicians and a stage. If only.

Without thinking it through, Tanzaa tapped into magic to conjure up a music hall in her mind, identical to the one in Umzulio, where she had first heard Dayvian perform. She perched it right there on the lip of the mountain above her sealed home. Tanza relished the gilded opulence there and the sheen on the stage. In her imagery, Dayvian sat on a stool to the side before the blue velvet curtains after they had been pulled open. In the music well below the stage, other musicians waited to accompany him, but he was the star, dressed in a fine suit, carrying a glossy guitar she did not recognize. He had made it himself, of ice and time. His snow-white hair drew the light and the blue velvet caught the color of his eyes. The orchestra had expanded, playing the prelude that set before them, billowing and majestic.

In her dream spell, she still waited in the wings for the music to include her. She wore her favorite dance outfit, white and glossy, with her best fit shoes, ready to dance. And then the Dayvian of her dreams began to play. His fingers flew like a blizzard over the icy guitar, with precision and joy. She gloried at the skill and beauty he brought to his arias. She took her cue, leaping out onto the glossy stage, powerful and thrilling in her ability to find meaning in the music. She flew, floated, and spun more freely than she could ever remember. An unseen audience wept before the grace.

Then, unlike ever before, Dayvian added his voice to the lyric, bringing the performance to a new level, sharing the story she enacted. She had always found Dayvian's voice attractive, like everything else about him, but she had not known that magic dwelt there too. It moved those that did not even know him. He had designed this piece for his own voice, velvety and warm, a rich baritone. He sang of lost love and the magic lost when one of the two drowned. Tanzaa listened as she danced, in awe at the power here. Had Dayvian become a magician? His voice mesmerized her, the audience, even her imaginary musicians to the point that they fell away into the background for a moment. As a whole, the magic in the music lifted them all like water in a desert. It sparked as a tangible glitter in the air, almost as if they were together again.

When the song ended, the vision ended too and her conjuring faded into the Land's power well. Tanzaa came back to her tent on a mountainside, with only the fire to warm her. Unashamedly, she wept for the end of the powerful song. She sat in her orb-light, sobbing, and was not sure why.

Finally, when she eventually regained her composure, she straightened and flipped through the music in her hands. She found the sheet music for that particular performance. Dayvian had titled it 'Reaching'. The word made her smile. He still thought of the drowning man analogy she had given him months ago. Of course, he was reaching toward her. He had not given up on her, so she had no right to give up on him. He had made such wonderful progress if he could send her these songs from clear across the continent. There was still hope.

And coming at such a perfect time, at the cliff of depression that she had reached, she acknowledged the miracle there. Dayvian was going to find the Heart Stone he needed to join her. They could be together if she would only cling to that hope. She just had to take the leap of faith and wait for him.

Tanzaa decided then, she would keep each piece of music as a precious pearl, pulled from deep waters, and open it only at need. Each night if the depression grew too much, she would 'play' a new song, as a reward for not giving up. Each day she would go Seeking toward becoming a Seated Wise One with the hope of a future exquisite performance to be held on the stage she knew awaited her in her palace. The music came to her as a gift to help her remember that he too was Seeking in another way. When he was at last gifted with a Heart Stone, she would be worthy of this man. And so, she drifted off to sleep in her tent, warm and content in knowing that Dayvian was coming and she could hold on a little longer.

At dawn, a voice woke her unexpectedly. "Tanzaa, it's Rashel. It's starting."

"What?" Tanzaa replied blearily. "What's starting?"

"I'm sorry, but there are absolutely no plants up in the mountains where you are or I would come talk to you in person. Can you meet me down in the valley and I can explain? We're going to all meet at the waterfall on the Don River."

Tanzaa thought she had wakened enough to now make sense of her friend's message and agreed. "I'll be there."

Moments later Tanzaa arrived at the base of the waterfall at the palace of Chiasm where Rashel, Yeolani, and even Honiea, Vamilion, and Owailion also had joined her. Someone had conjured a set of chairs and a table so that they could all gather around and look at a map for this war planning. No one bothered with a tent to keep the weather away, or a fire to warm them. They needed none of this.

This first meeting of all the Wise Ones when Tanzaa had been included surprised her. Did the Wise Ones often plan for war against an army? Perhaps Demion was sending both demons and sorcerers? How could the Wise Ones fight against such enchantments? Was she considered an equal even though she was still Seeking and not Seated? Could she take this time to privately ask Owailion how Dayvian was faring? Would he disapprove of the music he had sent her?

Owailion, who had been looking intently down at the map on the table abruptly looked up at her with an intense glower. Tanzaa turned away. She hoped her thoughts were not being read, right through her shields.

She was thankful for Yeolani's interruption as he addressed the map. "The main bulk of the Demion army is moving right up the forest road toward the north end of the Wall, toward Rayvgild Pass and we will stop them there. As far as we can observe, only their professional army is marching. We'll have to keep an eye on that. The army is bringing about ten thousand men, plus magicians to supply them. Their navy is meanwhile sending out ships, presumably to either the Don or Laranian Rivers...or both, but they are flagged as merchant ships, not war vessels."

Next, Vamilion, King of the Mountains took up the narrative. "I went in disguise to Umzulio to listen in on what the motivation and feelings are among the people," he explained and then added for Tanzaa's sake. "I'm also originally from Demion, but I've lived here in the Land now over two hundred years. No one there would know me. I get the sense that this is completely a political war. The common people have no idea why it's being fought and could care less, which is why they've not bothered including any conscripts in their army."

"Their justification, such as it is, has to do with the insult done the King. They've told the people that Tanzaa was kidnapped by the Wise Ones. People probably know better. The demons the king summoned knew that Tanzaa would be a great magician, and I think they wanted to possess that power.

184

Now that you've touched the Heart Stone earlier than they expected, they're going to attempt to steal you back."

"Why?" Tanzaa didn't ask it as a question but in amazement.

Rashel replied, carefully wording it as if she knew her friend might be hurt by this explanation. "We think they want the Heart Stone, not you. They might think the Stone gives someone their powers and if they can steal one from you, they will possess the magic of the Wise Ones. They're wrong, but that won't keep them from pursuing you."

"And for that reason," Yeolani continued as the primary strategist for the Wise Ones, "We think it best that you are not there at the pass where the army is going to attempt the crossing into the Land. Instead, we need you to protect wherever their navy is going to come ashore. It could be either at the mouth of the Don or the Laranian Rivers or even both. You have already mastered moving from place to place without any limits and you speak their language. You can read the thoughts of the captains and judge their motivations. That may be the only way to tell the difference between a ship set on invasion and one coming on legitimate shipping business."

Tanzaa nodded, wondering if she should be hurt to not be invited to face the main army of her former homeland.

Yeolani continued, "This should be something you can do without risking the demons attacking you specifically. It is probably more important than being at the actual battlefield and if you aren't there at the pass, they cannot meet their goal of catching you and bringing you back to Demion."

Tanzaa sensed Yeolani's hope that she would not be offended by being left out of the main conflict. He didn't know her very well. As a concubine, she had learned long ago that behind the scenes she could manipulate the true power. She knew where to place her influence best. She held no need for glory in war. Instead, Tanzaa decided that now was the time to bring out her bracers, to explain what she had discovered when she had protected that village against an avalanche.

"They are shields," she said by way of explanation and then pressed a vision of the incident with the howling dog into their minds so they could witness how it had worked. She added the subsequent incident, turning the hound into a second bracer.

After her colleagues absorbed the vision, they universally smiled.

"You made...you made a Talisman too?" Honiea murmured. "I thought only Owailion could do that."

"Nonsense," Owailion barked. "You did it with the Life Givers, Vamilion with the Wall, and that tree at Halfway is still absorbing and growing on demon magic. Any time you convert one kind of unwanted magic into another, it becomes a Talisman."

"Nevertheless, the bracers are perfect for the kind of protection we need from you," Rashel said, changing the topic back to the immediate needs.

Yeolani agreed with his wife hastily to make use of the new weapons. "There will be few people to protect there at the mouth of the rivers. Plant one bracer at each river mouth and it will act as a movable shield or seal. Your task will be to block anyone from Demion from coming up the river to attack the inland towns. You can still permit innocent traffic upriver. Demion cannot get a foothold here. Now, there's a sealed palace at both sites, but that seal doesn't keep specific ships from coming up the river. You can move between rivers, lifting the bracer when the traffic is checked for ships that should be allowed inland. How do you feel about it?"

"I can do this," Tanza affirmed. Then she considered the other fronts. "What of the army of the Land? What of their support?"

Vamilion had the grace to look embarrassed. "The Land does not have much of a standing army like other countries. Just our three garrisons. Gardway, Right, and Wallward. We've started asking for volunteers and they're gathering at Wallward." He tapped the spot on the map up against the Wall that formed the Land's southeastern border. "That site was closest to either route the Demians decided to take; north of the Wall or south around the bottom edge. We have about five-thousand volunteers and only about one thousand are trained. There are garrisons at Wallward, at Right and at Gardway where we're mustering, but the men are all gathering at Wallward. We weren't sure which route the land forces would take, so they began marching north only yesterday. We'll join them, protecting them magically once they reach the pass, within a few more days."

Tanzaa sighed with a bit of stress. So, she would be alone, defending two possible attack sites. At least she wouldn't be at a battle where she would be called on to use magic against the army of her native country. She wouldn't be required to learn how to fight with her magical gifts quite yet.

Then she thought of the Heart Stone that the Demians coveted. Without consciously thinking about it, she brought the orb out to gaze at it again. She kept it with the bracers, in an invisible weightless pack along with all the other things she had conjured for her convenience. Staring into the swirling shape made her think of Dayvian's blue eyes. The pulsing glow fascinated her and almost hypnotized her.

"Why?" she whispered to no one in particular, wondering what value a Heart Stone could hold to someone who could not use it. The other Wise Ones sensed this war they faced would be difficult for her, having never fought for her magical existence before. They wisely allowed her to think through things. She lowered her shields for them to read her thoughts. She shared with them her inclination when she severed her ties with Dayvian, to challenge him to find out everything he could about Heart Stones. What had prompted that suggestion? Had it only been the desire to have him find a Heart Stone for himself or had there been something more? How valuable was a Heart Stone?

As if he could reassure her, Owailion finally found something to say. "Dayvian has been doing as you suggested. He has been learning all he can, but there's only so much to be done. A Heart Stone is a gift from God, not something that can be earned."

"Dayvian sent me music," Tanzaa replied, startling them with the almost random observation. "Magic music. Is it a path to his Heart Stone?" She then pressed her memory and understanding toward them of the beautiful piece she had experienced the night before and stored in her mind.

For long, luxurious moments the music washed over the group, fully played by a fine orchestra within their minds. They witnessed her dancing. It lifted their souls as it had hers. She drew them down paths they had never considered before, imposing emotions on them, gently carrying them down a magical river of someone else's creation. The Wise Ones sat in stunned silence after the music faded from their minds, in awe of the impact and beauty they had been plunged into, like hot steel into a forge bath. There was no doubt that it was magical.

"Do you mean you think this is what the Demians are seeking, the power to create something like this if it can indeed lead Dayvian to his Heart Stone?" Honiea suggested. "What good would such...such power to move the human mind give them?"

"Power to move the human mind," Rashel replied. "It's the power both Tanzaa and Dayvian have, whether they have touched a Heart Stone or not; the power to move a human mind to do anything. He uses music and she can use dance.

That kind of power...it's what they want, not the Heart Stone itself, but the magician who wields it. The rest of us, we don't have that kind of magical gift. We do not influence whole groups. Neither do demons. They can influence only those that they inhabit. This can change whole audiences."

All the Wise Ones thought about what Rashel claimed. Slowly they began to feel the theory held merit. Demons would covet that kind of power. It would be seductive to them; the ability to manipulate an entire group rather than one human at a time, possessing them all to force them into evil.

"And what if Dayvian's music coming out of thin air or Tanzaa's dance works on demons as well as humans? They'll fear it all the more," Yeolani added. *"They'll want to control it for themselves or destroy it."*

"Demons, yes, I dance for them," Tanzaa confirmed, and as was her growing custom, she passed her memory of freeing the child from the little fish/rat demon. Her audience absorbed that memory and took note of how little 'dance' was required to put the spell on the demon and persuade him to let loose of the child.

"It's like name magic, but without the brute force of having the name...more like hypnotizing them," commented Honiea. "Have you tried the dancing magic on a larger demon? On a group?"

Tanzaa shook her head. She had barely explored her capabilities and had not sought out an audience. She remained mostly to herself in the smallish villages, trying to blend in rather than working with large crowds. All of them felt the confirmation of the truth; this theory fit like a final puzzle piece.

"Well," Vamilion summarized, "just because we now feel this could be their true goal, to take back Tanzaa for her ability to enchant an entire crowd, it does not change how we will meet them. Dayvian is safely up at Gandoy and Tanzaa, you can stay away from the main battle by protecting our frontiers from the sea. You can test your shields and dance magic on approaching crews. Our plans have not changed. Are we agreed?"

CALLING SPELL

*D*ayvian had no intention of remaining in a deserted palace at the top of the world. War breaking out in the east was his fault and responsibility. He would not be left out of it simply because he couldn't do magic. Moments after Owailion disappeared, Dayvian bolted back to the room where his host had stored him and began packing his bag. Most important: cauldron and guitar. He threw everything else haphazardly into his pack, then remembered it would be cold outside. He dug out the pot again so he could at least get a decent coat. Only moments after Owailion had left, Dayvian departed Gandoy as well.

"Be sure to lock up," Dayvian mocked in Owailion's gravelly voice, as he closed the cut crystal doors. "How am I supposed to do that?" Dayvian wrestled the doors to the palace closed and then looked for a latch, found nothing, and gave up. He ran through Owailion's project graveyard and then through to the outer doors where he was hit with a wave of late winter cold and put on his coat. He looked back at the outer doors that also bore no latch. He gave up at that point, trying to follow Owailion's mandate. Instead, he closed them behind himself as he could. They had to be pushed open from the inside so they essentially were locked to anyone but a magician, so he felt he could leave with goodwill.

But he turned to the bleak landscape and realized he once again faced a long march alone through a barren wilderness with little hope. At least this time spring would probably make it this far north before the end of his trek and going down the river would be faster than going up. It might be slightly warmer now than when he'd come north, but he still was looking at a month's walk before he even saw another human being. There had to be a quicker way to travel.

Why was he so anxious to get to a battlefront? Owailion would not have lied about the war starting. It was also clear Dayvian was part of the reason it had started. But that didn't explain Dayvian's almost manic need to go south and find out what had happened. Curiosity tortured him. Could he pull a horse out of the cauldron? He wanted to know, to the point he felt willing to try even riding. He did attempt bringing a horse out of the pot, and of course, his experiment failed.

So, Dayvian began running. Predictably his pace as he trotted across the tundra lent itself to a nice military march. He set words to it by the second week of jogging and found that he was wishing for a magic quill that would write out the score while he ran. With the ending of winter, he found he could move farther each day and his energy did not flag. Maybe he had improved his endurance by dueling Owailion every day. Perhaps this was another way for him to show his dedication and effort toward the Heart Stone. That thought had him picking up his pace and that produced another song, far harder and grim, almost frantic. With that faster clip, he arrived Savone in three weeks when it had taken a month to do it going north.

At Savone he spent a single night at an inn, hoping for news and was rewarded with a night in a real bed. He also received an offer to travel with a half dozen men who were heading due west to the coast to catch a boat south to make it to the war before it ended. Everyone had heard about the war but no one knew what had happened in the last few weeks. Dayvian declined the offered trip by sea. He wanted to be more than a scarecrow when he arrived wherever he was headed. As it was, he would still take some of his trip by boat down the river, but the less time on the water the better.

The next day he reluctantly bought a horse now that spring had arrived and he could feed the poor thing, forking over his last earnings from playing on his way north. He clung like a pack to the saddle and rode frantically through the Fallon Forest down to Lara cutting a week off that walk. He then found someone who would buy the horse there. Dayvian sat on the dock looking for a ship going down the river. It was full spring and flooding water brought many boats flocking down from Meeting like birds migrating. Getting them to stop to pick up a passenger took more time. He sat on the dock playing the military songs he had crafted, refining them so he could commit them to memory and eventually paper. After two days a barge carrying cattle down from the mountains took pity on him and picked him up.

This boat trip went far quicker than his voyage upriver earlier in the fall thanks to the spring thaw and going downstream. It did nothing to help Dayvian's seasickness. The only relief was that he didn't have to work his way downstream because he could pay and then be left alone. Except for two stops on the way to on and offload goods, Dayvian did not come out of his berth, and only then to gather news about the war.

The news, sparse and contradictory, did little to reassure him. He confirmed that Demion was the aggressor, but not where the front formed. Dayvian returned to his berth to be alone with his misery and indecision. During the remainder of the voyage, when his stomach allowed him, he used the idle time to set the marching songs to paper and tried not to be depressed.

Three months after leaving Gandoy, Dayvian stepped off the barge on the dock at Lolar once again. Now in full spring, the swamp that filled the Lara River's delta made the whole village stink of salty water and fish. The barge was about to go on to Gardway, a much better port, but Dayvian's money had run out and he didn't want to leave the mainland. Gratefully he left the ship and immediately felt better, despite the permanent rotten smell that pervaded the sinking village.

Dayvian made his way, stepping stone by stepping stone down through the only main road of Lolar, keeping his ear open for news or gossip about the war.

"No, sir, I'm full up and cannot trade music for what I don't have," claimed the innkeeper. "If you want supper, I can manage that. There are dozens of ships docked here, more than normal this time of year. Perhaps you can berth there."

Dayvian blanched at the possibility. "I'm also looking for news. What have you heard of the war?" Dayvian begged him.

"Most of the men from here have already joined up and not returned. I suppose you could ask among the foreigners," the innkeeper suggested. "They'll know more than I would."

Dayvian shifted to the men who crowded the evening's gathering. He heard the tongue of Marwen and Malornia, but a decided lack of travelers from Demion. It made sense no one would be traveling from an enemy's shores. Dayvian took his guitar to the hearth nearest a set of sailors from Marwen and listened in on them discussing their navigating woes.

"We were stopped at Gardway for a week before we could get permission to come upriver," one captain grumbled. "A ridiculous waste of time. I'd have been better served to sail for Malornia."

"That's strange," commented the second mate off another ship. "We weren't stopped at all. Got past the shield with no problem and permission to go all the way to Meeting. What were you carrying that you got stopped?"

"There's a shield?" Dayvian echoed aloud in wonder. The two men turned to him. He hadn't meant to speak, but now he was engaged in the conversation. "There hasn't been a shield around the Land for hundreds of years."

"Well there is one now," said the captain who had been stalled mid-river. "Guards stop and search every ship at Gardway. They made us wait even then until their lady magician had approved us. She was working on the Don River and we were quarantined until her to return."

"Which means we got in because she was here on the Laranian when we arrived," added the other sailor. "We were searched and then almost immediately allowed to sail on."

"This lady magician, did you see her?" Dayvian asked eagerly.

Both men looked at him like he had lost his head and thrown it down the river. "Not up close. I just saw a few ladies on the docks. The harbormaster waved us through past that big grand castle out in the middle of the river. He's the one that said, 'she let you pass'."

Tanzaa...it had to be her. She was guarding the rivers?

"But why are they blocking ships here? Is there going to be a battle here?" Dayvian asked, just to see if these men knew more.

"Doubtful anyone would fight for this swamp. Maybe at Gardway, but there's so little of value up the Lara River until you get to the forks in the river. No, the Demion army is going..." and the second mate dropped his voice to a whisper since he must have sensed Dayvian's keen interest, "to Rayvgild Pass. That's where the soldiers are being sent. The real attack is over land. The rivers are just being guarded, not manned."

"Unless you count one of the ladies on the docks. No one could stop a single ship if one was determined enough," the captain argued.

Rayvgild Pass. Dayvian had gone through those mountains less than a year earlier on his ill-fated final meeting with Tanzaa. "So," he asked with interest. "How is this lady blocking ships?"

"It's just like the shield around them palaces all over the Land. A ship simply cannot go forward. My mast and beams shook with the water and wind both pushing one way, and something else resisting. We could go no further and had to make port at Gardway. Lost a full week's sailing. I tried to tell the harbormaster that I was carrying silk and fruit, but he would not even help me sell the fruit before it went bad. I've lost so much on this trip, I'm swearing off any more trades with the Land...at least while this war lasts."

Dayvian tried to quell his excitement. Certainly, a Wise One was involved in blocking shipping up the river. They represented the only benevolent magic in the Land powerful enough to guard an entire region. He had to stay and investigate. Although he had planned to head east to join the war, this mystery tantalized him. If he could see her in action...

Dayvian would remain in Lolar. During the days, he worked unloading on the docks for money. At night he played at the one inn that provided him a bed in return. Staying in Lolar, he could tell when the river was blocked. All shipping completely stopped going up-river, although it did not block the traffic leaving the Land. He watched the pattern and every three days the flow opened up and trade moved inland again.

Dayvian often walked downstream through the swamps to

see if he could catch the magician that was blocking and then opening the river. Be honest with yourself, it could be Honiea or Rashel, but he hoped to see Tanzaa. Was she protecting this area? He yearned to ask her about receiving the music. If she was the Wise One protecting the ports, maybe having her nearby, she would recognize he was there and would contact him.

Either way, a week after he had arrived, Dayvian was asleep in the garret of the inn where he played. That night, when he plunged into one of those alarmingly memorable dreams. He walked through the marshy delta, up to his ankles in mud. His legs became cut with the sharp grasses that seemed intent on drawing blood. The thin spring air chilled him a bit, but nothing like in the far north at Gandoy, so he didn't complain. Instead, he opened his mind, letting his magical music come to him. Some of the reeds in the wind stirred a whistling tune that tickled at his instincts. He brought forward his guitar and harmonized with the simple music easily. Together the piping and guitar invoked a spell to call Tanzaa out into the marshes with him, or so his dream self hoped.

He could see her off on the edge of the marsh, with white-blonde hair blowing in the wind to which he played. He yearned to call out to her, but she skipped away, reveling in the haunting song rather than answering his call. Grief fell on him that she ignored him. Instead, he began to sing to her, hoping to lure her to come to him. If he walked toward her, she flitted away, dancing across water and marsh, almost lightly enough that the reeds she trod upon sprang her into the air. Dayvian watched her in fascination, keeping his fingers meeting strings, but with little attention to what he created. The song crafted the dream and the dream invoked the song. Together the two conjured a spell.

The enchantment seeped over moorlands like a fog, drifting

into the village, creeping toward the inn, through the neighboring shops, down the stone steps driven into the walkways to keep them from sinking, out toward the farms and stilt-bound fishery at Lolar. Finally, the fog wafted out into the navigable river channels. It spread like a coppery mist at dawn, low to the ground, drifting away with the night, pervasive and filmy.

For some reason, Dayvian did not fear this spell, although he knew he had not created it. Yet this mist could not be Tanzaa's either. He could not predict the effect of the gaseous spell, drifting, and twining about his knees. The longing in it rippled from him and out toward Tanzaa. Or was it the other way around? She knew where to find him, and so the message of the spell sufficed. He called with it, using what the marshes gave him. He only enhanced the magic of the spell with his melody. Dayvian let it spread, breathing in the gas, gazing through the fog, mesmerized by it himself until it had drifted over the entire delta and the night had grown light and hazy green with its power.

REUNION

*T*anzaa checked the bracer she had driven into the marshy earth at the river's edge. She peered suspiciously at the early morning mist just outside the village of Lolar. Something felt wrong here. This feeling had scratched at her Wise One instincts and she intended to find out exactly why. She could smell it as decay and rot over and above the fish that usually pervaded this area. She almost saw the magic like gas seeping up through the muddy ground. Something had gone wrong out here away from town and farther down the river than she cared to admit. It tickled on the back of her neck and made her twitch, as if her legs grew restless, needing to dance just to ward off the clinging magic on the air. Had something demonic snuck past her guard?

Over the last few months, she had spent her time flitting between the deltas of the two major rivers, keeping a keen eye on both places. The bracers didn't need to be watched constantly to do their job, but she had to keep aware of changes in both places, so she rarely spent time even monitoring the bracers. Mostly she had surveyed the boat-traffic that the bracers blocked and then let them through.

For the most part, she remained invisible or disguised in her counter-invasion work. She presented herself as a common woman, walking the streets, buying fish off the boats, and listening for word of craft movements. She also tapped into the perspective of the clouds overhead to know of any ships coming in that needed to be blocked. When that happened, she had learned to wrap herself in a spell of invisibility to go out to the ship itself to study if it truly carried soldiers from Demion. The enemy no longer used the actual navy ships since she sank a few by forking some lightning through their hulls. Instead, the Demians had begun commandeering fishing boats or cargo haulers so they didn't carry the Demion flag. This made a personal investigation necessary. Most of the sailors aboard were innocent men and women, forced into piracy.

She had even caught some Demion soldiers trying to swim to shore at Left which was uninhabited now that the entire garrison had departed for the war and so she was not looking just for ships now. The bracers could block quite a bit, but she was responsible for the intentions of those who came to both river deltas. She didn't want to block legitimate business, just invaders from Demion.

Twice she had come to the captain of such ships in her garb as a Queen, wearing silver and white silk with diamonds in her hair. In awe, the captains would speak with her. She warned them with a looming storm cloud that they were not going to be allowed to approach the shore. In both cases, the captains had turned back. At first, she feared that they might have to throw the Demion soldiers overboard, but it hadn't come to that yet.

She had not yet tested her ability to remove demons from any of the men. Tanzaa wanted to try her hand at that skill again, this time against a stronger demon. Her experiment with the little rat/fish latched on the child could be very different from a willing Demion captain, used to manipulating men with his power and rank.

Tanzaa had also heard from Rashel how the battles at Rayvgild Pass fared. While the Queen of Storms might have been helpful, she was infinitely grateful that she didn't have to deal with actual bloodshed. The soldiers had met in battle, and while the Wise Ones still held the pass, they had not been able to drive back the invaders. Tanzaa grew heartsick at the thought, and her depression loomed again, although she had not since resorted to listening to one of Dayvian's songs.

Now, something new had drawn her back to Lolar. She had sensed a spell being set here, something intriguing and strong enough for her to feel it seven hundred miles away on the Don delta. She could smell magic in the air, like a copper coin set in her mouth, pungent and metallic. Within her limited experience with magic, she had not encountered taste as an indicator of power. As a cloud of smoke on the air, she knew it meant fire and had leaped to the marshes to investigate.

She found the swamp disturbing, but the presence of a Wise One's palace, still sealed and sturdy in the middle of the river helped reassure her. It wasn't visible from her landing spot, lost in the early morning fog and the dark, but she felt it there behind her. If she walked out onto the river, she could only get within fifty paces of its walls. However, that wasn't what she came to see. Instead, she began tracing the coppery spell that had disturbed her.

Her sense of this magic grew stronger as she approached the village. It was too early for anyone to be on the streets, hopping between stepping stones in the road, so Tanzaa elected to travel invisibly and followed the spell's scent to an inn. She opened her mind to identify who awaited her if she went inside. What she sensed froze her in her boots.

Dayvian?

The place was filled with his presence. Tanzaa hadn't sought him out, but there he was...or at least the memory of him lingered here. Was this calling spell his handiwork? If so, Dayvian had changed. She could not be sure. She had never directly sensed Dayvian's magic. She had left him before he even awakened after he was rescued. However, this essence bore music throughout its underpinnings. She never would have anticipated his magic to be so metallic and green. She could almost dance to it, but what was the spell's purpose? To draw her in? She didn't dare reach for Dayvian's actual mind to investigate. It could be a trap? Would a Demion sorcerer be able to duplicate Dayvian's essence and superimpose a spell over it to lure her in? She very much doubted it.

On another line of thought, Tanzaa questioned if Dayvian were even capable of coming here to find her. Could he have made it all the way here to Lolar given that Owailion had left him three months before, stranded up north? The thought that he had come, without magic, down to face the war, chilled her. She couldn't ignore this spell. Whether it came from Dayvian or not remained to be seen and she had her doubts. Nothing about the magic here bespoke of his love. Surely that would have been Dayvian's main motivation for mastering any spell.

Well, she couldn't *not* investigate and if she happened to see Dayvian again...well, she would face her emotions when she had determined the purpose of the spell. Invisibly she made her way through the common room of the inn, navigating by the glow of the embers in the hearth and then up into the rooms above. She didn't have to guess which room was his; it almost glowed with the aftereffects of this spell. Notes floated visibly, at least to magical eyes in the air. Dayvian's pleasant scent drifted in her mind, almost making her dance rather than walk to the third door on the left. She wanted to reach out to his mind, but she had sworn an oath and no matter that she wanted to see him, she could not break her promise just to know if it was truly him behind that door.

Carefully she strengthened her shields against this unknown magic, removed her invisibility, and then turned the knob. The room, lit only by a few embers on the hearth, was simple. Only a pallet with a rush filled mattress and a single blanket. Sprawled under the blanket Dayvian laid asleep, his white hair gleaming in the light she brought with her. She looked at him in wonder, frozen in awe that he had come all this way and learned to craft a spell that drew her to him.

Yet, she felt nothing.

She felt no longing, no love, nor desire. Oh, his face would always be attractive and his long fingers, draped down the side of the bed still held some mystery for her, but the compulsion was gone. She no longer felt the magic pulling her toward him. He was any other man she might have met and known in her past. The Wise One compulsion to love him was gone.

At that thought, Tanzaa swallowed a column of aching emotion for what might have been. It was gone and she grieved; not for him, but her love lost. He would never become a Wise One. She didn't close her eyes. She knew she needed to control herself or the tears would flow, and so she waited, breathing slowly until she could close her eyes without the pain of wasted emotion.

So, it was true, the magic would help her fall out of love with him.

Part of her felt amazed at how quickly this break had formed. Another small part of her felt a flash of interest; who would come next? Still another portion felt a stab of fear, for she had no way of knowing how Dayvian would react to this altered state in their relationship. They had last spoken in the park in Umzulio at midsummer, and she had changed so vastly she wondered if anyone from her old life would even recognize her.

She almost didn't recognize Dayvian as well. He must have lost weight, and despite the spring that had finally arrived, he looked sun-worn and fierce. He had been staring into the eyes of a storm, battling it tenaciously, not unlike herself. Both of them had been crafting themselves into sharp weapons as best they could, and the room rang with his efforts.

Distracting herself from the sleeping face of the man she once had loved, Tanzaa looked at the traces of the spell that hovered about the room. It seemed rich with layers, green and copper. Strange, the flavor wasn't what she would have anticipated from her understanding of magic. Green wasn't Dayvian's color. The fiercely determined music she heard was truly his. She wondered briefly if this spell might be an emerging song, like one of those that he had sent to her three months before.

Strange, now that she had seen Dayvian here asleep and had acknowledged she felt no longer tied emotionally to this man, she still wanted to hear his music. It floated through her mind from time to time even now. Was she in love with the music more than ever the man?

Tanzaa forced herself to examine the spell once again. Yes, there was wind and music but now she saw the militaristic layer within. Below that she sensed something more, hidden. A thin layer of pain lined the edges, hemming him in, tying his soul to the spell like a chain. She had no explanation for that part of the spell, nor could she identify its purpose other than to draw him to her. Was Dayvian capable of this magic even though he hadn't found a Heart Stone? If so, he too had changed mightily.

Finally, Tanzaa reached out to wake him. She didn't dare touch his face or hands. They would be too intimate to him.

Instead, she shook his shoulder. Dayvian started, gasping like a drowning man coming to the surface and squinted at her in the dark. Helpfully Tanzaa brought up the light at the fire and he blinked in amazement, sitting up in shock.

You came," he whispered. His blue eyes opened wide and then he jumped out of bed and scooped her up and gave her a passionate kiss.

She did not return the embrace.

"Dayvian, no." Tanzaa pried herself out of his arms, suddenly uncomfortable with the intimacy she gladly would have basked in a year before. She felt like she was being unfaithful to someone she didn't even know.

"But you came," he replied with a hurt look in his eyes. He put her back on her feet, stepping back with puzzlement. "You came..." His voice faded as he recognized something was wrong, that she did not share his joy in their reunion.

"I came for the spell?" she replied. He seemed surprised that it had worked. "You'll bring other sorcerers with that call."

She had no idea what kind of things his calling spell might attract, but she could not be the only magical being to sense his handiwork here, spread over the entire delta. If there were Demion sorcerers or demons nearby, they would certainly be attracted by this.

Dayvian sat down with a thump on the bed, disappointed and upset. He seemed distracted, almost in pain. "But you heard me, and that was my intent. If I brought others... unwanted visitors, I'm sorry. I'm new to this."

She could tell. He maintained a shield around his mind, but he seemed too scattered to hold it with any strength. His frustration and curiosity flared occasionally, impinging on her shields. She could have pressed right through his walls with little effort, though she did not do so. It would be an inappropriate invasion and distracting to them both. Instead, she studied him from without, wondering about the link between them that had faded for her but had not stopped for him. Painfully she acknowledged that Dayvian still loved her and this confrontation would only bring him regret. Tanzaa slowly sat down beside him on the bed, hoping to change the subject to something other than her disinterest.

"Your Heart Stone?"

"No," he shook his head. "I've tried, but it's not easy. It's ... it's..." He seemed to have lost words.

"A gift," she supplied. She wasn't accustomed to being the one with words, but then she had changed since becoming a Wise One.

Dayvian nodded, accepting her explanation. Instead of declaring all he'd learned, he changed the subject as well. "So how can I help you? You're the one defending the rivers, aren't you?"

She nodded a confirmation. "Not with you here. It's not safe."

Dayvian took her hand, gripped it with his strong fingers. "You have to let me help. This war is my fault. If I had ...." but he let it die. They both had enough guilt about the war and neither would want to let the other share it. "How does the war go in the east?"

"The others fight. We keep them out, not drive them back. Wise Ones can only defend the borders," she admitted, and then, after a moment's consideration, she decided to reveal why this had all happened. "Demion wants us, you and I."

That surprised him and his head lifted, eager to look her in the eye again instead of carefully studying her hands. "Why us? I'm not even a magician yet and you're the newest one. What good comes from getting everyone killed just to snatch us?" he asked.

Rather than doing the speaking, Tanzaa pressed her memories of his beautiful musical compositions and the reaction of the war council at the waterfall.

The Wise Ones sat in stunned silence after the music faded from their minds, in awe of the impact and beauty they had been plunged into, like hot steel into a forge bath. There was no doubt that it was magical.

"Do you mean you think this is what the Demians are seeking, the power to create something like this if it can indeed lead Dayvian to his Heart Stone?" Honiea suggested. "What good would such...such power to move the human mind give them?"

"Power to move the human mind," Rashel replied. "It's the power both Tanzaa and Dayvian have, whether they have touched a Heart Stone or not; the power to move a human mind to do anything. He uses music and she can use dance. That kind of power...it's what they want, not the Heart Stone itself, but the magician who wields it. The rest of us, we don't have that kind of magical gift. We do not influence whole groups. Neither do demons. They can influence only those that they inhabit. This can change whole audiences."

"And what if Dayvian's music coming out of thin air or Tanzaa's dance works on demons as well as humans? They'll fear it all the more," Yeolani added. "They'll want to control it for themselves or destroy it."

Dayvian's grip on her hand eased as the vision unfolded. He still held her hand, as if he were a little gosling that he might crush, but dare not let loose. He nodded, understanding now what the war was truly about. "And can you control demons with your dance?" he asked carefully.

"I have."

"Then what can we do with it?" Dayvian wanted to know. "We cannot let the Land fight to protect us from Demion simply because they want our gifts. There has got to be some way to drive them away or make them realize that we are not their possessions, that you'll never use your gift to manipulate them. What can we do? They'll keep coming if we cannot convince them."

"I only protect," Tanzaa replied frankly. "Both rivers have had no invaders."

"For three months? You cannot do this forever," Dayvian insisted. His voice grew stronger, more frantic with each word. "What if we confront them? Or is there some spell to make them forget us. Maybe you 'die' as I did before, and they think we're gone and so they give up. Have you tried to...?"

Tanzaa stopped him with a lifted finger to his lips, but it was the magic of her movement that bewildered him, forcing him to stop with his suggestions. "No, we don't go alone. A Wise One does not need to work alone."

Reluctantly Dayvian nodded, taking a calming breath. When she felt he was stable again Tanzaa reached her mind across the continent, locating Rashel's presence.

"Rashel, we have a problem. Dayvian is here at Lolar. He created a calling spell. I answered it." Tanzaa projected her mind's voice toward her friend. She also spoke aloud, letting Dayvian hear her advocate for him. "Also, he wants to challenge Demion."

It didn't take long to get a reply. Only moments later Rashel had arrived at the inn right outside Dayvian's door and walked in. She shook her head in person, rejecting every impassioned suggestion before Dayvian could get it out of his mouth. Tanzaa had invited her friend to the inn to ask her opinion of how to deal with Dayvian's passionate magic as well as his recklessness with the music and all his suggestions to bring an end to the hostilities. He was almost manic and Tanzaa wanted another opinion on how to deal with his sudden need to throw himself into the middle of this war.

"There's no way we're going to let either one of you near the

Demians. If they want you two, why even let them see what they want?" Rashel said.

Rashel's face grew stern and she failed to conceal her disappointment that the two former sweethearts had been reunited. She withheld speaking her judgment aloud and instead addressed their immediate concern; how to end the war using Tanzaa and Dayvian's gifts.

"We can help," Tanzaa insisted, recognizing as did Dayvian, that the Demians would not give up unless something changed. After all, the war had been going on for three months with a stalemate at every front; Rayvgild Pass and both rivers.

"There's got to be a way to put a spell on them to make them forget Tanzaa and I exist," Dayvian clarified. "If we test our abilities, to make them forget, I'm sure we can force them to end this war and let us go free."

Rashel sighed. She had been witness to battles during these three months and dreaded more escalations. She wanted it to end just as much as Tanzaa and Dayvian, but not at the risk of losing either one of them to the Demians. If the enemy thought for a moment that Dayvian was alive, they could kill him with a word. Tanzaa wasn't quite so vulnerable but there remained the possibility. The enemy coveted Tanzaa's gift terribly, enough that they had singled her out even before she became a Wise One.

"I don't think it's wise," Rashel repeated. "Perhaps if we spoke with the others together we could come up with a plan where we can utilize your gifts and still keep you safe. That must be our main priority, even over ending this war."

Dayvian dropped his head in frustration and for once his shields held tight. Tanzaa, for her part, stood up and spoke privately to Rashel as she left the room, considering the interview finished. Even standing out on the stair landing, they spoke only in their minds.

"You should know," Tanzaa clarified, "He still loves me, but...but it seems to have faded for me. I don't understand it. He drew me here with this calling spell, but I won't give in to him. I didn't break my oath."

"I know that," Rashel reassured her. "If you had, you would have been blocked in your magic. Be careful. Something's not right here. Perhaps it is his calling spell, or something else. You're being tempted to help him and I don't know where that's coming from. Let's speak to the others before we do anything else. Maybe there is a way to break this enchantment without exposing you both to more danger."

"It's not me," Tanzaa declared. "He's the one drowning. I'll be sure not to drown too. Let me settle him first and then I'll come."

Rashel nodded sadly and then departed the inn, returning to the battlefield on the other side of the continent. Tanzaa solemnly turned back to Dayvian's room.

TRIAL AT THE RIVER

*S*he doesn't love me anymore, Dayvian thought painfully, swallowing the burning pain behind his eyes. He stared at his hands, forcing them to not tremble. Tanzaa has passed on, outgrown me, left me for her Wise One friends. That he had done this to himself only added to the emotional misery. The loss had not hit him yet, but the haze left in his brain from the spell, and the splitting headache only added to his malaise. He wanted to curl up on the bed and never move again. How could he have thought he could do anything here?

Dayvian had not expected much, but he had always held faith that Tanzaa would support him. She would always love him, he thought. But instead, she stood on the other side of the door, saying goodbye to Rashel. Tanzaa showed reluctance in supporting him about the Demians. She had doubts. She should have been thrilled with the magic he had displayed. He had sent the songs, the calling spell, and even had come this far south in so little time. All of it showed potential and great power. Surely she saw this.

His mind ran aground once again on how she had been lost to him. It sank in, filling the empty deep where his heart had once dwelled. Dayvian had to do something or he would drown in grief. Without thinking, he picked up the fallen guitar and let his fingers wander the frets, tunelessly playing. It would comfort him or open up something to grasp. He felt himself drowning in his grief and bewildering pain. He didn't hear Tanzaa come back in, or when she closed the door behind her and turned to face him.

"Dayvian, you need sleep," she whispered. She had never seen him so upset and overwrought about anything. The tearless grief painted his face gray, washing him way. His aimless music filtered from the pale guitar, distracting her. She knew this, but she resisted the harsh, out-of-tune melody. He couldn't influence her if she resisted. "You're not well."

"Tanzaa!" he shouted suddenly, so out of character. He leaped to his feet. "I have to *do* something."

His stormy temper made her all the calmer. He couldn't rile her up with his music, his magic, or rash emotions. However, she needed peace to think, so she did something she never thought herself capable of. She put Dayvian asleep. One minute he was ranting at her, and with a twist of her wrist and a gentle lift of her arm, she danced him into a deep slumber. She caught the guitar as it slipped from his fingers and lowered him down into the bed. Gently, as if he were a child, she pulled the blanket over his shoulders and brushed that strange white hair out of his closed eyes. She didn't want to notice the pain written on his face.

Instead, she forced her mind toward less painful puzzles. How could she help him overcome this strange obsession? To start with, she would confiscate the guitar. If he had no instrument, he wouldn't be able to craft more magic and draw the attention of unwanted observers. She would be a fool to assume her bracer would keep the sorcerers from Demion sensing the calling spell that drifted here at Lolar. In the meantime, she would leave him here and go meet with her fellow Wise Ones about how to deal with this newest wrinkle in their war with Demion.

Vamilion took the proffered guitar from her when Tanzaa arrived at their meeting place beside the waterfall. "I made it for him," he explained to her. "I thought I was doing something good for him, but it seems to have made him a little manic."

"Manic is good," muttered Owailion. "He is trying his best to show he's worthy of the Heart Stone. If that doesn't leave him slightly insane, he's not working hard enough."

"But he's putting himself in danger by doing these musical spells," Rashel confirmed. "I don't even think he knows what they'll accomplish. He's just crafting magic without thinking about what his spells do and so they go wild, like a weed in the garden."

"He's drowning," Tanzaa reiterated. "Can we teach him to swim?"

"This is hardly the time to be giving lessons in magic," commented Honiea. "This war is taking all our attention. Do any of us foresee an end any time soon?"

"Not unless we change our strategy," Yeolani grumbled. He hated this war too; slow feints of spells with little military forays and nothing to show for it other than bloody injuries to both sides and no progress. "Maybe Tanzaa and Dayvian are right. Maybe we need to force the Demians to forget them. Is it possible, Tanzaa?"

The Queen of Storms lowered her head, wondering that herself. "Can we experiment?"

"What do you mean?" Rashel asked.

"Disguise Dayvian, let him play, let me dance and see what happens to whomever we try to enchant."

Yeolani stirred in alarm. "Not at Rayvgild Pass. If we fail there, we've lost the war and we'll have to fall back. We should try it someplace where the Demians are trying to get in, but there are a limited number of forces or people to protect."

"Not Lolar either," Tanzaa agreed. "Away from Dayvian's other spell. It still drifts there."

"That's all well and good that we test him, but can we help stabilize him?" Honiea asked. "He seems to be...what was the word you used, my love...manic? Is that safe?"

"He still loves me," Tanzaa added. "But for me, the tie is broken. The curtain is closed."

This comment got Owailion to stir. "Wait, you're saying you no longer feel the draw toward him, but he still feels it for you? When did you realize this?"

Tanzaa shifted nervously, alarmed by the first Wise One's intense questioning. "At Lolar. No love, just....just worry for him," she replied.

Owailion shook his head, not disagreeing, but in sudden anxiety. "It's not supposed to work that way. If it has faded for you, then it should have faded for him as well. Dayvian hasn't given up, so the pull should be there for you still too. Something's very wrong."

"Well then," Vamilion commented, "what's the nature of the bond you created between us as Wise Ones?" He reached out and took Honiea's hand, recognizing the tie between them was originally purely magical but had evolved beyond that with time. It happened for all of them as couples, but for Tanzaa and Dayvian it had been altered and warped.

"Creating those bonds was never my work," Owailion growled. "Don't you think I would have severed it by now for myself? No, that compulsion is completely God's handiwork. He makes the ties and doesn't unmake them. Something is wrong if Tanzaa doesn't still feel the yearning toward Dayvian, and he's still bound to her."

"Then we'll have to test that as well," Yeolani summarized. "Let the drowning begin."

Tanzaa reached out to Dayvian, waking him with a gentle shake. All six Wise Ones crowded into cramped garret in the inn at Lolar. No light but the thin stream of dawn through a window lit the room. Dayvian sat up, startled at his visitors. He recognized them all but Honiea, the Queen of Healing, of whom he had heard the legend. What had changed that all the Wise Ones of the Land had come to join him for breakfast?

"We need to talk," Yeolani pronounced, no longer his jovial self.

Dayvian nodded obediently and reached for his boots. Then he noticed that his guitar was gone. The pit of fear he'd been nursing since Tanzaa's appearance the night before now burned deeper. They didn't trust him. Well, he didn't trust himself either and his hands shook unaccountably as he pulled on his boots and then rose to face his visitors.

He reached for his pack but Vamilion lifted that from him and Tanzaa took his hand. "We're going," she said in her gentle voice and he couldn't resist. He held on tightly and waited for the magic to shift them. He saw a blinding flash and suddenly the little room at the inn disappeared. Tanzaa had brought him to someplace he recognized only from maps.

The morning was more advanced, with the sun summer high with only a few fluffy clouds over the west side of a long river. To the south about five leagues, he could see two dark towers, Right and Left, standing guard over the green water. They looked like what they were; stout, heavily-armed fortresses, and an intimidating guard to the inland passageways. Farther downriver, beyond the two towers stood a white palace of a Wise One, glistening in the sun. It lifted resolutely into the sky atop an island right in the middle of the waterway. The open plains on either side of the river whistled with the wind and he wondered why they had brought him here, far from all other civilization.

"We want to test how your music works and this seemed a safe enough place," Yeolani explained in reply to his unvoiced thoughts. "Tanzaa has been able to tame demons as well as people with her dancing. She believes that your music can do so as well, even without a Heart Stone. We want to test that theory. In a few hours, a ship from Demion is going to try to come upriver. They always come and until now Tanzaa has blocked them with her bracer. We don't know enough about them at this point, so we are going to use this as an experiment. We want to see how your magic will influence them. Can you get them to surrender without bloodshed? That is the plan."

Dayvian's eyes bugged out a bit. He scanned the riverbank and the span of water that at the moment had no sail to be seen. "I can try, but I'll need..." he admitted, but couldn't seem to tell them he wanted the guitar back. He sensed their distrust, even Tanzaa's. He couldn't tell from where it stemmed. Wasn't his calling spell a good thing? The music he had written and sent to her had been benevolent. What had caused this sudden mistrust? Well, he would just have to do his best and burn away their suspicion. "I don't suppose I can have breakfast while I think about this?"

That comment at least got the Wise Ones to smile and relax a bit. While Honiea magically conjured a breakfast for them all out there on the western shore of the river, Tanzaa did her typical reconnaissance of the nearby sea lanes. She tapped into the presence of clouds that drifted over the delta. She passed over the palace of the Wise One, set on a lush island right in the middle of the river just before it opened up into the ocean. She then looked down at the far smaller guard towers. They had been built to protect the mouth of the river until the Wise One's palace could be occupied - its owner not found yet - but in the meantime, they seemed to have taken on another purpose. Soldiers manned the towers all the time, whether there was war or not. The people of the Land still did not trust the Wise Ones to protect them.

Well, she thought as she scanned below the clouds for a suitable ship, there were so few Wise Ones. A common man could go his entire life and never encounter one of them. Certainly, the palaces might engender some jealousy or suspicion, but the Wise Ones did most of their work outside their homes. Also, morally they could not misuse their magic, but the citizens of the Land rarely had an opportunity to witness it in action. Maybe the distrust of the Wise Ones was simply a misunderstanding...a little like the problematic magic of Dayvian.

As Tanzaa's cloud got farther over open water, she began to look more closely at what passed below her on the surface. Light flashed in her eyes, reflecting off water and marsh, like shadows moving when she spun in her dances. On the bright lines of the river, she spied boats, both small and large. Some must have been legitimate shipping, taking goods north up the river to the cities of Reflection, Next, Too, and First. These had been the original villages settled by immigrants when the Seal had been lifted on the Land. The Wise Ones' palaces had been there before, but empty and mysterious. That might have fed the distrust, she thought; an empty land but with exquisite preexisting architecture. It could engender fearful speculation at least.

The stream of legitimate traffic approached slowly. Few boats made it through the delta and upriver without her inspection. She saw that often they hesitated to even make the passage. As she flew overhead, Tanzaa's mind with the cloud, her thoughts dove down to the surface, seeking out the presence of captains great and small. Some sounded simply intent on getting their goods to market and sailing through the channel safely. Other captains harbored more profit-driven pursuits, intent on keeping their schedules. With all their open minds Tanzaa could tell perfectly well they didn't hide any enemies either. Yet one boat, a schooner carrying a flag of Malornia had a captain with a closed mind. Tanzaa needed to know more of his intent.

She swooped closer, at surface level and noted how low in the water this boat rode. Perhaps they did carry cargo and had legitimate business on the Don River, but Tanzaa would have to investigate before she could know for sure. This would be their test case, she decided. She took note of the details; flag, crew, rigging, the weight of cargo, and then left the presence of the cloud she had commandeered. She returned her awareness to her body that had remained on the bank with the other Wise Ones where breakfast was now being served.

"I've found a ship," she announced. She sat down to eat and shared with the others the vision and things she'd noted about the schooner. "The captain's mind is closed," she added by way of explanation.

"Very well," Yeolani concluded, "we can have Dayvian see what he can do to persuade the ship to come to shore here and we will remain invisible. If he cannot bring them here, we'll do a more...insistent search."

"It's got a deep draft," Owailion commented after seeing the vision in Tanzaa's mind. "We'll need to give them a dock so they can draw up." He put action to his words, waved his hand briefly toward the shore and a dock with pilings deep into the muddy bottom stuck out into the water twenty-five paces. "That's your goal boy; get them to want to dock there. Do you think you can do it?"

Dayvian knew enough not to equivocate with Owailion. "I do," he confirmed. "But I'll need my guitar." He had finally managed to ask for it, despite the palpable suspicion around the table.

Vamilion produced the instrument and Dayvian took it, strumming a bit to be sure it was still in tune. Then without further worry, he stood and began walking toward the magically created dock. What better stage, he thought, open air and a dock to an empty shore. Meanwhile behind him the Wise Ones erased any trace of their breakfast and made themselves invisible, all except Tanzaa who walked up to join him as he approached the dock.

"Do you think you can do this?" she asked.

It wasn't that she didn't have faith. She just wasn't as in tune with him now. She didn't have the heart to delve deeper into his mind to find the roots of his magic. She wanted him to succeed, just as she had wanted him to find fame in his music. Tanzaa would always want the best for Dayvian, no matter if it turned out he could do nothing with the music. If this worked, he would have gone a long way toward regaining the confidence of her protégés. With his music magic, he could craft a future even without being a Wise One. She wanted that for him.

"I have to, Tanzaa. It's the only way I can win you back," he whispered. Dayvian then stepped out on the dock, but not without the sense he was walking a plank out over the open ocean. He wanted to regain Tanzaa's love and he would have to be a magician to do that.

Tanzaa's heart sank as she overheard that thought. Dayvian had assumed that the magic was what would restore her love? He still didn't understand Wise One imperatives. The compulsion that had drawn them toward each other long before she had touched the Heart Stone would not hold forever. Dayvian becoming a magician had nothing to do with it. If he did not find a Heart Stone, the compulsion was wrong. No amount of magic would make it right. It was a misconception she didn't have the heart to correct. Owailion was right; something had gone awry with him. However, she had too little experience with the mysteries of the Wise Ones to puzzle it out at this point. She could only help Dayvian demonstrate his good-will and hope for the best.

"You need a disguise," she reminded him and put her hand on his arm to stop him. "Like my father?"

She concentrated on having Dayvian's age change ten years older, sandy instead of white hair and a few inches shorter, with brown eyes and a more earthy skin tone. She smiled at the results and Dayvian couldn't resist. He went to the edge of the dock to look at his reflection. His eyes startled him in the water. He felt how his jawline had shifted. He had never met Tanzaa's actual father, but he could see a faint resemblance to the lady he loved, and that satisfied him.

"You'd better go," he turned back to her. "If this doesn't work..."

"Have faith," she reminded him. I'll be..." and she motioned away off the shore, out of the range of his influence. Then she shimmered into the flash of water on the river, leaving him alone in this test.

Dayvian walked the remainder of the dock and sat down with his legs over the edge, almost able to dip a toe in the water.

He felt a bit queasy as if the dock moved like a boat. He wondered briefly if it were the water instead of the movement that made him ill. The planks where he sat seemed rock solid, but still, he kept swallowing back bile. To distract himself, he addressed the guitar, hoping it would still be in tune. Not that the brief walk over to the river would have altered its precise adjustment. Then he looked down the river, focusing in his mind on the boat he had seen in Tanzaa's vision. The vessel had barely passed the two guard towers and was only a speck on the water. What message could he produce that would bring that boat upstream to speak with him?

Always the music had come to him when he needed it. However, he had never done this on command, under pressure to perform. Now Dayvian regretted this test. How was he to call on the music when he knew his life and bond to Tanzaa was at stake? He leaned his head down over the guitar's body. He rested his cheekbones against the warm wood, sensing the fine grain, smooth as Tanzaa's face under his hands. He left the fine strings at rest and hummed under his breath, feeling the responding vibration of the hollow shape under his cheeks and passing into his facial bones.

Try as he might, he could not get the guitar to guide him to the music he needed. Instead, his voice provided the impetus. Dayvian experimented with his range, droning as low as his voice would go and the guitar's body amplified the sound, sending it oozing over the green ripples. Then he remembered that sound carried over water. And the higher the tone, the more it carried. Dayvian left the low note, letting it reverberate and then added another note a fifth higher, more comfortably in his range. Both tones meshed and the hum became a vibration on the flashing surface, a background to the music, like the bass to a dirge that refused to fade away.

Next, he lifted his head and felt his fingers take hold of the guitar's neck, but his right hand would not strike the chord. Instead, he felt his voice go higher, void of words but setting another layer to the echo the guitar continued. It rumbled and floated across the river. He kept the schooner in his mind, though his eyes refused to look out over the water to see it. Instead, he saw his altered appearance swimming in the reflection before him. His mouth opened to sing a strange haunting lullaby, or was it a dirge indeed? The sound grew stronger, not softer with time. Then his left hand shifted to another chord although he had not struck a single string. The chord shift set his hackles off. The new notes clashed horribly with his former music that still lay across the water like a thick oily film.

He didn't dare look up as he began to see silt swirling in the water, marring the reflection of his stranger's face. The music added ripples in the water not caused by its natural flow. Fish began flopping on the surface and then disappearing into the suddenly murky water. Dayvian kept the two notes in the body of the guitar and then his own higher note from his voice, plus the two clashing chords. Now he set his right hand to the strings and began plucking out a frenetic trill, over and over the same six notes, out of rhythm, as a background to all the other sounds. His gut carried the note firmly and he found he didn't need to breathe to sustain the tone. The song, if you could call it such, lacked any discernible rhythm, sounding more like an orchestra tuning up for a performance. Dayvian hated what he heard, but he couldn't *not* play it.

Then a distant echoing rumble caught his ear and he looked away from the water. The schooner was almost at his knees, heaving too. However, far down the shore, almost to the horizon, he saw something else so horrifying he thought the world was coming to an end. The great dark stones of the Left Fortress tumbled like a child's blocks. It fell in ruins.

The crew on deck had seen the tower collapse also. They

scrambled to the aft deck to get a better look. The echoing rumble of the fortress's fall came across the water seconds after their actual collapse. Dayvian jumped to his feet taking the music, even the low droning notes with him, and the water in the river settled.

The captain of the ship, however, stood at the port side glaring at Dayvian as the ship drifted up alongside the end of the dock. He ignored his men who had abandoned their duties to gawk at the disaster. The skipper appeared like any other man of the Land, arms on his hips, a week's beard, and a snarl on his face. It wasn't that he didn't see the tower falling. What he saw before him on this dock meant more to him. The captain knew a spell had brought his ship to this unexpected port.

"You," he snarled.

Dayvian couldn't say anything, his attention torn between the horror of what he feared his spell had done a few leagues downriver and the real danger of a ship captain close enough to slit his throat with a thought. Fortunately, he was spared both scenarios, for Tanzaa and then Yeolani and Rashel all appeared beside the musician on the dock. They all wore the glorious regal clothing of Wise Ones.

"What cargo do you carry?" Tanzaa demanded and her arm moved, her hand set in a strange angle with her fingers held in a graceful, almost impossible position. "You will tell us."

The captain opened his mouth with a pop, struggling to not reply. He had eyes only for Tanzaa. He paid no attention to Dayvian, who was leaning on his guitar to stand up, nor Yeolani who had drawn a sword of steel and gold, nor even Rashel who looked like she was a drowned bride, lilies in her hair and her green silk dress wet with the drink. No, the captain's had eyes only for Tanzaa who lifted her other arm, encircled with twining silver, luring him in. He almost started to try to step over the rail even though the ship remained several paces away from the dock.

Tanzaa halted him and asked again. "What is your cargo?"

"Men and sorcerers to infiltrate the Land," the captain replied to Tanzaa's dancing spell.

She cast her eye toward her fellows, now fully concerned. "What is your goal?"

Without missing a beat, the captain looked at her and replied honestly.

"You."

SHIP BOUND

*D*ayvian stood on the dock, heartsick but that one word got him to straighten up. He gripped his guitar's neck as if the instrument had suddenly become a club. He might have just leveled an entire fortress, killing anyone inside, and yet the only person he could think of was Tanzaa.

However, she didn't need defending. Instead, Tanzaa did a pirouette, attracting the eye of every man on deck. She spun lightly and they all fell asleep directly onto the boards, cluttering the deck, a few twitching like dying fish.

Without hesitation, Yeolani and Rashel hopped aboard, now in their more rugged clothing, and then Tanzaa followed. Dayvian wasn't sure he dared join them. He turned to the south, looking for the fallen tower, fearing the tumbled stones and smoke now drifting from the disaster far away. Had he caused that?

Guilt burned in his throat and he couldn't look away.

"You can't do anything there." Rashel saw his concern and called back to the dock to reassure him. "The other went there.

They'll take care of them and look into what happened. You should come and see what you've accomplished here."

Unwilling to be left behind, Dayvian set his guitar on the dock and jumped over to the deck of the schooner. The others quickly crafted magical ropes to tie up the crew and Dayvian helped with binding them up. All four of them found they had to scurry to the side to throw up at least once. It was an unfortunate magical trait.

Finally, when the crew was secured, Rashel went to the hatch and lifted it open and Tanzaa went down first. Dayvian nervously watched the girl he loved go boldly down into the hold, but Yeolani reassured him. "She's got her bracers and no one down there is going to think of harming her. Just look at her."

To that comment, Dayvian had to agree. Tanzaa beamed in his mind, bright, white, and scintillating. He could watch her move for hours, and now she was climbing down the hatch to face 'men and sorcerers' that had come to take her back to Demion. She had absolutely no fear. Magic had changed her tremendously. He found it intimidating, to say the least, but he wasn't going to let his lady go down there alone. He jumped forward to go second, followed by Yeolani and Rashel, all of them still feeling queasy.

Below decks, the hold had been set up as a transport ship with bunks and hammocks for at least a hundred men and arms. In the dim light, Tanzaa had tossed a few blazing magical lights that hovered up against the roof, lighting the way. She had danced down to the far end of the hold, putting everyone there under the same spell she had utilized above on the deck. Every man was asleep or had dropped to the floor unconscious, oblivious to their four visitors. The soldiers' weapons heaped and left trailing out of chests along the boards witnessed to their military nature. The captain had spoken the truth.

Rashel looked at Dayvian and warned him. "I'm going to use that truth spell again so you can see how these men truly are," and then she moved her hand subtly over the soldiers. One could easily identify which men were magicians or demon driven, and who were just military.

The regular fighting men appeared almost normal except for the blood on their hands. Many of them now slept transformed into full armor, with shields and swords in their lax hands. Thanks to the truth spell, the half dozen sorcerers wore black and bloody clothing. Snakes twined around their bodies. Maggots covered their faces or gross deformities that stank or oozed, mostly from their mouth, nose, ears, or eyes. This did little to help Dayvian's sea-sick stomach. Then there were the three men who carried a demon physically attached to their bodies in some way. Great sucking monsters clung to these men. The creatures resembled pieces of various animals but put together in strange ways. Huge claws or suckers had latched onto their human host's face, neck, or chest. Thankfully the demons themselves also slept on under Tanzaa's spell, oblivious to the Wise Ones' presence.

"Can you wake just the demons?" Rashel asked, covering her nose against the smell.

Tanzaa thought about it and then shook her head. She didn't have that kind of control. They needed to be awake to see her dancing. And these were bigger, more fearsome creatures than the little rat/fish she had subdued up in the mountains. Dayvian interrupted her thoughts. "If I keep the rest asleep and then can you wake just the demons?"

Tanzaa's eyes grew wide with speculative interest. "Maybe."

"And what will you do with the demons once you wake them?" Yeolani reminded them before they tried something experimental.

Tanzaa knew what had worked before. "Put them in boxes

and then bury them," she explained, reminding them how she had dealt with the demon she encountered before. "Dayvian, keep the rest asleep, but be careful, just the men."

Dayvian nodded his understanding and then realized that he had left his guitar on the dock. He debated going to get it, banging it down the ladder, and finding room to play it in these crowded quarters in the hold. Going on instinct instead, he sat down right there in the passageway between the berths of their prisoners. He closed his eyes, concentrating solely on the men he wanted to remain asleep, and lowered his head. Even asleep they could hear his music. That was why his gifts worked differently than Tanzaa's.

He found the right tone in his head and began to hum the low droning note again. He didn't layer it as richly this time, and his voice was only capable of making one tone at a time, but his hands moved into the chords he wanted to add. It must have looked strange, with no instrument on which to play, but his fingers formed the shapes and magically the guitar chords added to his voice. He pushed the men into an even deeper sleep so that some even stopped snoring.

He didn't flinch when Tanzaa began to move. She delicately wakened the demons one at a time. First, she roused the iguana with legs like a horse that had its tongue wound around the neck of its host. With a flick of her wrist, she lifted its eyelids and met its cat eyes. She smiled winningly at the monster and then lifted her arms into the improvised dance. Her hands beckoned to it and the creature lifted free of the magician. It barely stirred as it moved away, floating as the mist demons could also invoke. Hastily Yeolani conjured a metal box all set with a wax seal and a lid that he held open for a new occupant.

"You want to sleep forever," Tanzaa whispered to the creature and it gazed longingly at the box. She lured it toward the casket and it willingly drifted inside and closed its eyes, falling asleep again under her gentle, graceful persuasion. Yeolani snapped the lid down and sealed it with a thought. He set the box on the floor like luggage they must remember to take with them before they left.

"Brilliant!" Rashel whispered, cheering carefully to avoid waking anyone. In much the same way they quickly made luggage of two more demons. Then with a flick of his wrist, Yeolani sent the cases out into the prairie, burying them several yards under the topsoil of the open plains. Years of grass and passing cattle would only deepen their coverage.

Dayvian looked up now, wondering if he could stop his portion of the spell and Tanzaa nodded. Rashel helped him to his feet and the four of them now looked at the men they had left with which to deal. Now what? They could not leave the entire crew and 'cargo' sleeping for eternity, even if the spell would last that long.

"You were saying something about making them forget you," Rashel reminded, still speaking quietly for fear of waking the hold full of napping warriors. "How would you do that?"

Dayvian looked over at one magician who still literally dripped with blood and evil. "I don't think I can do anything permanent. It wouldn't be right to just release some of these magicians. They're evil by the looks of them. The regular troops, we should try to make them forget why they came here. Can you send them back with cargo and they'll simply think they are supposed to guard it all the way home."

"I agree with it being limited, but with you involved, it's uncontrolled" Yeolani commented. "You did well there...but you saw that tower falling. Was it a result of what you've been doing? Your...I can't call it a spell...your...whammy is kind of strong."

"Use my magic," Tanzaa interrupted. "Mine is short and near. Dayvian's spreads."

Dayvian thought about what Tanzaa was implying. His ability to work a spell spread beyond where it was supposed to go. It affected everyone within his range for as long as he could sustain the music, but he couldn't narrow to one subject as Tanzaa had just demonstrated on a single demon. Tanzaa's gift had limited effect simply because the subject of the spell had to see her movement. It made sense. More people could hear his music than could see her dance, but hers became more precise because of it.

"In that case," Rashel summarized, "Dayvian's magic can be directed at the crew and most of these soldiers, but we need to remove very specific memories from the sorcerers...or we kill them. They are the leaders and will have no reason to be on this boat if not to do evil here in the Land. They won't be fooled by a simple memory of guarding a cargo ship through a war zone."

"So, we use a different whammy on different men," concluded Yeolani. "Let's separate them. Regular fighting men up on the deck with the crew. Sorcerers down here."

Magic accomplished the sorting easily enough. Dayvian waited down in the hold, fighting back his nausea while Yeolani, Rashel, and Tanzaa used their magic to move the soldiers up onto the deck and set them out like cordwood. He stood alone guarding the remaining sorcerers. With that isolation, he began wondering again about the falling tower. Was he to blame for the fortress's destruction, as well as the war itself? No wonder the Wise Ones have shown distrust of his magic. How could he hope to be worthy of a Heart Stone now? If he had a single death on his hands, especially by using what little magic he possessed, would God forgive him?

Could Tanzaa forgive him? He wondered briefly how well his gift would work on her. Could he possibly get her to love him again? Then he rejected the thought immediately. It would be immoral to manipulate her that way. Anyway, she would hear his thoughts and instantly stop him.

Maybe that was the problem with him now; the music came so easily he didn't try to control it. His wants and desires simply translated into the melodies. He never controlled them by resisting the urge to play his wants into his songs. All he did to send his music to her far across the continent, was play his desire into existence. Dayvian had wanted to call Tanzaa to Lolar and the music had come to do it, even in his sleep. Later he had yearned to impress the Wise Ones, especially Tanzaa, and so he was able to lure the ship with that yearning.

So why had the tower fallen with that particular use of his magical desires? Dayvian concentrated on that for a bit and explored his motivations. Because it was not just Tanzaa he was trying to impress? Or was his magic not as purely motivated as it should have been? Trying to persuade Tanzaa or the other Wise Ones should not have been his main reasoning. He should have wanted to do the magic out of a desire to help in the war, not to get his girl back. A wave of shame at this realization made a dull ache in Dayvian's already unsettled stomach. So magic was easy; the morals were where the true burden of good magic resided.

Dayvian sat in the dark of the hold contemplating his failure and didn't notice whenTanzaa found him miserably chastising himself. She moved so gracefully to stand in front of him. She had heard his thoughts and she waited for him to process what he had done. He knew his shields would never hold Tanzaa out now and he didn't try to. He could not ever keep Tanzaa out of his mind.

"I'm sorry," he whispered in shame. "I did the magic for the wrong reasons," he confessed aloud. It wasn't her forgiveness he would need, but it was a start.

Without comment she reached down to him, pulling the drowned man to his feet. "Come help," she instructed and then turned away to go back up the ladder to the deck. Reluctantly Dayvian followed her and surveyed the damage.

Forty soldiers and twelve crew members littered the deck, all in various stages of dreaming, snoring, or both. Dayvian wondered briefly what a man under a spell might be dreaming about, but then thought better of it when he remembered it had been Tanzaa's dance that had put them in their vulnerable state. He shook his head to dispel the unwanted imagery and turned to the others.

"So, what's the plan?" asked Yeolani. "What cargo do they think they'll be taking back to Demion? Or are we sending them back to Malornia where they're flagged?"

Rashel had thought of that. "Wheat. It's no trouble to give them a hold full of it and while it won't hurt the war, it won't help either. We can let them decide where they want to sail once they're out of our waters. Wheat is easy for me to conjure. Then we simply have to empty the hold of its occupants and get rid of their memories. Which of you would be better at that?"

"Dayvian," Tanzaa provided. "His works better when they're asleep."

Rashel and Yeolani both tilted their heads identically at that thought, and Dayvian almost laughed. That was how Tanzaa and he used to be, reflecting each other's actions, thinking the same thing at the same time in the same way. As he recalled this, he swallowed a burning pit of regret. Tanzaa didn't love him anymore. He sighed bitterly and then looked out over the horizon, seeking the wreckage that remained of Left. Its fire no longer burned on the horizon so he could not blame the tears in his eyes on the smoke.

Rather than wallow more, Dayvian hopped over to the

dock to get his guitar and then brought it back to the ship. He wasn't sure he would need it, but better to be prepared. He sat on the railing and concentrated on making his motives pure: not to impress the Wise Ones or winning Tanzaa back. He must want to do this to keep her safe. Send these men back to where they came from, forgetting there ever was strife between their countries. Have them recall episodes of trading for wheat to bring back home. Make them forget the sorcerers that remained in the hold. Help them sense a desire to go back home. Those were the thoughts and images his music spell must give these men. He briefly tuned the guitar and then lowered his head over the instrument.

Nothing came.

A trickle of fear burned behind his eyes. Why couldn't he think? Something was blocking him? He lifted his head, puzzled at the strange fuzziness he felt, for he had never sensed writers - well musician's - block before. He looked up at the Wise Ones with sudden alarm. Then right before his eyes, Tanzaa danced, only for him, as if she were his muse again and his heart leaped. He had hope? Did she? But he forgot the thought before the guitar fell from his hands and he sank to the planking in a stupor, asleep just like the crew, dreaming of Tanzaa's dancing.

AMONG THE RUINS

"$\mathcal{A}$re you sure you can do it?" Rashel asked. "We can probably manage if you don't think it's right."

"No, he's mine," Tanzaa affirmed. "Not here though."

A ship was the wrong place to attempt this, not with the sea-sickness. None of the Wise Ones would be at their best on the boat either. Yeolani was down in the hold, dealing with the sorcerers. Tanzaa had just allowed the crew and soldiers to waken, then promptly danced them into forgetfulness.

That still left Dayvian, the most troublesome piece of all. How could they help him without killing him? His magic was corrupt, toxic, and growing in power. They had ample evidence that it was going awry and without understanding why they dare not let Dayvian touch another instrument or sing a single note.

"Well, wait until we're all together. You might need our support and let's hear what the others have to say about what happened at Left," suggested the Queen of Growing Things.

None of them had experienced something like what Dayvian was undergoing. As a person, Dayvian was not evil or he never would have been eligible for a Heart Stone. However, with spells going amiss and turning destructive, the other Wise Ones must study his magical gift and learn how to dampen or eliminate the corrupting influence. They wanted to be careful in how they handled it without harming Dayvian himself. First, the broken bond to Tanzaa and now the tower; he could not be trusted. Was the falling of the garrison at Left just a strange unrelated coincidence, or was it a symptom of their overall problem with Dayvian. Either way, all the Wise Ones should be together to control the situation.

Yeolani, Rashel, and Tanzaa swiftly finished their dealings with the hijacked boat. They removed Dayvian's sleeping figure from the deck, floating him to shore on the air. They then magically filled the hold with a cargo of wheat and wiped the memories of every person on board. Then they magically pushed the vessel farther out into the stream and finally released them from all control. Invisible and standing on the shore, the three Wise Ones witnessed brief panic on deck as the sailors realized they had fallen asleep on the job. The crew righted themselves and after a few moments' confusion, the ship began sailing south, downstream toward home.

Once the Wise Ones felt assured that the ship would do as expected, they magically shifted five leagues south to the tumbled ruins of Left. They brought Dayvian with them, limp as a rag doll. Tanzaa didn't want to see her former lover so vulnerable, so she concentrated on this new scene. She had only observed the tower from afar, on her first trek into the Land. It had been identical to the one where the garrison had challenged her entry. Yet this tower's black stones laid scattered about the shoreline like a giant had been throwing bricks. Whole stones as tall as a man had fallen all across the muddy bank and even into the water, up to a half league from its former foundation.

Among the grass of the prairie and the fallen stones, Tanzaa saw the charred remains of household items, furniture, and the carcass of an ailing horse.

Owailion stood near the edge of the destruction and explained. "Fortunately the entire fortress has been emptied for the war. All the men are away at Rayvgild Pass. The cook and washerwoman had remained behind but had been outside the tower, setting up their garden. They escaped being crushed by running for their lives. Honiea is comforting them. They probably will be welcome at Right, on the other side of the river."

Then Owailion took one grim look at Dayvian's limp body on the ground and made a judgment. "He failed?"

"No," Rashel clarified. "He was able to keep the men asleep while Tanzaa danced the demons into submission. And he also did some serious thinking about why he brought down the tower when trying to bring the ship in."

Yeolani added thoughtfully, "Dayvian was probably correct about it.

He thought it was his motives. If they weren't completely pure, he got these kinds of bad results. I think Dayvian is convinced he is the cause of the problem here and has no idea there might be something else involved. Then when we asked him to wipe the minds of the men on the ship, he couldn't do it. He was completely blocked because he insisted on pure motives. It's now obvious that an outside force has taken him over and won't let him do his magic without its permission. So, we put a shield over him and put him to sleep so we could discuss it privately and analyze why this happened."

Owailion grunted his approval of their plan and then added. "When we arrived here, the smell of magic covered the stones, but it wasn't musical. Dayvian might have initiated the spell but this wasn't his magic that brought the tower down. I think it was...well, Yeolani. Do you recognize this smell?"

Surprised, Yeolani looked at Owailion and then out at the fallen stones. "It isn't like it was then," he mused. "It was foggy and...metal and the mist. You think it's the Siren?"

Owailion nodded. "Remember, we found Dayvian in Lolar, right near the marshes where you encountered the Siren all those years ago. Did you ever investigate her later?"

Yeolani shook his head. He had not wanted to fight that elusive magic again, for she had almost killed him back when he was Seeking. If Rashel had not rescued him, he would not have survived the Siren's song. If that alien magic had changed form and now had invaded Dayvian instead, then this was very dangerous.

To save Yeolani from such painful recollections, Vamilion and Honiea came wandering out of the fallen stones, and now all together they could study what magic had truly caused the fall of Left. Owailion waved his hand over Dayvian's lax form, placing a complete truth spell over him. Tanzaa looked on with curiosity. She had never witnessed Dayvian under this spell and wondered what she would see.

His appearance changed dramatically before her eyes. He now wore the regalia of a Wise One: white leather lined with rabbit fur the color of his new hair but stitched with intricate silver embroidery and a gray velvet cloak with a silver lining. Over his back, he carried an ivorywood guitar, probably a future Talisman. He looked like a prince. Privately, very privately, Tanzaa admitted she wished his eyes would open so that the blue would shine and she could say she had never seen anything so beautiful. So, he had been destined to be a Wise One after all. She pulled herself away from what might have been and directed herself back to the other matter at hand.

However beautiful he seemed, something strange had layered itself over Dayvian's image. Tanzaa felt like she was looking at him through murky water. His form seemed out of focus or covered in thin, slightly oily slime. It almost glistened in the spring afternoon like oil on water, an oozing haze. She recalled how puzzled she had been, thinking that green could not represent Dayvian's magic. And the flavor of copper in the air burned through her mind. It seemed poisonous and alien to him.

"What is that?" Honiea asked in a revolted tone. Indeed, all of them could see the substance marring the vision. "It's not a demon, is it?"

"No," Owailion confirmed. "I've never seen it. Demons should be misty or look like a monster. He didn't have this film on him when I left him at Gandoy. I suspect it is the residue of the Siren that Yeolani met in the marshes above Lolar."

Tanzaa had no idea what a Siren was, but surprisingly she had seen this green film before. "It is agor," she proclaimed.

"What?" all the Wise Ones queried at exactly the same time, all looking at her with amazement. That the newest of the Wise Ones had seen this completely new magical phenomenon surprised them all.

For her part, Tanzaa struggled to explain. Instead, as was her habit, she passed them a vision of what she knew of an agor.

In the courtyard where evil magic was performed at Umzulio, the entire court, retainers, courtesans, sorcerers, and priests all gathered for a ceremony. Tanzaa had attended as a twelve-year-old, forced to witness a variety of sorcery ceremonies, but this was different. The usually bloody altar, the only permanent structure in the courtyard, had been cleared, washed and polished for this event. The old king was dying and his son, the one who would eventually be her husband, was about to take the throne. With his new authority, he also inherited the residue of his father's magic.

In a grand parade, eunuchs entered the courtyard already crowded with guests. These slaves carried a jewel-encrusted litter baring a shriveled old man on it. He had been dressed in rich robes of deep blue indicating his royal lineage. The old king was alive, but only just. When the eunuchs put down the litter atop the altar, he groaned in slight pain. Behind him in the procession strode another younger man, also dressed in royal robes and carrying the scepter of Umzulio. At his side he wore a richly carved dagger and, on his hands, black gloves stitched with gold thread. The courtiers began chanting arcane lyrics as the frightened younger Tanzaa looked on.

When all this spectacle was staged to Crown Prince Zathuramin's satisfaction, he stepped up to the altar and rested the scepter across his father's stomach. Then the prince removed the old king's crown from off his grizzled head and placed it on his own. Prince Zathuramin stood tall and proud, looking over his court, not down at the old man, his father. Tanzaa remembered thinking he acted more like a high priest than a monarch. Then the heir grasped the weapon at his side and drew the sharply honed dagger. He turned back to the old man, and with his free hand, he covered the eyes of his father. Abruptly everyone began chanting in Demian, a spell they all seemed to know. Yet the prince's words were different, commanding. The congregation knew what was coming but even young concubines were not allowed to look away. Prince Zathuramin raised the dagger high and plunged it deep into the heart of his father. The prince became the king.

Then, to those with magical eyes to see, like the blood, greenish oil seeped out of the body. It moved up the dagger from the dead king and swarmed over the arm of the new king. He did not stir, letting the substance creep over his limbs, up over his head and crawl into his nostrils, ears, behind his eyes and finally down his mouth, open to receive it. The liquid eventually covered him completely in the film. Then it absorbed into his skin and became invisible inside his body.

There it would become part of the magic the new king already possessed.

"Agor," Tanzaa the adult reiterated. "Magical spirit that cannot die, but also will not live on its own. It has no body. It passes one to another to add to his natural magic."

"It's a kind of parasite," Vamilion whispered in horror. "I have heard the word, but never witnessed the phenomena. It's the remains of a magical soul that has lost its body? Why does it not pass over to the other side? Each successive king must have added his power to those that came after. How many generations of magic that must be. And which agor is this one on Dayvian? Is the agor also the Siren?"

No one had more ideas on that point. Instead, Rashel began proposing more questions. "And what powers does the agor give to Dayvian? How much of his magic is derived from the agor, as opposed to his own gifts? Is it evil? We've learned a lot about how to contain demons, but this isn't the same thing. How do we remove it, other than the way that ceremony did?"

"Not to mention how do we contain it once we remove it?" Honiea added. "And what damages will this cause him? Is this why he hasn't found a Heart Stone yet? Is this why Tanzaa is no longer linked to him?"

That thought stunned Tanzaa, who excitedly looked again at Dayvian, trying to concentrate on the man beneath the film. She too wondered if she had lost her love for him because she wasn't really sensing the man himself.

Yeolani pointed out practically. "I'd love to go tramping through Dayvian's life with all these questions, but right now we've got a war to fight. We can't allow this...this agor anywhere near a battlefield, or even near us for that matter."

Owailion raised a hand to calm the stem of commentary. "I will take Dayvian and investigate. Meanwhile, Tanzaa, your gift with making everyone think the way we want them to should turn the tide. I have faith in your ability to convince the Demians that they do not want to fight us anymore."

Tanzaa looked up startled. "I...I want to help Dayvian."

"Yes, and the best thing you can do to help him is end this war, so we are all free to help him without interruption," Owailion replied impatiently. "I'll take him to Lolar, to that inn where you found him. It's out of the way and I can guard the river while I'm there. That way you won't have to come all the way north to find me. When you five have finished the war, come to Lolar and we'll settle Dayvian there. Maybe forcing it back into the marsh from which it came."

Tanzaa didn't like it. Deep down behind her shields, she hoped that what Honiea had suggested, that she no longer felt the binding to him, was because of the agor. May that be true. She wanted to love him. Dayvian obviously was a Wise One underneath the coating of the alien presence. His royal regalia proved that even if he had no Heart Stone. However, Tanzaa also realized she must again put the welfare of the Land above her love for Dayvian. This helped her decide. She would go to war and then come help battle the agor.

Mournfully she looked around the bleak stones of a toppled tower and wondered at the agor's power if it could do this by utilizing Dayvian's minimal magic. Then she turned to the mountains beyond the river, somewhere beyond the horizon, where the pass to Demion awaited her. Again, she was leaving Dayvian behind. Indeed, for the past ten years, this had been their fate. Leaving each other every time grew more difficult and painful. Now she found no hope whatsoever in it. Perhaps it was the memory of Dayvian that she was leaving behind with Owailion. She still didn't feel the yearning toward her childhood sweetheart, not with the agor covering him, but would it return if they could rid Dayvian of the effects? It didn't matter, she reminded herself. She had her duty and the rest would sort itself with time. At least that was what the Wise One instinct within her claimed.

As she turned to weave her way out of the fortress's grave-yard, following Yeolani and Rashel into battle, Owailion stopped Tanzaa with a word. "One more thing. The music that Dayvian sent you, do you still have it?"

Surprised she stopped. Owailion knew about that?

"It was the last act of magic Dayvian tried when he was at Gandoy before I left. It too could be poisoned by the agor. There was one song he didn't want to send to you. It might be a clue to how to free him from the agor. May I have it?"

Tanzaa feared she knew which song he intended, even though she had only glanced at the sheet music briefly. The impression of the songs resided in her mind still. She knew the simple piece of paper would be no loss to her. Obediently Tanzaa made her bag rematerialize and brought the composi-tions out. She would not miss them, especially since she dupli-cated each piece as she pulled them out of her pack for Owailion. He indeed went for the haunting one she had antici-pated, the one about Raimi, Queen of Rivers, and his lost wife.

Owailion nodded his thanks but didn't even look at the other music. He probably did not have a single artistic bone in his body, Tanzaa thought privately. Owailion made the offending song burst into flames and then without acknowl-edging her, he grabbed Dayvian's flaccid arm and disappeared without a trace in a magical shift.

22

BATTLE OF RAYVGILD PASS

*T*anzaa looked up at the looming mountains on either side of her as she entered the crack in the earth known as Rayvgild Pass. She disliked it immediately; maybe the name, maybe the battle scars or maybe the mists and cloud that obscured clear vision through the trees and tumbled rocks. It all combined to make her feel hemmed in. She felt like she must dance on a stage too small for her. The dark of the storm overhead felt like curtains about to be lifted off a performance. She must dance or die. For months the Demians had been ambushing, attacking, and otherwise forcing their way at the border between the Land and Demion. The five Wise Ones and the assembled soldiers of the Land had held the line with no intention of taking one step over it. But how did you convince a far larger force, with hundreds of sorcerers and twice the soldiers, that coming into the Land would not happen, ever?

No one on the west side of the pass assumed they could take over Demion. Why bother? You didn't kick a hornet's nest to see what buzzed inside. And besides, the Land had all they wanted; peace, plenty, and power fairly used. Of all the known countries on the planet, magic did not rule the people of the Land. Instead, magic resided in a few carefully, wisely chosen people who could not use it for evil. Was that why the Demians constantly attacked? Could they not tolerate the thought that magic did not mean ruling over others when it instead meant serving others? Was it really only jealousy?

"That and the thought that power such as theirs must grow until it encompasses all. Sorcerers will never have enough," Vamilion added to Tanzaa's unshielded thoughts. "We just have to convince them at this time that what they have is enough."

"How?" Tanzaa asked as she peered down the roadway that led into the pass, through the trees and into the dark beyond. She could easily sense the army lurking out there. She felt their clinging minds, swarming over her shields, trying to seek out any weakness, like a roach finding a way through the least crack. "If they come for power, won't they always want it?"

Vamilion nodded his head. "In Demion do they still use the old proverb? 'Greed is like a snake trying to swallow an elephant? It will consume itself trying."

Tanzaa smiled. She had heard the old saying, but not in the house of the king. "The seal of the king is an elephant," she commented dryly.

"Yes, but an elephant is also frightened of a mouse. We want to make them forget you and Dayvian exist. That's probably the only way to get them to stop. No one needed to die anymore."

"Can we make them believe they have what they want?" Rashel came forward, listening to the strange conversation of the two who had been born in Demion. "If they are intent on getting you Tanzaa, can a simple illusion satisfy them? They take the illusion home and then discover they have nothing. Would they give up at that point? Maybe pretend our illusion is real to convince their people they have won and they can leave us in peace?"

"Perhaps," Tanzaa agreed. "Most would be satisfied with such a story, but the illusion must be very convincing...able to dance and do magic."

"So, what do you need to create an illusion like that, one they would believe?" Vamilion asked, considering there were just the five Wise Ones. The Land's five thousand troops were hidden in the woods ahead of them waiting for the Demian's next move.

Tanzaa dropped her head, envisioning how she would convince ten thousand men, including sorcerers and the king who might or might not be within the units of men gathered on the far side of the pass, that they had captured her. The illusion would have to be more advanced than the horses she had conjured to travel when first she entered the Land. This illusion would have to walk, talk, interact, and perhaps even dance and perform magic. And she would have to spread this magic with every one of the troops on the other side. The prospect overwhelmed her.

No, she needed another plan, some spell that could be performed and then reliably last into the future without her monitoring it. Could she convince them all that there was nothing to gain here? Or would forgetting her be more beneficial? If they forgot about her, traveled all the way home, and only then discovered how they'd been tricked, would they come back for more revenge? Morally could she lie to these men? The Wise One magic hid certain restrictions here. An illusion was doable, but an outright lie, no. What would happen if the Demians forgot everything; the war, their reasoning, even their purpose for coming, everything but their way home? That might be more plausible.

And she could enhance the desire they probably already

held; to go home. Homesickness, she knew it and could amplify it until the assembled troops wept for their wives and children as they marched. Slowly the vision opened behind Tanzaa's eyes and it pleased her. The Wise One instinct had guided her true again.

But she needed the music. She could not perform on such a grand scale without the music. Dayvian always provided such a background for her, one that could spread until it reached every ear, made every eye tear up, and pierced every heart. Could she enchant ten thousand men without Dayvian's music? Deliberately she forced herself to consider her options, slowing her decisions down until she had looked at all sides. She thought again of the music Dayvian had sent her, wondering if among those songs might be one that spoke of homesickness. Could she find one to fit the occasion?

Without thinking about her explanation to the others, Tanzaa knelt on the ground in the middle of the roadway and drew her pack into existence. She began pulling out the duplicate music she had made of what Dayvian had sent her. She rifled through each score, hearing the melodies and a few words in her mind before she set it aside. She privately marveled at the range and magic that brought the complete orchestration to her just by looking at a few bits of ink on parchment. Yes, she could read the music, but his melodies pressed themselves into her mind just as she had been doing with her fellow Wise Ones, sharing a vision. And it was pure magic, not tainted by the poison of the slime spirit agor.

As she held one of the scores in her hand, Tanzaa, at last, realized she had been doing this magic all along. How many times had she shared a vision with the other Wise Ones to supplement the words she would not say? Dayvian's music could be shared in the same manner. She would force the men of Demion to hear his song, and the magical melody would form the background to which she would dance. Open their hearts and then she could dance into their minds, sending them home, forgetting all other desires.

She looked over all the music, picking the simplest piece, and settled on it to do the job. The Ballad of Raimi; the song Dayvian had not wanted to send to her, that Owailion had destroyed. The words would not be included. The Queen's name would not be revealed. Fate settled into place and she knew what to do. As long as the words did not go with it, the haunting lyric would suffice.

"I need a stage," she declared, holding the music up. Then she pressed into their minds a vision of what she proposed.

Dusk fell in Rayvgild Pass like fire through the trees that choked the narrow valley. The setting sun passed through the clouds Tanzaa had conjured to feed the mood. Even though it was well into spring, an unexpected fog settled in the landscape, almost like smoke. It made it difficult for any of the soldiers to see each other. The mist hid many things happening. It acted as a signal. Under the cover of the dark and the cloud, the men of the Land began their retreat, back to the Wall, taking their weapons with them. Their movement, secretive and quick, must finish before dawn or they too would fall under Tanzaa's enchantment. Yeolani led the retreat, assuring the commanders that they were not abandoning their posts, just clearing the battlefield. The soldiers left reluctantly, giving to the Wise Ones the war and the complete defense of the pass.

Then at dawn, when Yeolani returned, with the mist still thick and eerie, something moved through the trees, flickering behind the stones. Like a ghost, seen only out of the corner of an eye, or with the movement of a head, a deer flashed down the narrow roadway. None of the Demians who thought they saw it, could say exactly what they saw: a doe or a buck, antlers or tail. Every one of the warriors claimed the creature glowed, white as bone and silent as it moved, leaped, or danced through the trees.

And they all wanted to hunt it.

The Demians dropped their weapons and reached for their bows, leaving their stations. The officers and sorcerers too caught her spell just like the lower ranks. And each thought he alone would catch the deer, glowing in the misty moonlight before she faded into invisibility. Each soldier herded her toward the eastern mouth of the pass before they all lost their pretty prey in the fog.

When the sentries on duty had pursued the deer right into the main Demion encampment, confusion abounded. Now the entire army had gathered, all of them seeking an elusive animal, even though they stumbled over each other, crowding into the pathways between their tents as if none of them could recognize they had left the solitude of the forest pass. They saw only trees, heard only the careful, stealthy steps of a deer feeding in the forest. There were no tents, campfires, or other hunters.

Then gradually, as the warming sun rose, it burned into their minds as well as the fog. A melody lifted simultaneously in the morning air. The hunting men stilled and looked around themselves, confused and enchanted by the melting mist. A simple song blended with the light into an intoxicating brew of bewilderment. They stopped their hunt, bows pointed down, and heads lifted to gaze into the branches of trees Rashel's illusions had crafted. None of them could recall the exact tune, or even if it had words. What instruments they heard eluded them. Perhaps it was the wind that blew the music, like the last tendrils of mist into the morning sun. None of the survivors of the hunt could remember how the melody flowed precisely.

Instead, the only indelible memory all the soldiers clung to was of the lady on the stone.

Tanzaa stood on the last tumbled ridge at the mouth of the pass, as if manning a wall at war above the Demion camp. The wind caught at her dress of white satin and tulle. It washed through her hair that hung loose and gold on the air. Like a statue carved of marble, she looked over them imperiously, commanding their attention. Trees did not obstruct their view and the light did not blind their eyes. They all witnessed her pale arms lifted into the air as she stretched into the music.

Tanzaa danced and let her memory provide the music. She heard the entire score, more than Dayvian could ever hope to play on his own. The other Wise Ones helped by amplifying the sound and Vamilion had flattened out her 'stage', shielding her from being approached as she danced, but otherwise, this was all Tanzaa's magic. She danced her feelings of how much she missed her love for Dayvian. Then she forced the army below her to feel the same. Their personal loneliness fed into it until they could cut through the homesickness with drawn swords. She belonged with him, but she had been stripped of her home. Raimi wanted to come home, the soldiers wanted to go home. Her home was in Dayvian's arms. All three thoughts blended in Tanzaa's mind and fell on the soldiers like spring rain.

Then to top off her spell, Tanzaa began to spin away their memory. Gone, the war, their understanding of the magical woman they had sought, and the Land they had attacked. They would find their way home with a recollection of a wondrous hunt that ended with no success. They remembered only the beauty of the doe, the mist-shrouded forest in which they hunted and a whole season spent away from family. They would find their homes again as a welcome sight and have no desire to hunt again. Even the sorcerers fell under Tanzaa's enchantment. Never was there a magical dancer, never a gifted musician. Their time away was only to go hunting and return to Umzulio empty-handed, wiser and more content. That memory burned into their mind with the mist.

Tanzaa continued to spin and stretch long after the soldiers turned and left the field. For her own sake, she needed to express all her grief, washing it away to a finale no one would see. She could not stop until it had all flown from her.

Perhaps her efforts, completing the spell on herself would witness the need for a Heart Stone. She must prove to God that she had tried as well and as devotedly as Dayvian. She would let go of her love for the memory of the man if it would keep him free from the taint of the agor. He must be free to move on with his life. She had to let go and so she put a spell on herself. Finally satisfied, she stopped her spin and waited patiently for the world to stop moving too.

Meanwhile, Vamilion followed the departing Demion soldiers, listening to their thoughts for several leagues, and seemed satisfied that the entire army of Demion would wander south and east until they reached their homes some weeks from now. They had been defeated. Meanwhile, the rest of the Wise Ones walked unmolested into the abandoned camp of their enemy. Rashel was the first to congratulate Tanzaa when she jumped down off her 'stage' and came weaving her way through the tents.

"Masterfully done, Tanzaa," she announced. "You've performed magic I don't think any of the rest of us could manage. We would have to do it one by one...ten thousand men. We were wrong not to bring you in at the first."

"You couldn't know," Tanzaa replied. "I didn't know."

"Well," Yeolani interrupted, "We know now. Don't get angry with the Queen of Storms or she'll have you gnawing on your own boot just for the fun of it. That song, it was..."

"Dayvian's," Tanzaa redirected him. "His music, pure music, and powerful."

Yeolani had wanted to ask how she could have made a song about something that had occurred so far in the past, back when Owailion had been the only human in the Land, but then Rashel stopped him with a look. It said very clearly that the subject of a Wise One's death should be avoided.

"I was going to say haunting as well but...but that's not the right word either. It's as if Dayvian walked with the Queen of Rivers."

Honiea lifted her head from peeking inside one of the abandoned tents.

"Maybe he tapped into someone who was there, with first-hand experience. Demons were here in the Land then. And now Dayvian's possessed by this agor. What if the sorcerer that destroyed her is this creature? Did Owailion ever defeat him? What if an agor is a sorcerer who simply refuses to die?"

That thought terrified Tanzaa. Nowhere in the song had it speculated who had taken over Raimi's magic. Tanzaa's unrest transitioned into her hands and feet, urging the other Wise Ones to wrap up their investigation of the abandoned camp quickly. While she didn't consciously speed up her friends, they all left behind their war with Demion before the sun reached its noon height and they abandoned Rayvgild Pass to rendezvous with Owailion at Lolar.

23

AGOR OF LOLAR

*O*wailion sat on a stool he conjured out in the marshes at Lolar and considered his situation. Off to his right, Raimi's palace stood tall, glittering, abandoned, and stark against the blue spring sky, surrounded by the waters of the Laranian River. The village of Lolar rested on the far shore from it. The town eked out a living in guiding ships through the ever-changing passages, or they worked with fish, but nothing was going to bring this place to its potential. Owailion remembered this land before settlers came, with a deep verdant valley lined with trees and waterfalls casting mist into the air. Now Raimi was gone and the huge marble walls he had finally built for her only looked like a gravestone over the marsh that had formed at her death. It was Raimi's graveyard, especially since he created that palace himself the year after he failed to save her life.

At his feet, Owailion had laid Dayvian, still sleeping out on the grasses. The King of Creating didn't care much beyond that. Hopefully, the musician didn't sink. Everything here, except perhaps the pervasive mosquitoes, sank or stank of bilge water. He hated this place. It seemed sad to consider even the stench was his fault too. If he hadn't let his lady die, she would have healed this land and lifted the marshes. Her gift with the rivers would have been invaluable here. Instead, Owailion had to build pumps to keep the people and the buildings from sinking lower.

Quit sinking lower yourself, Owailion ordered himself aloud. He had become quite adept in the last few hundred years, at avoiding painful thoughts like this. He usually dodged misery by posing puzzles or challenges to himself and working on them until he had a non-magical solution for the situation. Now, lying in front of him he had just such a puzzle. With latent curiosity, Owailion tossed the truth spell over Dayvian's figure once again to examine the agor. Why hadn't he heard the term before? Probably because here in the Land there were no such creatures, he guessed. It was alien to this Land and his dragon-gifted Memories, but not, apparently to other nations. With a flick of his wrist, he flipped Dayvian over onto his face and saw the glossy green film completely enveloped the young man.

Curiously Owailion tried something else. He flipped Dayvian back over, set him up, and then with a snap of his fingers he woke the musician. Dayvian gasped, but couldn't say anything. Indeed, Owailion kept him completely immobile, able to breathe but nothing else. Dayvian's eyes bugged out in alarm at sensing himself completely paralyzed.

"Relax, I'm testing something," Owailion tried to reassure Dayvian. From the panic on his face, this comment didn't help much.

Rather than dwell on yet another failure, Owailion changed his audience. "Agor, can you hear me?" he asked. The agor had not inhibited Dayvian's use of magic or his body, so it had not taken over completely. It was the magic in him that the agor chose to manipulate. Owailion had deliberately ignored any thoughts that came roaring out of Dayvian. He wanted to speak with the invader.

"What are you, agor?"

To show who was really in control, the creature put Dayvian back to sleep, letting him flop back down in the marsh like a puppet with its strings cut.

"Why do you care?"

Owailion heard this reply only in his head. The mental voice scraped and scratched at his shields. So, the slime didn't need Dayvian to do the magical communication. If what Tanzaa implied was true, the agor was a magical spirit in its own right. But not a demon?

"Are you a demon?" Owailion asked in a mental voice, wondering if Dayvian's consciousness was needed for the warped creature to hear.

Alarmingly Dayvian's mouth began to move. "Of course, I can hear you. Am I a demon? Only if you make me into one." The young man spoke but never opened his eyes, demonstrating all the agor was capable of doing with access to a human body.

Owailion tried not to react to that reply. He strengthened his personal shields and thought hard about his next questions. So, the agor spoke in Dayvian's voice when it wanted to do so? This was a disconcerting problem. Dayvian's speaking voice tapped the same potential magic as his instrumental music. This creature was powerful; far more powerful than Dayvian had been on his own up at Gandoy.

"So, explain yourself to me. Are you the Siren that the King of the Plains encountered? I've never met one such as you," Owailion said aloud, hoping not to allow thoughts to pass, at least from his end. Until he knew definitively how Dayvian had been infected it was best not to allow closer contact.

The agor laughed harshly and then left off using Dayvian's voice and continued under its own powers. "Why would I explain myself to one such as you? A failed magician, corrupting your work, then abandoning the world. You're a hermit at best. You used to revel in creating. Everything you touched was a wonder. Then you chose to abandon the magical. And so evil happened, because of you, Owailion."

The agor knew his name.

He was horrified, even if it wasn't his real name. The agor knew of his past. It knew how to hurt him. Owailion stood up and squelched off into the marsh a few yards before he could even stomach turning back. His impatience, long his fatal flaw, now simmered and boiled, for he had always been overeager to know the truth. However, he didn't want this entity to point this out to him.

"Did I create you?" he finally asked, still fearing the answer. He had long ago sworn to look evil in the eye if he must. And a Wise One's oath must be kept.

"After a fashion," the agor replied. "I could maim you terribly if I wished, for having a hand in my creation. I might harm you as I have been harmed. No one can kill you, Owailion, but no one can kill me either, as I am already dead. But then you would ...well, let's just say, you deserve the suffering you've brought on yourself. Nothing I could do would harm you worse than you hurt yourself."

A niggling little thought warned Owailion to wait for help. He should not continue this line of questioning. He would only exacerbate this problem, but he didn't listen to the impression. The agor represented a puzzle, like an itch that needed to be scratched, even if it opened old wounds. He had to ask.

"What are you if you aren't a demon?"

Owailion had not expected a nice pleasant conversation, but he also wasn't prepared for what happened next. Dayvian sat up again with his eyes glowing magically green. With a wave of his arm, the musician sent Owailion flying, landing thirty feet away, with a roaring in his ears.

"I am anger, fury, rage. I am thwarted desires." Dayvian's voice erupted over every sense Owailion possessed, washing over his shields like they weren't even there. "I am betrayal, disloyalty, abandonment."

Then the magic hit Owailion. With another flick of his arm, Dayvian sent a wave of invisible power against him, pushing the Wise One away, crushing him into the mud.

"You will leave the boy," Owailion pushed back, his voice low and fierce, but with perfect control. He could not fire against the agor, for he might do the young musician harm. The agor, on the other hand, chose not to protect Dayvian from damage, and he was eminently human and killable.

"What?" the monster replied mockingly. "To return to the mud and swamp? No, I want my body again and this one will do for now. Dayvian is mine and I will do with him as I please."

"Your argument is with me. Leave him now," Owailion said again.

"Shall I use name magic on him, as was done to me?" asked the agor, mockingly. To emphasize the threatening point, the agor made Dayvian hold out his hand and he conjured a fierce-looking dagger into his palm. Its serrated edge gleamed in the sun more than the crystal hilts. With a maniacal look in his glowing eyes, Dayvian turned it tip first and pressed it against his chest, drawing just a drop of blood. "You see, I have complete control of him. I know his name," boasted the agor in Dayvian's eerie voice. "I have the evilest magic at my disposal with no Heart Stone to stop me."

Owailion's horror sank lower but he did not dare react. This Agor of Lolar knew name magic and understood Heart

Stones. What kind of sorcerer comprehended these kinds of things? Only a Wise One.

Since the threat of killing Dayvian outright did not get the desired response the agor tried a different tactic now. Without hesitation, the musician directed the knife to a new part of his body and stabbed himself in the thigh. Dayvian's mind, as well as the agor, shrieked at Owailion in overwhelming pain and emotion. Owailion struggled to keep the stony grimace on his face.

"Why kill the body I have just acquired," the agor taunted. "I'll just rip him to shreds, heal him, and do it again.

Owailion looked away as Dayvian took another swipe, this time across his chest, laying his ribs bear, mixing blood with the mud he had lain in. Obvious pain didn't seem to disturb Dayvian's mindless drive to cut himself slowly to ribbons.

With a wrench to his soul, Owailion knew what he had to do but it grieved him. She would rage against name magic being used on her once again, but if his suspicions were true, it would be the only way to block the agor.

"Stop Raimi!" he demanded, still pushing against the wave of pure power crashing down on him like the depths of the ocean. "Don't hurt him. It's me you're angry at. What do you want of me?"

The controlling spirit stopped slicing at Dayvian but instead replied with a snarl. "I want you to suffer."

Rather than push up against the furious pressure the agor forced down on him, Owailion shifted tactics. If the agor was truly Raimi, he did not want to use more name magic to fight her. None of the others needed to know his wife's horrific past or how low she had fallen. Instead, Owailion magically shifted to the other side of the river, behind Dayvian, and then opened up a rift in the ground, hoping to bury the agor in a grave, right along with the musician. Better Dayvian die than remained possessed by this monster. Perhaps Raimi would leave the body, and they could bring him back from the dead again.

The rip in the ground began shaking into a canyon deeper than Owailion's intent. The fissure started draining not only the marsh but the nearby river as well, swallowing the anchoring trees on its banks. Would the chasm begin drawing in even the ocean beyond? The gash threatened to swallow the surrounding Land itself. Dayvian fell sliding down the mud-fall into the chasm. The river followed him down into the opening, pouring overhead and burying the musician along with the agor in a deluge of water and mud, taking them down into a black hell.

"NO!" shrieked Tanzaa's mind.

She had arrived in a bright white flash from the Rayvgild Pass, along with the other Wise Ones. They all landed on what had once been the western bank of the river. Now only muddy swamp slid like some tremendous sludge away from them. Tanzaa's fury at seeing Dayvian go down under that black wave overwhelmed her. Storm clouds formed instantly, roiling with her anger. She couldn't control herself. Lightning without her direction rippled through the air, lancing toward Owailion, but none of it managed to hit him. He guarded himself with an invisible shield, deflecting it just as he resisted the agor's fury. The power Tanzaa threw at Owailion went instead to feed the waves of magic directed at the pit he had created.

"No is right," Vamilion called over the thunder and the roar of a river falling into the abyss. He wrapped his arms around Tanzaa's, holding her down, preventing her dancing magic directing lightning at Owailion. Honiea moved in front of her, forcing the dancer's silver eyes to focus on her rather than Owailion across the chasm.

"Look at me Tanzaa. The agor is doing this. Wise One cannot fight Wise One. You need to control yourself," she murmured, trying to mute the fury she saw snapping there in the metallic eyes.

"Let me go," Tanzaa still cried, straining against Vamilion's hold. "Both drown...he's drowning."

Then she performed magic she had never conceived of; she melted right through the King of Mountain's arms, into the soft earth. He was left grasping at the air and seeking where she had faded.

Yeolani and Rashel meanwhile did their best to lift the chasm that Owailion had started, but nothing was keeping it from spreading. "Are you doing this?" Yeolani called to the King of Creating through the protective shield Owailion had built to defend himself.

"Are you daft?" Owailion shouted back. "The agor took him over and was killing him. If we don't stop this, the whole world will go with it. I think I've got hold of Dayvian's body but I don't dare bring him back up if the agor is still manipulating his magic. It spreads, remember? Any magic, he makes it spread. A crack becomes a canyon."

"Well, Tanzaa's gone down after him too. She intends on drowning as well." Then Rashel added in concentration, "I've got her in a bubble. She won't go farther. But we've got to control the agor. Any ideas?"

Meanwhile, Vamilion shifted his focus, concentrating his magic on sealing the seam in the earth, but the earthquakes were pervasive and kept snapping open new faults. Yeolani and Honiea flitted to the village of Lolar and began evacuation efforts, transporting people magically out onto the plains, away from the river that would swallow the village whole without a word of explanation.

"It's a spirit," said Owailion even as he struggled against the lightning, the agor's pressure and even the ground that slipped under his boots. "You can't kill what's already dead. We have to convince it to leave in peace."

"Then that's Tanzaa and Dayvian's gift," replied Vamilion who felt like he was sewing on the earth's fabric so fragile it crumbled in his hands. "If we can bring Tanzaa up here, she can enchant the agor, instead of fighting you. She might be able to persuade it to leave Dayvian's body in peace. Is Tanzaa sane enough to convince anyone of anything?"

Rashel nodded, "We have to try. I'm bringing her up now." The Queen of Growing Things put words to action and slowly, out of the half-league wide rip in the earth, a bubble of mud lifted free of the river turned waterfall. It hovered in the air, dripping away slime and then floated to the west side of the slash. Rashel brought the bubble containing Tanzaa right in front of her and very calmly tried to reach some sanity in her friend's mind.

Covered from head to toe in mud, Tanzaa hardly looked the part of a Wise One. She pounded her filthy fists against the magical barrier and her silver eyes flashed in anger. When she recognized Rashel bringing up her cage, Tanzaa pulled away from the shield and straightened up. Rashel wiped at the mud on the outside of her barrier so she could see her friend a little more clearly and then explained.

"Tanzaa, you've got to listen to me. We are going to bring Dayvian back out of that pit, but you've got to dance the agor into submission. Are you in control enough to do so? I will not release you until you can concentrate on that."

It took a moment and Tanzaa had to brush her muddy hair away from her face before she nodded. "I'll do it," she declared. The thunder overhead rumbled an affirmative and began to direct itself toward the outer plains rather than specifically at Owailion.

Rashel nodded and let the bubble rest on the trembling

ground before she allowed it to burst open. Tanzaa stood a moment in the mud not reacting to her newly restored freedom. Then she turned and looked with pain down at the waterfall of the Laranian River crashing into the abyss where Dayvian had fallen. Then her silver eyes shifted toward Owailion only threatening a little and she nodded.

"Bring him up."

Owailion had created much the same magical prison for Dayvian as Rashel had to encase Tanzaa. It had fallen far lower into the earth and with the strain of leagues of river and mud pouring over it, raising it back out took time. Like the earth itself was giving birth, the bubble rose and hovered over the cascade of the river that washed it clean of the mud.

Owailion didn't pop the bubble as Rashel had. The agor continued controlling Dayvian from within. The musician laughed maniacally and beat on the barrier with abandon. The dagger he had conjured under the Agor of Lolar's command still stabbed at his flesh as well as the inside of the transparent barrier. No one seeing Dayvian this way would question that he was completely under the power of the evil spirit.

"I knew you couldn't resist," the agor shouted using Dayvian's physical voice that also rippled with its magical influence. "You Wise Ones are doomed to fight me forever and lose. I can't die and so you cannot stop me. Dayvian is mine and you will never complete the Sealing of the Land. His Heart Stone has become a millstone around his neck."

Tanzaa didn't listen to the eerie two-toned voice. Instead, she surged with magic and conjured a stage that lifted at her feet, hovering out of the mud. Then she flared again, with lighting to lift the gloom as she put herself into her regal clothing. She glowed in white and silver, clean and brilliant, shining in the lightning that flashed against the horizon. She raised her arms and the music of Dayvian's final song thundered against the clouds.

Tanzaa began to dance. She leaped, spun and the clouds reflected her movements, dipping low and swirling in a bewildering pattern that mesmerized everyone. Subtly the magic gripped them all. Vamilion didn't notice that the earth had stopped shaking. Owailion lost concentration on Dayvian's prison and it began to sink back toward the river before Rashel elbowed him to concentrate.

The agor stopped its shrieking through Dayvian. Instead, the musician stared slack-jawed in wonder and dropped the dagger. Then he began swaying to the music that cut through the still roaring river. No words accompanied the music, but they all knew the lyrics. Tanzaa's dance easily told the story of a Wise One committing suicide rather than being forced to continually hurt the man and the world she loved. Owailion found himself weeping uncontrollably where he stood. Every emotion echoed and reflected, off the water, off the storm above, even off those witnessing this dance.

But Dayvian's torturer was not going to submit. A calculating look came into Dayvian's glowing eyes and then he closed them, cutting off the dance and its influence. He raised his hands and began to play counter-music with no guitar in evidence. His clever fingers and subtle voice made the sound and his magic crafted an attempted antidote to Tanzaa's dance. The agor's song echoed hollowly against the insides of Dayvian's invisible cage and then spread, creeping across the chasm like fog, drifting toward the sinking village. The Wise One's palace, flashing in the lightning began to vibrate like a tuning fork. The humming palace trembled on its foundations and added yet another set of notes to the competing songs.

Rashel put her hands over her ears rather than endure the dissonance. The earth began shaking again, startling

Vamilion out of Tanzaa's spell. Belatedly he began again sealing the gash below Dayvian's trap. He forced the river back into its former channel. The roar of falling water eased, but this only aided the spread of the conflicting music. Dayvian verses Tanzaa. The majesty of Tanzaa's refined and crafted music of Raimi's Ballad carried more power but Dayvian's blunt, droning dirge crept farther downstream. It covered the countryside with thick, oily magic. The Wise One palace that would have been Raimi's, set in the middle of the river, trembled under the weight of the agor's terrible music of despair.

Owailion broke himself away from Tanzaa's spell just in time to turn to the south and witness the crumbling of the palace he had built so many years before. It could not withstand the sonic stresses and began to crack. The walls trembled and the foundation began sinking in the liquefied earth. The echo of its snapping hit the gathered Wise Ones like the thunder. The marble crumpled and massive chunks of wall impacted in the marshes, crushing the village of Lolar and setting it ablaze. Then the whole island in the river shook convulsively and then sank away. Looking on, the Wise Ones, horrified by the destruction, could think of nothing to do. There was nothing to be done against magic like this.

Except for Tanzaa who still locked eyes with Dayvian. He was her spinning point, the spot she would always find every time she came back around in her pirouette. She saw his eyes, blue as ice beneath the cold, green glaze of the agor's influence. She danced as a hawk would fly, with fierce joy, complete power, fearing nothing. If she could battle an army, she could make one broken spirit leave the man she had once loved. She would die trying. She would drown in the Agor of Lolar if she could not save him. This she swore as she moved to the music she crafted from her memory.

"I will take his soul and join his magic with mine," the Agor of Lolar swore.

"You will leave him," Tanzaa insisted, forcing Dayvian to open his eyes again. He might play his counter-magic, but if he could still see her, Tanzaa could reach him. He would not drown if she reached for him. Tanzaa spun faster, becoming a blur, a tornado of power forming about her, assuring her that she could dance forever. Then she began speaking directly to the agor, for these words could not be blocked.

"You wish to go back to where you've been. You wish to sink back into the waters of the world you have known. You do not want to live with magic. It has been a bane to you. Leave the musician and go back to where you have made your home. Go back. Release him."

The Agor of Lolar growled and it wasn't in Dayvian's voice. Instead, Dayvian began pounding on the inside of his prison, but this time it was with desperation to escape, not in rage and frustration. Owailion saw this, drawing his eyes back away from the rubble of a fallen palace and willingly now brought the bubble closer, toward Tanzaa's dance, away from the river. He gently rested it on the rebuilding shoreline.

Dayvian stood within the bubble, beating on the walls. The counter-tune ceased and instead began to encourage the dance. His music began to swell with synergy rather than competing goals. Dayvian's wordless notes provided a base, another layer added to the ballad he had prepared months ago for this time. Released from their grief over the fallen palace, the other Wise Ones turned to the musical battle still to be fought. They started to join in the chant.

"Go back and release him."

Then, to everyone's surprise, Dayvian began to sing along with the song. His voice, pure and exquisite, worked against the Agor Lolar, forcing it to listen. Now instead of conflict, the two performers complemented each other. Accompanied by the amplified memory of the magical Ballad of Raimi, sung by its composer, and danced with the God-gifted grace Tanzaa could bring, the Agor Lolar began to melt away from Dayvian. He didn't dare look down to see the ghostly green film began to ooze off him like the mud. Dayvian could sense it dripping though he could not see it. The freedom to breathe and think clearly returned to him. He felt the presence pooling, blending with the mud at his feet in the containment Owailion still had not released. Instead, Dayvian watched Tanzaa's dance like it was his lifeline. Perhaps it was.

Now the Agor Lolar began to make its own sound, gurgling and furious, completely free from Dayvian's voice. He continued to sing the lyrics to the Ballad of Raimi out of desperation. Without a body with which to sing, the mental voice of the betrayed spirit sounded feral and enraged, but it didn't use actual words. Instead, it tried to overwhelm Dayvian's song with sheer volume. It raged against its impulse to leave Dayvian. Its fury scraped harshly over magical ears, but it failed to mask the grace and powerful beauty of song and dance.

In an ugly liquid, the Agor pooled at the bottom of Owailion's enclosure and carefully Dayvian tried to step free of it. Now he could look down, still singing the words that seemed to only repulse the monster. Tanzaa continued to dance, but now she wasn't concentrating on the spirit, but more on Dayvian, who seemed to have changed. She felt again the bond with him now that he was free of the slime. That thought, that she could hope to love him as her mate again, gave a swing of joy to her movements. She watched him, wondering why Owailion didn't release Dayvian and collapse the shell on the liquid spirit.

Looking down Dayvian saw something in the ooze of the agor's presence that demanded his attention. Carefully, avoiding as much as possible contact with the liquid creature, he bent down and reached his long fingers into the green substance that was agor. He pulled something free, even though the slime clung to it. He flicked his wrist to get the sticky substance to release a globe of blue swirling light that he discovered at the bottom of his magical cage.

In triumph, Dayvian held high a Heart Stone.

It pulsed to the rhythm Dayvian's racing heart. Every time she spun, Tanzaa looked at it now, unable to stop yet, but still focused on that blue, exactly the shade of Dayvian's eyes. He had done it. He had forced the power of the universe to admit he had made the effort to become a Wise One. God had forgiven him for the brashness of not allowing her a choice. He had won.

Acknowledging that miracle, Owailion reached out his hand and 'squeezed' the prison globe he still controlled. Accordingly, the enclosure popped Dayvian out, retaining the Agor Lolar in its cage. The newly minted Wise One fell a few feet to the ground, staggered a bit, and then straightened up in the free air of spring.

Relieved and suddenly exhausted, Tanzaa stopped her spinning and also staggered before Dayvian swept her up into his arms, covering her in mud again. She could care less. They clung to each other to keep upright. Both recognized that their magical bond had been reestablished, now that the agor no longer existed between them. At last, they were free to be together and the world was right again.

24

CLEAN

"So, what do we do with it?" Rashel asked of no one, looking at the green film in the bottom of an invisible cage where it hovered just over the water of the river. Above their heads, the sky had grown clear, free from Tanzaa's emotional influence. Somehow even the agor looked new and young in the spring air.

"It has destroyed an entire village, brought down a garrison tower and even a Wise One's palace. There must be some way to contain it," Vamilion reminded them all. He remained grim, feeling the pain within the earth. Despite his magical efforts at the bedrock level, the area still rumbled and needed healing.

"The Agor Lolar can't die," Owailion pointed out as he washed on the banks of the now fresh flowing river. "She said as much and I doubt she can lie. She certainly didn't spare me some brutal truths."

"Well," Vamilion asked, "If she spoke to you, where has she spent the last few centuries that we are only meeting her now? Was she the Siren that Yeolani encountered when he was Seeking?"

Yeolani shrugged absently. "All I remember of her was the light and the burning; nothing so green and slimy. The voice was different too. The Siren was seductive, not secretive. This was the same territory though, so it was probably her, just in a different form. She couldn't invade me at that point the way she did Dayvian. I was already a Wise One by that time, so she attacked differently."

"I felt her influence only after I came here," commented Dayvian from further out in the river where he was practically bathing albeit fully clothed. "I had a dream that she was Tanzaa and she tricked me into making that summoning spell. Was the Siren what you were trying to avoid last summer when we were arguing about how to go north?"

Yeolani nodded. "That and news of the war. Both things would endanger you, but you attract danger like a moth to a flame."

"You all keep saying she," Honiea pointed out. "Do we know it was a she at all?"

"Her voice...it was female," Dayvian provided. "That's why I could have such a vocal range when she took over my body. She was naturally that much higher than I am and so she could hit every note needed. I'm sorry about the garrison...and the village and the palace. How many..."

"No," Tanzaa interrupted him comfortingly. "Don't sing in a minor key."

"She's right. No one was killed," Rashel reassured him.

"The palace was empty, for some Wise One still to come. Owailion, whose was it?"

Owailion sighed with regret and looked south toward the now empty horizon where the river now guarded only rubble. "It was the palace of the Queen of Rivers."

"Raimi," Dayvian shuddered. "If..." but Tanzaa's admonition to 'not sing in a minor key' stopped him.

Honiea, who had already healed Dayvian's extensive wounds, stilled him. "The garrison was emptied for the war. The village, we managed to evacuate everyone. Lolar is a loss, but it can be rebuilt."

Yeolani rolled his eyes at the prospect. "Why are we rebuilding a village in such a vulnerable place? Besides, it stinks. Too many sirens and demons and dead fish lurking about."

They all looked downriver at the crumbled ruins and smoking ashes of the village of Lolar. Absolutely beyond Dayvian's control when under the agor's influence, he still felt a sense of guilt. Owailion who knew more of it than any of them refused to speak of it. No one else had an answer.

Yeolani asked curiously. "Where do we need to plunk it if we cannot kill it? This cannot happen again."

"We'll send it to the sea," Owailion announced. "We all avoid the ocean already...until we find the Wise One of the Sea. In the meantime, she will find it difficult to locate another magician to invade. At sea, we need not deal with her. The sea will have to be her prison."

None of the others argued his logic. The King of Creating took the offending monster in its crystal cage, strengthened the spell he had crafted around it, and threw it with all his considerable magical might toward the south. He saw that it flew past Gardway Island and out into the deep of the Open Ocean. Eventually, the cage might weaken under the agor's influence but she could not return to the Land unless she invaded another magician or crafted a body of her own. And with them all wary of her influence, no magician of the Land would fall prey to her again.

The Wise Ones made repairs to the broken land over the next few days. Rashel raised trees to stabilize the soft earth along the river's channel. Vamilion sealed the underlying bedrock once again. Yeolani and Honiea worked at relocating the homeless villagers farther up the river, building them homes around the base of Yeolani's palace. Tanzaa and Dayvian were married on the very stage where she had danced him free. Owailion officiated and also managed to keep his peace about all that had happened. All of them avoided speaking about the Agar Lolar.

Just before they were all set to depart, Owailion asked Tanzaa an important question. "Do you think you know enough to guide Dayvian and get him Seeking, or shall we find another way to teach him magic, rather than having him grope through it as he has done thus far?"

Tanzaa looked at the King of Creating, startled by the offer. She hardly felt she was trained herself. "I...I found my home and one Talisman, but..." she said hoping that would provide evidence that she could serve as a teacher.

"But you two are the only ones of us who have the power to influence whole masses, humans and demons alike. Dayvian must learn control from you and you alone can teach it," Owailion insisted.

Honiea came to her rescue. "Yes, but you also can keep on Seeking too. There's at least one more Talisman and then the pendant and another Heart Stone to find. You've got years still to go."

"Don't let that intimidate you," Rashel added. "Yeolani and I were both Seeking at the same time and it worked well. Or maybe Yeolani and I can go with you again for a while if that would make you feel better."

Tanzaa nodded, relieved to have a solution. Dayvian had always been an equal and she didn't feel right trying to teach him. It disturbed their dynamic and they had only just reestablished their equality. She had rescued him and he had rescued her often enough. Thankfully neither had drowned, although it had been close several times. Out of the corner of her eye, she saw Dayvian smile at something and she wondered if he was testing out a newly found skill of listening in on her thoughts. His smile deepened as a confirmation.

"So, you said you found your home," he began, hugging her. "Where?"

"In the mountains," and she pressed the memory of the summer garden into the minds of all the Wise Ones.

"It's called Wyndyvilorion," Owailion provided, referencing the memory. "The garden at the top of the world, in the language of the dragons. We often take names based on where our homes reside. Or you could stick with Tanzaa since it isn't your complete name. Either way, you should never make known your true name. And Dayvian, you should change yours immediately. The Agor Lolar knows yours but I don't think she's vindictive enough to kill you with it, at least not at this time. I'd be more concerned that someone from Demion will see you and know you're still alive."

"Can we think about it?" Dayvian asked, feeling a little flustered by the quick changes Owailion was suggesting. What happened to the King of Creating being a hermit, far more interested in his machines and the quiet cold of his home far away? Why now had he taken such an interest in the challenges of Dayvian's world? His physical wounds had been easily healed by Honiea. However, the mental invasion of being possessed, forced to harm himself, and being used as the tool of so much destruction, would take more time and Honiea's gifts could do little for those pains.

"Take your time," the Queen of Healing admonished. "Just please make sure you tell us when you've made your decisions. We will leave you now and wish you luck in your Seeking."

Honiea and Vamilion, hand in hand, departed in a flash of light. Owailion looked at the two remaining couples and sighed. He wanted to go home as well, but there would be no relief there either.

Yeolani piped up, "If I don't want all the refugees from Lolar taking over, I think I have a good activity to teach Dayvian some conjuring work. Come on. Let's get away from this miserable place."

Rashel rolled her eyes and reached for her husband's hand. They too popped out of existence, disappearing magically. And still, Owailion stood on the river's edge, unwilling to move.- Thinking he wanted privacy, Tanzaa reached for Dayvian's hand to take him with her, since he didn't yet have a way to travel magically. Davian willingly took her hand and then hesitated, turning back toward Owailion.

"Thank you...for everything," Dayvian whispered. He knew Owailion would wallow here for a little while longer and they might not see each other for ages more. Dayvian wanted to share at least his thanks for the rescue, the lessons at Gandoy, and his willingness to face the evil of the Agor Lolar despite the pain. Dayvian couldn't verbalize it, but he knew that somehow the monster had been more of a wound to the King of Creating than it was to the newly minted King of Music. And he didn't know why. Nor was he likely to learn that secret simply by asking his mentor. Perhaps if he wrote Owailion a song of forgetting. No, the King of Creating would not want to forget his pain. So instead Dayvian simply smiled and took Tanzaa's hand, leaving the oldest Wise One to his memories and misery.

Tanzaa leaped and then they too were gone.

EPILOGUE

Owailion wandered through the spring rain among the shards of marble left of the ruins. It soaked an already wet land where Raimi's palace had once stood. Perhaps his sourness attracted clouds naturally. It had been raining ever since Tanzaa left. It fit his mood and Owailion wasn't complaining. This had been about all he had left of Raimi and he wanted to preserve what he could. The split and scattered ruins would eventually sink away and the entire island would become uninhabitable, he knew.

He thought hard about many things. For instance, the Agor Lolar would eventually come to exact her revenge against him, he was sure. He knew her name and could torture her, just as she would torture him if she returned. Perhaps one day she would learn his true name and kill him. He had often wondered in the past hundreds of years if he would eventually come to such an end. Death would be welcome. The Agor Lolar knew him too well and had the power to match his. The world would not long survive a pitched battle between the two.

In his fist, he held a parchment, Tanzaa's copy of The

Ballad of Raimi. The music itself might be magical but that didn't keep the rain from blurring the notes, washing them into illegibility. He must remember to speak with Tanzaa and Dayvian about making that particular song disappear. He didn't think either of them would find a desire or need to spread the words of the song, but it gave Raimi's name and he wouldn't have it out in the public ever again. Why risk it?

Without quite knowing how he would manage it, Owailion drew a set of pipes into existence. They had once been Raimi's, a Talisman. He had buried them next to her body and being magical, they had not decayed. This kind of magic would be better performed by the King of Music, but that would require explaining and Owailion would not do that. He lifted the pipes to his lips and concentrated on what he wanted to do.

Somewhere offshore, out at sea, in a magical cage, the soul of Raimi floated. He would keep her offshore, away from the Land where her bitterness would not interfere. Now was not the time. He had been promised that she would one day return and the Wise Ones would be complete, but that was still a long way off. In the meantime, he must protect the Land from such as her. He must remove the memory of Dayvian's name from the Agor Lolar or she might just destroy him yet again. Owailion played away her memory of all that she had done and learned in possessing Dayvian. The Pipes of Forgetting served again, though Owailion knew he could never forget.

Owailion then dropped the pipes in a puddle and watched them sink again in the marshes where he had buried his Raimi's body. There was a reason why he must live forever. It would take that long for him to do his penance. An eternity might eventually open a door as to how he could ever make it up to the woman he loved, that he had allowed this to happen to her. She had become a corrosive spirit, without a body and no way to leave the Land she was sworn to protect. No wonder she was so angry. And she wanted him to live with that knowledge. Well, now he knew how Raimi fared, and with the knowledge came new pain.

With regret, Owailion turned to another duty that must be done. He magically forced the shards of marble the size of houses to sink into the soft ground as if they had been pounded down by the hammer of the rain. He used them to reinforce the sides of the delta, perhaps clarifying the river's channel a bit more. If the people did return, they would have a clear path. It was the least he could do.

Dear reader,

We hope you enjoyed reading *Heart Stone*. Please take a moment to leave a review, even if it's a short one. Your opinion is important to us.

Discover more books by Lisa Lowell at

https://www.nextchapter.pub/authors/lisa-lowell

Want to know when one of our books is free or discounted? Join the newsletter at

http://eepurl.com/bqqB3H

Best regards,

Lisa Lowell and the Next Chapter Team

ABOUT THE AUTHOR

Lisa Lowell was born in 1967 into a large family full of hands-on artists, in southern Oregon. In an effort to avoid conflict, her art of choice was always writing, something both grandmothers taught her. She started with poetry at six on her grandmother's ancient manual typewriter. By her teens she moved on to pen and paper and produced gloomy, angst-ridden fantasy during adolescence. Her mother claims that Lisa shut the door and never came out until she left for university. During this time she felt compelled to draw illustrations throughout the margins that helped supplement her neglect of adjectives and consistent story lines.

A much-appreciated English teacher, Mrs. Seghetti, collected these moody musings and sent them in to scholarship foundations. Lisa got a scholarship for that rather poor writing, escaped Oregon and went to university. While she loved her family, her only requirement in a school was anywhere too far away to come home on weekends. She got as far as Idaho, Utah and then even Washington D.C. before she truly launched. She traveled to Sweden (Göteborg, Lund and Sundsvall) for a year and a half during college where she also reconnected with her heritage.

During college Lisa also fell in love and then had her heart broken. Suddenly she had something to write about. Every story written since harbors a romance and a tangled journey; a *saga* as it were, where the tale comes back to the start. She started to tap into Scandinavian myth and overcame fears of writing conflict. All her earlier failed starts and fascinating characters now molded into an actual story. Completing her degrees in Secondary Education and Masters in English as a Second Language at Western Oregon University, Lisa continued to travel and read favorite authors; Lloyd Alexander, David Brin, Patricia McKillip and Anne McCaffrey. She graduated with a teaching degree 1993.

Then, when she came back to Oregon, like a fairy tale, she met Pat Lowell. They met on Sunday, played racquet ball on Monday night and were engaged by the end of the date. The sense of peace in meeting someone with the same goals and values made it right. Four months later they were married. Lisa began reworking childhood manuscripts into credible stories, and this was when Sea Queen began. When children did not arrive as expected, the Lowells adopted three children, Travis, Scott and Kiana. At that point, Lisa chose to ease off writing actively for a time to focus on her family. However, she kept all the ideas and honed her skill while teaching Middle School English. Storytelling remained her true talent and made her a skillful teacher. In 2011 she was named VFW Oregon Teacher of the Year.

In 2012 a friend asked for manuscripts so he could learn how to get a book onto Amazon in e-book form. As she had several half finished works she could contribute, Lisa gave him one and when she saw how easy that seemed, the idea of publishing snuck up on her again. Her children were moving on, and she felt she could again begin to write. She reworked the first book in the Wise Ones series, Sea Queen, and began sharing it with beta readers. However, her friends wanted to hear the back-stories of some of the other characters so she started writing those into full manuscripts and realized that a series was born.

Publishing became more important when Pat had a terrible accident and developed Parkinson's Disease. Lisa had to stay closer to home to help him and he encouraged her writing. She continued to teach English in middle school (someone has to) and also experiments with drawing, dances while she writes, sings when the radio is on and reads a great deal of poorly written essays by thirteen-year olds. She still lives in Silverton, and dreams of Powells, the best bookstore on earth. She is still in love with her husband Pat and still loves writing tangled journeys.

Heart Stone
ISBN: 978-4-86751-581-5

Published by
Next Chapter
1-60-20 Minami-Otsuka
170-0005 Toshima-Ku, Tokyo
+818035793528

1st July 2021

Lightning Source UK Ltd.
Milton Keynes UK
UKHW041729080622
404097UK00011B/18

9 784867 515815